BORDERLINE FICTION

Also by Derek Owusu

That Reminds Me
Safe: On Black British Men Reclaiming Space (ed.)
About This Boy: Growing Up, Making Mistakes and Becoming Me (with Leon Rolle)
Losing the Plot

BORDERLINE FICTION

DEREK OWUSU

CANONGATE

First published in Great Britain in 2025
by Canongate Books Ltd, 14 High Street, Edinburgh EH1 1TE

canongate.co.uk

1

Copyright © Derek Owusu, 2025

The right of Derek Owusu to be identified as the
author of this work has been asserted by him in accordance
with the Copyright, Designs and Patents Act 1988

No part of this book may be used or reproduced in any manner
for the purpose of training artificial intelligence technologies or systems.
This work is reserved from text and data mining
(Article 4(3) Directive (EU) 2019/790)

[Permissions credits TK]

British Library Cataloguing-in-Publication Data
A catalogue record for this book is available on
request from the British Library

ISBN 9781838855710

Typeset in Bembo by Palimpsest Book Production Ltd,
Falkirk, Stirlingshire

Printed and bound by CPI Group (UK) Ltd, Croydon CR0 4YY

The manufacturer's authorised representative in the EU for product
safety is Authorised Rep Compliance Ltd, 71 Lower Baggot Street, Dublin
D02 P593 Ireland (arccompliance.com)

For Billie
and
for Berthy

I sit and listen to the sounds in my inner being, the happy intimations of music, the deep, earnestness of the organ. Working them into a whole is a task not for a composer but for a human being who, in the absence of making heavier demands on life, confines himself to the simple task of wanting to understand himself.

Søren Kierkegaard, *Papers and Journals*, 1843

Twenty-Five

So, yes, I was in love again, losing balance, stumbling towards an earlier phase of my life. It was a moment I thought I knew, one I thought I could distinguish from my grazed and swollen knuckles as I fought back vertigo, the peak of a desert where a person became a thing. I remember I was still, stood staring at the girl who had just walked into the hall. She had a unique fringe of braids, 8 that covered her forehead and then curled around to fall back with the others, hiding in plain sight, so stunning but shielded. She had the delicate face of a statuette, high cheeks that balanced light, everything working together to illustrate features that could be shattered if you weren't gentle enough, a face baked under the sun inspiring shadows. A nose she hated for its European shade – though only in the light of the colonial could it cast such doubt – and lips that looked thin until gently coaxed from between her teeth. I think her eyes were blue, purple in some lights, like poetry turning its back on the prosaic, but they would always change colour whenever I tried to remember them. As I stood there, she could have been on the outside of the universe and still touched me, her silhouette soaking up light and colour from whatever came close. I fell in love like I had never known the feeling, like the sudden intimation that the presence of God was real. I tried to imagine a life before her, before this moment, but then the vision came back to me and I could feel truer words trying to find me, concussive sentences falling over themselves to reach me. A slight turn and I saw a friend, I think, or a stranger – no, someone like me who was also unfamiliar with many faces and was trying to ingratiate themselves with the cluster of black students by means of being in their presence, students who were waiting for the seats to be put into place along the stretch of tables. I rubbed, put pressure on my eyes and then took a deep breath, rolled back my shoulders to widen my chest, to let the feeling spread. But then, a small split in the fabric of fantasy and I knew I had to be mistaken, had to convince myself. I turned away from her and settled back into my surroundings, my shoulders slackening, and I nodded in agreement, shook my head in dismay, watched the subtle changing aspects of my friend's – it *was* my friend's – face, and tried to decide on the most satisfying response – an expressed tremble from my chest or swallowed words to the same effect. He carried on talking while I thought without acting and what would have been butterflies burned in my stomach, their charred remains reminding my body of the anxious state I'd managed to find distance from. I remained quiet. Efe, his name was Efe, spoke like he didn't have time to listen. He smiled a lot as he spoke, a smile that showed 23 teeth and pleased whoever was caught in its wandering light as he turned left and right while speaking. I wondered if he smiled in the mirror, and then noticed he had a split in the middle of his bottom lip that he kept sliding his tongue down between sentences, winces so quick only a flash could capture them.

The flyer had said speed dating would last an hour and a half so I put my hand in my pocket, broke two more 10mg pills out of their blisters and surreptitiously popped them in my mouth, moistened up enough that I could swallow them down without an excess of spit. I felt around for one more in case I needed it but realised I'd forgotten an entire pack back at my dorm, and even with what I'd taken, panic tried to break the calm that usually insulated me from the instability of everything around me. No, I would be fine, I thought, and took to my senses: heard chairs scraping floors, smelled a body passing soaked in Tom Ford, then I rubbed my hand over my scar, trying to remember how it had felt before I needed to heal excess, and then, to the left, saw my friend, watching me, waiting for an answer. Sorry. Yeah, come then, I said. Come where? he replied. Bro, just sit down somewhere, man. One spliff and you're moving like . . . Just come, man. Sit there . . . I didn't smoke but embraced the undertone of my slow strides, unashamed, closed my eyes and let the echo run, follow me like trails of silver haze obscuring one path form another, one remedy from another. And then I turned, saw where he was pointing, to a seat opposite a light-skinned girl with her hair in a bun, lips soft and slightly wet. I imagined them against mine, would blood rush at the pressure, would she lean into the kiss indefinitely? Both her hands were under the table. The grey jumper she wore was being pulled from one shoulder to another, her hands likely swallowed by her sleeves, maybe nails being picked at inside. I walked over and sat down. I felt calmer already, though I knew the pills took a while to take effect, manifest, maybe it was all in my head but I've always reacted quickly and intensely to most things. My stomach felt controlled again, hardening. I could relax as much as possible and worry about the unfortunate side effects tomorrow.

Hey, I'm Marcus.

I don't think we're supposed to talk yet, you know.

Oh swear? My bad. When can we talk?

She ignored me and looked to the end of the tables where Gloria, one of the organisers, and her flock of students were standing and looking to us, telling us the rules and explaining that there shouldn't be any pressure, this is to make friends, not find love. Just be yourself. I remembered reading a book about boosting self-esteem and the author suggesting one of the best ways to overcome insecurities was to imagine a person you think is charismatic, charming and full of confidence, and then see yourself walking into their body and becoming them. So I imagined someone I met years ago standing in front of me, looking down at the girl opposite. I stood up into his body, took a deep breath and sat again, crossing my legs. When I stood up the girl turned back to me and lifted her hand from under the table as if to reach over and stop me leaving. The cuff of her jumper was chewed up, threads hung loose and there was a visible dampness around most of it. I glanced at it and knew she was watching me. Her hand was gone again. I looked into her face, focused on her nose and said, I used to bite the skin off my knuckles. Look, you can see where the skin has healed. I leaned forward and offered my hand but she recoiled.

Ew, allow it, she said.

Then the bell rang for the speed dating to begin.

Nineteen

You know what, I never thought to work in a gym before you know, like, I never thought it was a job man could do, which is a weird one for me because I've been banging gym since I was like 10 or 11, tryna look like Ahmad Johnson and them man, shoulder pressing my dad's living room sofa with all its threads hanging loose, hearing all them coins and other random shit shifting away from you when you lifted it off the floor. I never flexed, though, and only really clocked my body was changing when the birthday beats from my cousins wasn't slumping me like they used to. But yeah, man, gym, I won't lie, I actually loved my job. True, sometimes it pissed man off but these days what aint gonna piss you off at least a little bit? Gotta take the poison in your paradise, get me. It was a bit of a trek as well but I actually preferred them long-arse journeys compared to walking and standing in line at job centre. Don't get it twisted, nothing wrong with signing on, like, usually it's nothing to feel shame about and bare man are on it, but it's when you're actually caught up in there or queuing outside for the P's. Everything just looks different when you're actually seeing it happen instead of thinking about it, get me.

Anyway, got this job now and yeah, I actually can't believe I worked my way up from receptionist to personal trainer, a proper big man ting, the freedom felt so good and I didn't have to worry about line managers preeing when I was on my break or operations managers asking about where I been and who I was coming out the pump room with. When I first started, I won't lie, it was a bit long, worst part's when you had to say hello to everyone when you weren't feeling it, acting like you were bare happy to see members even though you know say they weren't happy to see you on their lunch break grinning bare teet, but yeah, anyway, what else, yeah, I had to take cards, swipe them in and offer towels, sometimes even having to pick up used and dutty ones too, upsell some shit protein bars, locker hire or electrolyte drink. I used to hate the entrance too, the button never worked properly and people were too eager so they'd slam into it and look at you in your face like say them trying to make it back to work before a meeting or a call or whatever had anything to do with you. I was gonna say before their manager gets onto them but those lot never really had managers like that. But nah, you see them turnstiles, they were always in man's dreams, one on each side of me, locked and I'd be trying force my way through so I could do a chlorine test on the pool while people were screaming and melting in it. A mad one. Anyway, I think I was a fitness instructor for like 4 months after that, and I won't lie sometimes I think fitness was better than personal training, it was sorta like chilling in the middle of the gym and reception, glorified cleaners someone must have called us once, and fair enough, but more time you just worried about what you should do when a new member's blood pressure was above 140 over 90 or whatever, or how you could give unsupervised PT sessions on the sly, or even just trying to dodge them drops of sweat coming at you like say your forehead was the only place they wanted to land when you were cleaning around the treadmills, those hardcore cardio heads always going nuts. Then I qualified for PT. If I'm being honest, I only managed to finesse it because my boy and I came up with this system, basically just me listening to him tapping his pencil a number of times that matched the letter in the alphabet. I mean, it was multiple choice anyway so even without those morse code antics I might still have passed. Maybe. Because reading was always long for me. Hard, even. I'd just be bored or understood the words on the page but not what it meant when you put them together, get me? And even with writing, I remember I'd get the letters the wrong way round so sometimes it looked like I was trying to spell a word backward and forward at the same time. I've still got some homework from back in the day, in those little blue notebooks with your name on the front, remember them ones? And even on the front of that I've spelt my name wrong, with the 'a' and the 'r' backwards looking like say they were squaring up with the 'M'! All mad. So because of that now, when I was a yout, my dad used to slyly call me stupid, talking bare slow to me and asking if I was okay and if understood what he was saying. True, sometimes I was slow with the Twi as well and I would zone out, but I weren't so dumb that I couldn't understand stories about rabbits and Ghana and everything else he was trying to tell me, like c'mon. And I got over them things anyway, but still, when it's time to read or write something I make sure I take my time, make sure everything is in the right order, get me. And I don't think what my dad said was an insult, like, I don't think he saw it as him being rude or anything, mostly because he'd told me before how when he was in Ghana his parents had shown him too, making sure he would only focus on the things he could do, like the things he could control instead of failing at the other stuff or whatever. You know what, I don't even know if my dad can read, you know, even though man had bare stories. And my mum, I think she actually felt bad for me. She would always ask – nah, actually, not asking, telling me – she'd be telling me, it's too hard for you, isn't it, son? Can't lie, at the time, they were right. Believing in yourself and all them other random thoughts going through your head are probably the only real things you're dealing with in childhood. But yeah, man qualified, and I actually passed the practical bit without help, so there was no way I was going to bruk up one of my clients, I just didn't know where the infraspinatus was and how many muscle heads the bicep had. Really though, who cares about them things when all you're trying to do is gain muscle or tone up? Actually, nah, tell a lie, some do. My first paying client, a member I gave a health check to once, asked me how long it took me to become qualified. Obviously I didn't lie but after that he'd always ask me if I was sure when I told him which exercise we'd be doing next. Joke man. I know he thought I hadn't clocked what he was doing, that he was probably just trying to sneak in a few more seconds rest before the next set. Minor, though, because I knew how I got here so no one could chat to my confidence or tell me I didn't know how to build muscle or drop weight. I was in good nick, as the other PTs told me, good genetics reh reh reh but I remember when I was actually skinny even though I was bussing like 100 press ups every night and ate nuff chicken and potatoes and white rice. I was always active, always outside. To the point where you'd even catch me skipping dinner sometimes as well. I didn't really like food like that. My dad clocked this at some point and started watching me and one day pulled like 8 potatoes out of an empty bin, it was mad, and dashed them at my feet. I knew he weren't gonna do nothing but tell me some long story about wasting food and how he couldn't afford to munch air when he was young. My dad was one of those people where it's like as soon as they start speaking it feels like they gonna go on for time trying to get to the point with some long annoying story. Like, even when he weren't actually trying to tell a story the explanation was always longed out and it just felt like he was trying to school you like some village elder with some shit he just made up. Anyway, these days I was eating as much as I could. There was a Tesco just down the road that sold a whole rotisserie chicken for like 4 pound and I'd eat that with raw broccoli throughout the day, robbing one two protein bars from the reception stand as well. I don't know how much I weighed but I knew my body fat was about 6.7 per cent. One of the PTs hit me with some callipers and I swear I'm not lying when I say everyone in the gym was waiting for him to call and tell us what my calculated body fat was. Makes sense why so many members would shout me for sessions. Because obviously they thought if I could do it for myself, I could do it for them. And why not, though, alie? I know this pissed off some of the other trainers because they thought they knew their stuff and I didn't, I just looked good. Oh well. No beef or anything like that but I'd clock them watching me when I was with a client, checking to see if I knew how to instruct the proper technique for a deadlift or was spotting a squat the proper way or whatever. Some of them tried to take my clients, too, chatting to them and putting things in their head about nutrition and technique when they'd see one of them waiting for me in reception, but it never worked. I must have been making about 4 bags a month easy. And I only took cash, stacking it all in my locker. Reckless. But I liked to look at the money in real life. Before all this the most money I had ever had at once, like, proper cash in my hands, was like 400 pounds, 8 weeks' pay from some part-time job in one supermarket. I quit after that first pay cheque hit my account because they made us work with frozen food without any gloves and cos they made man work for like two months without seeing any P's. Imagine. Sometimes I stood in front of my locker and just counted all the notes, stacking them on top of each other. I knew exactly how much I had so if I finished counting and had a different number, I'd begin all over again, making sure each note was the right side up.

Oi oi, Marc counting his money again.

Marc, mate, are you a fucking builder or what?

Weren't you a builder before you became a personal trainer, Marc?

No, he was a carpenter.

Stripper, mate, you've all got it wrong.

I let them chat shit and just focused on the P's. The gym took rent from us every month, and I'd wait until like the last hour to pay mine, trying to make sure I had a new client or old ones had renewed or I had at least a couple numbers I could cold call. The money always had to make sense, feel me.

Opposite the reception area there were these leather seats that were really for members to chill before or after a session, for the sales team to try and sell memberships sitting down like a proper business transaction but mostly we all used them to sit around between clients and chat shit, the receptionists and fitness instructors coming to chill too if there were no managers about or they were on their break. You weren't allowed to eat out there but obviously I did because the kitchen was nasty most the time so I'd break off a piece of my rotisserie and cover it with kitchen towel, taking one, two bites every now and then, rolling residue tissue into a ball with my tongue and spitting it out behind the chair, making sure Rafiq, the gym manager, wasn't looking. Them lot chatted bare. More time I just sat back, munching and laughing when they did, watching new members and running up to reception when I clocked they were asking about training. But I picked up a lot of gist chilling in between them man. Mostly what trainers were pressing their clients, which gym members were on it with basically anyone, apparently, which PTs were using cocaine as a pre trainer and who they thought was on gear. Obviously my name came up. They keep trying it but they'll never catch man out like that. I've never dealt with any of my clients like that, because how can you charge them for sessions if you were laying with them tryna catch your breath the night before? Only when I was a PT, though. As a receptionist? Bare tings. The pool area was the best place to chat to them. As well as swiping in members and handing out clean towels and all that other stuff, you also had to do pool checks which was basically making sure the chlorine levels were alright, pool was clean, no dirty bits floating and the scum line was decent, that the sauna and steam room were the right temperature or whatever, that the safety stuff was working and that no one was doing anything they weren't supposed to be doing. Listen, we were the ones doing what we weren't supposed to be doing, like, I can't even tell you how many times I'd be talking to a member by the pool and then next thing I'm showing her how the pool tests work and then quickly slipping into the pump room and sliding man's hands down her underwear, lifting up her bra and sucking her breast, fingering her and then licking my fingers and lipsing. I don't think I ever fucked anyone in there but definitely ate couple members out even if they didn't give me brain, I didn't care. More than anything, I just wanted to kiss them, especially the brownings and dark tings. I hate saying it, like I know it sounds moist, but I can't even lie, I just loved it, that shit was spiritual for me. But eventually I clocked that a lot of them would pull away and look at me like, is that it? At first I thought they'd suddenly clocked how mad we were moving, but then I'd realise what they were really on and start kissing down their body just to build it up and then I'd be squatting on my tiptoes with their pum in my mouth. They'd see me the next day and act like nothing happened. That's one thing I liked about them corporate types: it's like everything was just business. It's like sucking their lips and eating their pussy out was just part of the membership package. Can't lie, though, I was a bit pissed when I qualified, because those people were straight away struck off my potential client list. Oh well. But yeah, as a trainer, not on that. And anyway, almost as soon as I became a PT, I was loved up. Not loved up like them man out here buying flowers and perfume and thinking it's some flex to swap sides with a gyal when they're walking along a road. Nah, this was a proper love ting, like, there were moments when I'd stop in the middle of some convo or joke or just watching her or whatever and just think to myself, yeah, I fuck with you, grinning bare teet, can you believe it, like, that was actually my bedrin. It was a member, though, still, I won't lie, but it wasn't someone I trained or had dealings with. She was my boy Anton's client. He's the one who even got me the number. The first time I seen her now it was one of them moments where you're like I swear I know this person from somewhere, but obviously that's the deadest bar you can drop when you're trying to move someone up, even if it's true. So I just watched her. She walked up and down past the reception then stopped and asked me if I'd seen Anton.

I think he's around here somewhere. If I see him I'll tell him you're looking for him.

Say Adwoa is looking for him.

Aight, cool.

Thanks.

And that was that. But she'd given man her name on a sly one so I thought okay, let's see where this goes. I was a bit shy, won't lie. It's mad, though, because even when someone is proper sexy but you aint on them like that, it's so easy to chat to them, even small small flirting. But once it's like rah, this girl is actually nice, like I'm actually feeling her, then suddenly you can't even say hello and goodbye properly. That first time I met Adwoa, when she said thanks, imagine I almost said, Thank you too, like some ediat. When she turned away I could see she was smiling, though. I think we both clocked we were feeling each other from early so when it's awkward like that it's just like confirmation and one of them stories you keep loaded for when you're having those sweet conversations and saying who moved to who first or whatever, them ones where it feels like remembering these typa things keeps everything fresh. She said it was me who moved to her first but c'mon, why you telling me your name then? Anton knew what time his clients were and obviously so did she so all I needed to say to him was, your 4 o'clock is looking for you and he'd know who I'm on about. But yeah, I spoke to him afterwards and told him to tell her that I'm feeling her. I was almost 20, you know. Mad. But he said cool and when he came back to me, he had her number ready. I've never been one of them who likes to play games so I got at her quickly, as soon as I got home, even. She didn't even ask who's this, just texted me back, *Hey Marcus*. We both knew what time it was.

Twenty-Five

I tried to remember as much as I could about each person who sat down in front of me, anything interesting about them, one body forming as each slid out of the seat, a character pieced together with charming idiosyncrasies and obvious elements of personality I found appealing, then it all floundering in front of me, an ideal that then became repulsive, giving the person who sat down after I discarded this idea an advantage to take hold of my heart and level out my disorder. Jayde, she was a singer, taught to harmonise in church but found her faith in music stronger than the idea that nurtured it. I wrote down her full name and EP title and still listen to it sometimes when my thoughts are caught in a loop on the past. She said she loved seafood even though it made her nauseous, but having a cigarette after each meal evened things out and she could consume more until the nausea became sickness from overeating and she didn't know why she was telling me all of this but at least she was being honest. I agreed that honesty was the best way to start any relationship, friendship or otherwise, and then lied that I loved seafood too, lobster being my favourite, but the truth was it made me sick too but agreeing with her and saying, Me too, felt more like a lie than the truth. So, I was being honest in a way. She was light skinned with dark parents so hated to be called mixed, though she only dated mixed men, but said she enjoyed chatting to me and was okay with us going book shopping or something. I hoped I liked her music. Christiana took her place, slim, cheekbones that suggested a runway or an obsession with food, maybe both. I held on to the previous conversation and stretched seafood across our table. She said she was a vegetarian but found it difficult to adhere to because she loved shaki so much. I asked her if she knew what it was made from and she said she didn't care, that she'd even endure eating fufu as long as there was shaki in the soup. While she spoke, I began to wonder what her fingers tasted like. Her real obsessions were with singers Robyn and Amy Winehouse, who she mentioned as 'Amy' instead of her full name, and hoped I was joking when I confessed I'd never listened to any of her albums, but vaguely remembered *Body Talk*. Before her next question I felt myself push my foot against the floor, slide back an inch and then raise and lower myself on tiptoe so I was floating up and down without anyone noticing. Too much effort to lie I told her my parents were from Ghana and then watched as she raised an eyebrow that kept her eye wide until she left the table. I kept watching the distance, following students who carried on walking past seats meant for them, deciding instead to question those behind the bar, and then the others, the nervous or needing a break, girls coming from flushing nothing and the boys sideways stepping to disguise the pull to adjust themselves. And me, I kept telling myself no, shaking my head whenever I felt the urge to look down the loosely connected tables and find the girl I'd decided I didn't love any more, the one from earlier, the one touched and sculpted by God but probably set in the oven by the other. It was too soon but finally I thought fuck it and turned, the room pausing for me to nod to each body as I counted them and checked to see which one was her. None. I counted them one more time and imagined an additional number to create something even in my head. She had left. Relieved or bereft, I couldn't tell, but I held the emotion close so on my walk home I could either tear it from myself or plaster us both with it. But I wouldn't have to. The feeling was superseded immediately when I faced my next speed date. So I looked down at the sores on my knuckles before she could spread her elbows on the table, counting in my head again the number of braids across her face hiding who she was from me.

I've never looked at a woman and imagined what it would be like to fuck her, but I always find myself picturing a life with them, the good, the indifference, how we'd cut a path through the bad, how quickly it could happen, does happen, and the myriad ways I could perform what I thought was the desired intensity of love. San and I spoke for less than two minutes, a shorter period it seemed compared to everyone else who had sat down before me, but she was uncanny, appeared removed from everything, and though our time was compressed, everything around us collapsed as we spoke and our pocket universe contained an abundance of information, everything I needed to know, everything I needed to play and replay in my mind until there was no doubt I knew San better than anyone else. When she got up and left, her chair remained empty, an evening ending where it had begun, a parallel to so much of life. Drinks were being served, snacks about the room, and those who were rapt with feeling and hoping for harmony, the affinity cut short, hovered close to what might have been, not quite engaging but speaking words to another who was near enough that a fallen phrase would reintroduce them. And then those who felt nothing, who could turn and walk away, were able to pick up with ease where their conversation had ended with the bell. I couldn't drink because of the pills I had taken. Well, I could, but I wouldn't, not today. I found myself in a corner and kneeled down to tie the laces I always tucked into the sides of my trainers, looking up into as many faces as I could before I had to get to my feet again. I couldn't see my boy anywhere. Four more minutes, I told myself, then I would leave, enjoy the calm and real efficacy of the codeine and Xanax and fall back into my reveries and branching possibilities. San's face was clear to me even with my eyes open, her skin so delicate that two fingers down her cheek would stretch and smudge the work only just finished, gods justifying their existence with hers. While she'd asked me questions and I'd answered quickly, instinctively, I'd wanted to reach forward and lift her threaded fringe, be the first to see her all as she was, unbraided and secure. The room was becoming overwhelming, and I couldn't match the conversations I heard with the mouths they were coming from, so I took a deep breath and started walking towards the exit. I counted each of my steps and before I reached the open door, shortened my stride so the last step before I touched the outside was not the number 17.

Nineteen

First dates will forever be awkward so I wasn't even pressed when the silence dropped and she was just there staring at me. Obviously I couldn't be obvious like her, but every now and then I'd watch her for a bit when I was acting like say there was something interesting about the Wetherspoon's carpets or the people walking about on them. Her top lip had a cupid's bow. One girl I used to chat to back in the day said I had one and showed me what it was so now I always clock it on other people. Adwoa's one was deeper than mine, though, like God pressed her top lip too hard and now it looked like you could easily snap it in half with two fingers. I liked it, though, I wanted to slide my tongue up and down it. I loved sucking lips, man, seriously, it was actually a problem, suck them like I used to suck those ice poles I'd melt in my sink and just drink the juice from the tube. I'd have like 10 of those melting in my bathroom sink at the same time. It's mad, though, because if you start doing all that too quickly, kissing, I mean, it can put people off, so you gotta be patient, know how to style it out. It's funny because most man are going through all the motions of biting neck and squeezing breast just to get to the point where they can beat. If gyal were like, Aight, nah, fuck all that, just fuck me, you think man are gonna say, Nah, actually, let's build up to it and lips and touch each other first? Yeah, exactly. But me? I won't even lie, and I know it makes me sound like some sweet guy, but if I don't get to suck her lips, top lip, bottom lip, I'll even try put both in mout at the same time, yeah, If I can't do all that then the vibe is just dead to me. Obviously, I can still beat but it's like, in my head I'm just counting how many times I've clapped cheeks, like, how many minutes she gonna take to buss. Mayn listen, at one point I even faked my own. No shame, though, I don't care. Listen, hear this, one girl I met in Flashes, yeah, Flashes Before Your Eyes, that's where most people in Tottenham went these times because back then it was like every club had closed down or just switched up into something else the next day out of nowhere. I hear it, though, man did like to scrap outside and I know those bouncers were stressed but it's not like it was every night or whatever. Anyway, this girl I met in there, she was sitting on my lap in the garden area. It was a garden but no trees or plants, just the fences of bare people's backyards, actually crazy how they could have a club there, but I actually preferred it out there because inside the music was making man vibrate, them ones where the DJ hasn't clocked it's way too loud so when I get home now there'd just be this eeeeee sound in my ears and Skepta still chatting about we need some more girls and so of course sleep becomes even more of a myth. Anyway, I must have met her when I was waiting for my drink, waiting for time, actually, and I knew it was taking long mostly because I weren't tryna put my elbows on the bar and lean forward to get noticed. I knew nuff people had dropped their drinks on there and I hated the feeling of being sticky like say I could brush past someone and then we'd stuck together for the rest of the night. Actually, wait, you know what, I think that girl just came over out of nowhere you know and sat down on man's lap. I was talking to one guy I hadn't seen in time, telling me how I don't shout him again, but as soon as she come over, man got up and buss out and didn't even give me his number. Anyway, so me and this girl would be lipsing and then she'd pull away and start puffing on her cigarette. Like, this was all she was doing, nothing else was really happening. I don't really smoke like that but I didn't really mind it to be honest, like, I didn't mind just being there with her, for the whole night even, and I won't even lie, I'd actually decided it after the first time she kissed me. I just made sure I ordered sweet drinks like Baileys or Disaronno so it was the only thing I could taste. Obviously I was buying her drinks too but I clocked after like the third time I got up that she had about 4 drinks on the table near us. I think bare man were buying her drinks and she was shook to drink them or something because she even put my ones on the side too, even though she was sitting on man's lap. Anyway, most nights it was packed in there, like, the smell should have been unbearable but you almost looked forward to it, that mix up of body odour, Black Opium and Paco Rabanne, maybe some cognac in the air too if bare man were tipsy and spilling their drinks while reaching for their head to buss a skank. Yeah, you'd see people cutting shapes in their corners, but really the corners weren't even that, they were just groups of people all over the place, maybe you'll see someone catching a slow whine outside, the DJ barely even reaching them so you know the riddem was basically in their heads. Like, there was obviously a dancefloor but more time it was just used as a place to stand and watch, or mostly it was a passageway where people sometimes stopped before they reached where they were going because they'd clocked one ting, or wanted hail up their bedrins, buss one, two skanks with the cup in the air and spill one, two sips to the plastic floors, and see, that's the reason why when one tune dropped for a next one to come in, in that little piece of silence during the transition you could hear Clarks, Kickers and Air Max 90s peeling off the floor. Yeah, sometime you could get in with trainers on if you knew the bouncers. My cousin Sam, or DJ Kane, used to be the one to get me in, but now I could roll through on my ones, I'd been there so many times and always said wagwan to the bouncers so whichever man was on the door would low me in wearing whatever. I was rocking jeans and a slim fit in the garden with these TNs that had lightning bolts running through them. I was calm, weren't watching no face, but still, come see man try and barge me every time I went to the toilet or bar, rolling in their shoulders when they were walking like say every day they were banging chest. But I know them man never went gym. Just hype on coke. That's why they moved like that, but honestly it never really affected me. Even when I was sitting with this girl, one guy came outside and was like, You two have been out here for time, man. I was thinking, so? How you moaning and begging like that because you want piece? I didn't say anything, just carried on doing nothing with this ting on my lap. We weren't even talking, just sitting there looking at each other every now and then and lipsing. Listen, every time I came back from the toilet and she sat back down on man, I'd get a semi going on fully but she'd act like she couldn't feel it. I weren't trying to press it up on her, to tell the truth I tried to adjust myself a bit so it wasn't bait, but it's like she wouldn't even let me move it. She weren't grinding on it but she knew wagwan and didn't care. One thing, though, every time I tried to bite her lips, or put one of them in my mouth, she pulled back, looked at me and shook her head. It wasn't even one of those where you can tell they aint feeling being kissed like that, where they look at you like some deviant or something. Nah, I could tell she liked it but I think she was thinking we aint doing all that out here. Calm. We carried on and I got bare drunk, like I think I was even holding back tears at one point. Ask me why and see if I know. But I remember her twosing me on the walk back to mine so you know I was gone. All my cousins were in bed when we got in so we tiptoed up the stairs and over someone sleeping on the landing. I was one of the only ones with their own room because I promised auntie I'd pay rent once every 3 months. We get inside now and I lock the door and she starts undressing. I walk up to her and try do my thing but she stops me and says that's enough. Enough of what, I'm thinking.

You like kissing, don't you?

Yeah, I do.

A lot.

Yeah, and what?

Nothing. So you're not trying to fuck, you just want to kiss me?

What?

You heard what I said.

No, obviously I want to fuck you, I'm just a bit waved, sorry.

So?

So I get it if you're not on it.

Are you being serious?

Yeah, because obviously, sometimes it's like, if one person is drunk and like, even me, like, sometimes I'm not feeling—

Just take off your clothes, please.

Aight, aight, cool, one sec.

What are doin'?

Hold on, trying to find something. Okay, cool, aight. Lemme grab a drink quickly, though. You want one?

No thanks.

You sure?

I don't drink.

Oh swear?

Anyway, I got into the bed now and took off my clothes and she undressed in front of me. I know it was supposed to be sexy but I was already ready like, let's just do this ting. So hear this, she gets into the bed now and of course I get on top and try lips her again. I aint even ashamed, she had nice lips, bro. But she turned and gave me her neck so I just started biting her as she found and grabbed my dick under the covers and put it inside her. Listen, I was there and then I wasn't. Imagine, started thinking about a client who owed me P's, how many days until rent was due, vex that I hadn't hit my chest properly in the gym because I only got 7 reps instead of 8 on the incline. I was semi-hard still, though, and kept the same energy from when we started. To be honest, I don't even know if she came because when it got to the point where my mind started drifting to a next gyal, that's when I could feel myself going soft so I had to style it out, grunting, biting her shoulder and digging my nails into her arms and holding her close to man. I lifted up my head, arched my body a bit so my dick was inside her as much as possible, feeling like some idiot, and then closed my eyes but quickly opened them again when one thought tried to creep up on me, and then just relaxed on top of her. I wasn't even out of breath.

Did you cum?

Yeah.

Are you sure?

Yeah, little bit.

Hmmm.

When I drink, nothing really comes out.

Isit?

Yeah. You want some water? It's a weird one.

No. Can you get off me? I need to go toilet.

Oh shit, sorry.

I rolled and was on my back and put this dumb look on my face like tryna capture that post-nut happiness and clarity. I can't really fake those typa looks but I always try. Not saying man's miserable, I'm not, obviously, but just that I've been through couple things that made me look at the world in a different kinda way, get me, like, all you have to do really is watch the world or just look around ends to clock what people are like deep down, like, I know them bruddas ask God for forgiveness after they've stabbed someone but they still do it, and I'm not saying I'm on some Ozymandias thing and everyone should be rubbed out but sometimes being born just feels like a fuckree. Anyway, what am I saying, yeah, so yeah, after I pretended to buss I knew she was watching me, saw the side eye when she was putting on her underwear and the tracksuit bottoms I showed her were in the top drawer. Listen, if she knew, she weren't trying to say anything. Just staying mad about it or thinking I was some weird yout. Not like I did her dirty and was selfish. Fair, I could have paid more attention, but this shit just felt too ... like sometimes while I'm fucking it's like suddenly I'm up on the roof just watching how dumb everything looks, two people just smashing their bodies together like we're angry we can't just be one person. Or sometimes, wait, how do I explain this, okay, yeah, sometimes it feels like while I'm fucking I've been robbed, like say someone just took something from me one time, you know that quick shock like say your heart just pumped cold silver, when you've just clocked something is missing and you're rubbing your hands all over your body bare confused even though deep down you know wagwan, but yeah, it's also like this repetition and I keep forgetting they robbed me only for that shit to happen again, and by the end I just feel like all I got left is my bones chilling inside my skin, like nothing in-between. I don't even know what I'm saying but I feel like that kinda thing is alright at work because at least I'm getting paid. And honestly, where my head was starting to go, I knew I'd need to reach for something to sort myself out and knew she wouldn't like it, would probably be shook to be honest. But yeah, after all that I just felt like my body had been drained. In the end she came back in the room, got into bed without taking off man's bottoms and faced the wall, curled up like a baby.

You okay?

Yeah, I'm fine.

You want me to call you an Uber?

So what, I have to go home now as well?

Nah, nah, just saying if you want one, it's calm, I'll get it. Wait, what you mean, *as well*?

Let's just go to sleep.

Aight ... Are you upset?

No, why would I be?

I dunno, you just seem a bit off.

I'm fine.

Aight, cool.

Goodnight.

Goodnight . . . You want me to hold you?

. . .

Or not. Up to you.

. . .

. . .

Yes please.

So I got closer and wrapped my arms around both of hers like say I could break her if I wanted to. I dunno what she was on but I didn't mind, like I could sleep like this, calm. She started moving about and then I could feel her thigh against mine, and heard my tracksuit bottoms drop on the floor.

Anyway, I didn't kiss Adwoa on our first date. Sitting there in silence, I thought lemme just say something because I know most normal people feel weird when no one is chatting on a date, but I was so tired, I did like 5 sessions back to back from 2 p.m., but still here I was, just sitting there sipping my drink, double Henny, and preeing the people walking around us. We could of gone somewhere nicer, to be honest, obviously I had the P's for it, but this was the closest place to the cinema and I told her walking was long for me right now. In the silence I clocked one guy playing the fruit machine, his belly was a bit mad, still, and it reminded me of one uncle who used to run around a park near my yard and do half press-up on a bench. But yeah, watching this guy, it looked like it was bit of a stretch for my man to play the game, probably had one of those emergency pens too, he looked Ghanaian as well, and then Adwoa finally spoke to me.

Why do you keep going to the toilet? Are you nervous?

No. But when I start drinking I need to go a lot.

Isit?

Yeah? Why? You're not chatting to me, anyway.

And that's my fault?

Did I say that? I don't even mind it, but obviously I know some people think it means we aint clicking.

Are we clicking, Marcus?

Boy.

What?

I dunno.

No, go on.

I mean, when I first saw you, yeah, obviously, there was a click. That's why I was checking for you.

But you didn't ask me. You got Anton to ask me.

Yeah, he'd see you, init, so he was the best person. If it's me, I might not see you in the gym for time. I swear I'd never even seen you there before until you asked me about Anton.

You mean you hadn't noticed me.

Nah, nah, not even, probably just we been at the gym at different times. Why you tryna twist it?

I'm not twisting anything. I'm not offended. You've noticed me now so it's fine. Happy to be noticed by you.

Isit now?

Yeah, it is.

We finished our drinks and walked 42 steps to the cinema. I ordered popcorn I wasn't really hungry for because I thought maybe she'd want it but was on a budget or something and

I wasn't trying to come across rude, but I was right, though, because watch her ask if I could get a sweet and salted mix. When we sat down in our seats I knew there was gonna be this tension about kissing so I just asked her.

What, now?

Yeah, man. Just get it out the way so we aint worrying about it later and can digest this popcorn properly, no embarrassing belly noise while we're watching the film.

You mean so you're not worrying.

Whoever.

Does your belly rumble when you're nervous?

Sometimes, yeah.

Are you nervous right now?

Adwoa, what even are you doing?

I'm just playing with you. But no, I don't want to kiss you right now.

Okay, cool . . . Was I rude or something? Are you offended?

No. I just don't want to kiss you in a cinema.

Ah okay. Fair enough.

I can't remember what we watched because all I could think about was why the cinema was such a bad place to kiss.

Twenty-Five

On the train ride home, the carriage was full, but I'd managed to find a seat with someone looming above me preferring to stand, their knees buckling every so often, teasing a collapse into my lap, and I imagined them falling into me like a ghost inhabiting my body. His back was to me but I sometimes glimpsed the white of one eye followed by the dark pupil trying to turn and look at me. It was unnerving and to elevate the feeling I imagined the eye turning all the way round into the back of his head, watching me above the closure of his hat. I took another .25 of Xanax and leaned my head against the window, looked out onto Manchester racing past without much friction as it went by. I only came here a few times a month, anyway, to visit the Arndale Centre and a used bookstore opposite. Sometimes I'd walk along the road adjacent to one of the university buildings, examining the novels laid out down 4 long tables, hoping one day my words would be worn and beaten but still have the strength to take hold of a life and be meaningful. Between those visits to Manchester, Bolton was my home, a place I loved in the evening but couldn't hold eye contact with in the light. I turned away from it as frequently as it ignored me. In shops, in clubs, on campus. There were times when I sat in the university reception area reading for hours and not even a whisper drifted over the service desk. I could have been anyone, waiting for anyone. From the sofa I could turn and see the main road, imagining Sisyphus happy walking into the passing cars to relieve himself of the burden of a weightless existence. Staring out that window was how I met Ama. She asked me if I was okay and I fell in love with her. It lasted only a few months, ending when she took my medication from me and I told her she'd saved my life the day she spoke to me. But mostly I was alone. And I didn't mind it that way, a life without transference, and I could be consumed without holding out for someone to follow me down, follow me anywhere.

Back on the train, I kept sliding my hand down my leg, holding it over my pocket, feeling nothing then clenching my fist and releasing it. I did this 8 times and eventually forgot whatever I was waiting for. Then the phantom returned and this time I caught the shudder, pulled my vibrating phone out of my pocket and read the first few lines of a message from my mum. I put the phone face down on my knee, caught it as it slid off and then put it back in the exact spot again, preparing myself for another fall as if leaning into a loop, my restless leg stepping into an eternal reoccurrence, irritating but distracting me as I slipped in and out of wondering if self-preservation was selfish if you knew, if you were aware your current iteration was useless? The only thing to be taken from me was lethargy, and if I gave in to those messages from my mum, I'd end up drained, almost dead like the rest of those constantly around him, bra Nancy, friends and family who had blindly endured because they once felt their cold words were profound murmurs to a dying man, a man who then struggled to express he needed them. And now I was one stop away.

The train doors remained open on the platform even though no one else was alighting and the light of the carriage, I noticed, was brighter now that there were no more bodies cramped into the aisles. I looked down and blinked 15 times and when I lifted my head, there was someone sitting opposite me. If I listened to the echoes of my anxiety, I could have believed he'd just appeared, but more likely I just hadn't noticed him as I sat with myself thinking about my mum and wondering how much honesty could exist in so few words, questioning if she'd fallen back into the pattern of emotional blackmail that she liked to embroider onto her funeral cloth. She knew my fear, ignored it enough times in passing to make it significant when she finally acknowledged it. Life insurance envelopes were always left in places no one would have sat to read them and when she fell asleep in my room on days I spent the night somewhere else, she'd leave her bible open on my pillow, knowing I'd never read whichever psalm or promise the page was left on but hoping that the presence of God was enough to move me one way or another. And so she watched me as I carried the good book back into her room, the way I always picked up the smaller, pocket-sized ones, many accumulated over the years, lives as delicate as my dad's, and placed them just under a corner of her pillow. I didn't believe, but I knew. I'd seen, I understood. God. I knew what it felt like to be abandoned, knew how often we, *made in his image*, were so passionate about a thing that now lay one with dust and desertion, its conclusion a disappointment, everything after and before a waste of time. Feeling the absence of God, when existing became too real, when I could see life without it being lived, when I was without my meds for too long, I imagined how we float in space, many planets alike, stars, fragments of worlds, galaxies, possible universes, like the discarded words on the page of a frustrated writer, a watchful but tearful God blinking away the tears and thus flittering us all in and out of existence. Or perhaps just me. Or maybe this detour of being born was so we would come to understand the value of eternal life. Maybe. But it wasn't often I thought about things like this, wasn't often I allowed myself to. It was lucidity I could fall from, face first into a reflection where Nothing made sense, where a feeling of being ruptured from reality could creep in. I picked up my phone from the side of my thigh and pushed up a blister pack from my pocket with it. I looked at the black screen as I slipped the small pill into my mouth. I was about to light up the words of my mother again when the man in the seat mirroring mine spoke to me. I put my phone face down on my thigh and turned to look. I hadn't heard the voice but I knew he was speaking to me. When our eyes met, I could see his mouth move and this time I caught the meaning of the words. I shook my head, scattering the shards of reflection and rubbed my eyes to bring myself back.

You alright?

Um, yeah. Yeah.

Deep in thought?

Yeah. Something like that.

Sorry I interrupted you.

Nah, it's cool.

I feel like we're going to be here for a bit and the silence was stressing me out.

No worries.

Exhausting, isn't it?

Think the train just does this sometimes.

When someone tells it to.

What?

Tells the train to stop, I mean. Like at a red signal. It doesn't just stop on its own, always some instruction, course correction, if you will.

Right, okay . . .

Where you off to?

Home.

Whereabouts is home?

Bolton. I go uni there.

I didn't even know Bolton had a university.

No one does.

So how come you're there and not somewhere else?

My ex.

Your ex? That's interesting. You decided to go uni together?

Nah. She helped me get into uni.

Coincidence. What do you study?

What is? And English Lit.

Oh, I see. Not my ex, but back in the day my brother did the same thing for me. University of Manchester.

Yeah? I was just there.

Of course you were. What's in Manchester?

Just some ACS event.

You don't seem the type.

Yeah. Was meant to be somewhere else. To see my dad, actually.

This was more fun, I imagine.

Yeah, something like that.

I hear you. None of my business. Fair enough.

Nah, just not that interesting.

That what's on your mind?

What?

Playing the events over and over in your head?

Nah, not even.

I passed my hand over my head as if I had hair to brush back, clenching my teeth, taking a deep breath, holding it and then breathing out, recalling I'd already taken something for my nerves and just had to be patient. Calm down. He was looking at me like I was asking for something and he was disappointed he couldn't offer it, like someone else would help, he was sure, but he was saddened it couldn't be him. His face was reflective, light entering the topmost corner of his window illuminating whatever he used on his skin, handsome somehow, a face you couldn't look at for too long, though, without giving yourself away by the silence, something secretive in its appeal, one of them faces you would be hesitant to show to others because you knew they wouldn't see it. As he leaned forward towards me there was a ring swaying on a chain around his neck that caught the same window light at intervals and revealed an engraved snake around the outside with its mouth open towards its tail.

Do you always do that?

What?

Think sentences through in your head before you say them?

What do you mean?

Ah, finally. We're moving. That felt longer than it was.

Yeah, it did.

You ever had that feeling when you were a kid, like when you've been waiting for something so long, when it actually happens, it's like being dropped from a height, that excitement in your belly?

You mean anxiety? Yeah, sometimes. Don't really like it.

You had anxiety when you were a kid?

Everything feels like anxiety to me.

Right. Okay. Well, I'm seeing someone I haven't seen in a few months and I'm having that feeling now.

Is that good or bad?

I'm not sure yet. Anyway, let me leave you to your thoughts. Enjoy the ride back. Nice to meet you?

Kweku.

Nana Kwesi. Just Nana, mostly.

Cool.

These day names, always make me feel old. Like someone's uncle.

You think?

Yeah, image being called Wofa at this age. In Ghana, last thing, sorry, but in Ghana, your uncle on your mum's side is the person who's supposed to look after you mostly, not your dad.

Isit? Nah, didn't know that.

Don't think many people do.

I hear you.

Including my own family.

Yeah?

Yeah, I try remember because he always forgets.

Who?

My dad.

Oh, cool. Aren't you getting off here?

Nah, few more stops.

Cool.

Life did him dirty but we're all stained somehow, feel me?

Yeah . . .

What's your dad's name?

No idea.

Ask him. Might have the same name as you.

We approached my stop in silence but I felt our convo needed an end, it lingered rather than died and I knew it would be awkward to recall and so I turned to say something but he was looking away, like he was trying to avoid the unwieldly goodbye instead of shaping it himself. Fair enough. I'd have to weave my own conclusion. I stepped off the train and I walked up the back path of the station, crossed the road to my dorm village. I could hear music from a few of the rooms, drink ups or club preludes, shadows moving back and forth behind the sheer curtains, a piece of J2's dance floor cut for a kitchen. I'd been raving since I was 16 and was exhausted by my early 20s. There was only one club I'd ever walk into again, for complicated reasons, and it closed down before I came to uni. I was older as well, a student of maturity, apparently, but still seeing with eyes of my childhood. Almost 26 and I wished I could go back. I picked up a package from the halls security hut and felt through it to get a sense of the medication without opening it. My floor was quiet, everyone already out. Sometimes the students would knock on my door and invite me with them, a bottle of White Ace in hand and, I think, the hope that I would say no, a complaint it was too late. Beyond 21 can appear as the end to anyone in their late teens, but we still approach it regardless. But they soon stopped knocking when I didn't answer or told them to come in and cornered them with the insincerity of a literary soliloquy, awkward and consuming, touching Pierre Menard from Borges, a *Catch-22*, or the multiplicity of Niffenegger's Henry. Loneliness means you don't have to disappoint anyone until you develop the habit of talking to yourself.

Once I was inside my room, I stripped down to my boxers, using my feet to peel off my jeans like a stubborn layer of skin, my clothes a heap like shedding on the floor, threw the brown parcel into my top drawer, put my phone down and climbed into bed, searching under my covers for the book I'd been reading before I left. I reached to check my battery and wanted to glance at the message from my mum again, look away then look again, 4 times seeing it, considering if I should open it in full and respond, but it had been replaced by another, a text from the organisers of the speed dating about another event, a group trip to Thorpe Park. I turned off my phone and started again on the first page of *Slaughterhouse-Five*.

Nineteen

You fucked it, mate.

How, though?

Who asks *can I kiss you* on a date?

Okay, yeah, I won't lie, it was a bit corny, but at the time it seemed like a normal thing to ask, get me, like, let's just get it over with because of all the sexual tension.

What fucking sexual tension, you bell end?

So you've spoken to her?

Not much, mate, but from what I've heard there wasn't any fucking sexual tension.

So I was just imagining it then?

I fucking hope not.

Anton usually talks sense, but this time he was wrong. Because during my next gym session who do I see but Adwoa, not moving shy or like the date was dead and she was trying to avoid man, but actually being nice, like twisting and turning up her body while chatting to me like we're bedrins, asking if this is how I get my clients, walking around the gym in a vest that likes to show nipple. She kinda had a baby face but it was more like one of them faces where you look your age but still have that childish cheekiness, skin like say you could see yourself reflected in it because she just knew how to cream herself well, could clock this even without touching it and when I was close enough I could smell the shea butter, gyal that cream their whole body when they come out the shower, a ritual like, see them in their towel, one foot on the bath or toilet, rubbing their hands up and down their leg, no hair, it's one of those images where you don't even know where it came from, where you can just see it and it makes sense. Sometimes I'll think of something and the vision is just there in my head, even if I aint ever thought about it like that before or seen it before, still I'll just see this perfect version of an idea. Not saying Adwoa was perfect, though. But yeah, she smelled good, still. As for me, I was just on the baby oil ting and also, why waste time putting lotion where no one is gonna see? My mum loved doing that, she used to be bare aggressive about it, Vaseline as well so she had to use nuff force to get it smooth on man's skin, rubbing like she was trying to bun my forehead, bun me, even. Anyway, Adwoa didn't really have a forehead like that, and I loved how her top lip lifted a little bit so you always saw her teeth when she was talking without her lips pulling back. But yeah, so I seen her in the gym and we buss a little convo, nothing serious, and then she asked me to spot her on the squat – minor, Anton knew I weren't trying to take his client – and we ended up on treadmills next to each other for the cool down. We would have been in the steam room but she weren't prepared for it. I was gonna tell her to just rock a towel but it sounded a bit mad in my head. So I was there on my ones, towel around my waist hoping no one opened the door to come in. I always slid my finger down the walls and sometimes saw this yellow sheen with the water that the other PTs said was body fat but I think they were chatting shit. Round about these times it was usually busy with people who aint even been gym, just jump in here straight from work. But it was just me so I could deal with my nose properly, the steam helped and I could blow out all that nasty shit. There was a trick to keep the steam running, you had to pour water on this one tube that came out the wall, then it would start puffing again. That was one of the things we had to try and catch people doing when we did our pool checks because I think it fucked with the system, but yeah. I had a few clients left that day but texted Adwoa about linking up after. She was down. This was a spur-of-the-moment ting so between clients I had to run over to New Look and cop a slim-fit T-shirt and jeans, my trainers could run.

Here he is. Looking dapper, very dapper.

You might wanna iron that shirt, though.

Where you off to, Marc?

Not sure yet you know.

A date?

Yeah.

You thinking, food, something active, just take her back to yours?

Nah, not like that. Maybe food.

Take her shisha, mate – a voice from a locker. The door closed and of course Anton was standing there.

Shisha?

Yeah, mate, Adwoa's been on about it before. I'll put money on it.

I was thinking maybe Lobster and Burger or something?

Fucking hell, mate, that's a serious lack of imagination. Take her shisha, you bell end.

Alright, alright. shisha.

You're lucky I'm not seeing her in the morning.

Yo, Anton.

Yeah, mate?

Let me use some of that Black XS spray, please.

You're fucking useless, you know that, Marc?

Adwoa looked good. Her hair was Dutch braided, two of them, actually, so she looked even more innocent, but drop to the jeans now and then turn it around and the back was a mad ting. Made me wish she was on raving so I could catch a whine. Anyway, we walked around central for nearly an hour looking for a good shisha place, not even a good one, just any after a point, so when we turned onto one street and saw bare of them on each side of the road, bruh, we both started pacing like say we were outside and our riddem just come on in the dance. We sat down in the first one we came to, sat outside and asked for two hookahs, one with mint flavour and one with strawberry. I was thinking if I had to lips her later, I didn't want her tasting some fruity flavour, I'd rather it just be a breath of fresh air and mint kinda thing. We both fell back into these hench bamboo chairs. That walk was long and she was in heels so I know she was feeling it but she didn't say anything, just firmed it. The relief we were both feeling made sense of the silence while we were just sitting there, like even though no one was chatting the vibe was completely different from when we found ourselves in that pub. Then they brought out the shisha and I ordered a Long Island iced tea but knew say the waiter was gonna act like they might not be able to make it. He said he'd see. Bruh, they always say that as if they don't have the all the ingredients just chilling at the bar. Adwoa ordered a pina colada and I remember thinking, so she does drink, thank God. But she probably weren't on anything else. I went to the toilet and then bopped back out like say we hadn't just been on a mission from Piccadilly just a minute ago.

Are you gonna be going toilet a lot again?

Nah, probably not. Why? People go toilet when they drink you know.

Yeah, but are you actually going toilet?

What else am I doing?

You tell me. Anyway, let's look at the menu. You think we should eat?

I'm not really hungry, but I could eat something.

Okay, let's order some starters and just pick at them?

Aight, cool.

I started drawing the shisha now and man's head turned into smoke, like the rush was so mad I felt like I hadn't even breathed out. I'd never done this before and thought it was just about flavour but I clocked straight away that there was tobacco.

Do you smoke?

No. Do you?

Nope.

Why you asking?

Because I'm sure there is tobacco in this.

Yeah, I think so.

You done it before?

Yup. I'm sure it's not a lot, though.

Not a lot? Bro, it just blew my head off.

Don't call me bro.

Aight, sorry, sorry.

It's okay.

Maybe I just need to get used to it.

Yeah, maybe. Is it really that strong?

You don't think so?

I guess I'm just used to it.

Hard-core smoker, yeah?

Not really.

You don't smoke nothing else?

No, do you?

You mean like weed?

Is that what you meant?

Yeah, not just weed, though.

I see. No, just shisha. Sometimes. You?

Nope. Nothing.

Do you do any drugs?

Like what?

Like any drugs. You want me to name them?

Nah, I get you. Erm. I won't lie, sometimes. Like now and then.

I see.

Does that bother you?

Not really. But it might later on.

Later on when? Like in the future?

I dunno. How long you planning to do them?

Wait, why are you . . . ?

I'm just asking.

Nah, why you questioning me like this?

Marcus. It's not that serious. But this is our second date. Might as well be honest about things now? In case we're wasting each other's time?

I hear you. Okay, yes, I do drugs sometimes.

Which ones?

Coke, I said after a bit. Fam, I was getting hot and might as well have been drinking the shisha at this point. She was just watching me, calm, and that made it worse. Why was she grilling man like this? Then I thought, you know what, fuck it, if she wants to know then that's on her, I'll be real and if she wants to bounce, that's her problem.

Are you uncomfortable, Marcus?

Not uncomfortable but I'm just thinking.

We don't have to talk about it, don't worry.

Nah, I don't mind.

It's fine. It's your business. I shouldn't pry.

What do you mean?

I mean it's your business.

So you don't care?

That's not what I'm saying.

Then what?

Marcus, are you being serious?

What do you mean am I being serious?

Okay, you're making this a bigger deal than it is.

What's a big deal?

Nothing is a big deal. That's what I'm trying to say.

So you don't care about the coke?

Care in what sense?

You don't care if I do it?

Right now? Not really. But later on, like I said, maybe.

In the future?

Yes, Marcus, in the future.

I feel like you're trying to say you don't care for man right now.

Marcus.

Stop saying my name like that.

Why you getting defensive?

How am I getting defensive? You're the one saying you don't care what I do.

Oh my God. Okay, I care.

Nah, forget it.

Why is this such a big deal?

Nah, because I feel like we're feeling each other and then you—

And then I what?

See what I'm saying, now you're getting defensive.

Marcus, are you alright?

The waiter came over with the food, perfect timing because I was about to start saying some mad shit and I knew I shouldn't but when that feeling comes, I swear it's like my body just takes control and leaves man standing there. Like, I'll just be watching myself moving mad, the room getting bigger and smaller like say an eye was watching and dilating back and forth or whatever and then I start saying things I don't even mean, like say it wasn't actually happening, like say the real world had just dropped man out, but then it's also like the only thing I can do is try anything to climb back into reality again, my body or whatever, saying anything. Listen, it's so hard to explain, but in the end I just have to firm it, let the world do its own thing for a while until it's all forgotten, dashed away until the next time I remember this moment and it's happening all over again. Now I couldn't even go toilet to calm down because I knew she was thinking man was some coke head. I closed my eyes and listened, listened to my man putting the food down on the table, moving the hookahs for space, saying something I don't even know what, then listened to his footsteps walk away, 8 until I couldn't hear them any more. Aight, I was good. Not good, but I wasn't about to start telling her about herself.

Marcus, are you okay?

Yeah, yeah, I'm fine. Sorry. Listen, I wasn't tryna be rude. Just a long fucking day. I was gonna go straight home to sleep but wanted to see you so I'm still a bit tired.

It's okay. You want to go to the toilet?

No? What you trying to say?

I'm just saying. You do you. I'm not judging.

Nah, I'm good thanks.

But seriously, how often do you do it?

Do what?

You know what?

I dunno, few times a week.

I see. How do you contain the energy?

Energy?

Yes. Or maybe not even energy but you always seem to have this vibe, like you're having a good time? Actually, sometimes it's like you're looking for something that no one else can see. Like you're scared, maybe?

Scared of what?

I don't know, Marcus, it's just an example.

Of what, though?

You know what, it doesn't matter.

Nah, nah, it's cool. I think that's just me.

Okay, if you say so.

Trust me.

Alright.

So anything else you want to ask me?

Nope.

You sure?

Yup.

Nah, go on, I know you're curious.

Not really. If you say it's only sometimes, well, a few times a week, I dunno, is that a lot?

Not really.

Well then.

It's mad how it all started, though.

Isit?

Yeah, crazy story.

I can imagine.

Yeah, you don't want to know?

Sounds like you want to tell me.

What?

Nothing.

Why you being so rude, I don't get it.

I'm not trying to be rude, Marcus, but this isn't really a normal conversation for me.

Yeah, it's not normal for me either, but I'm just trying to be real with you.

Right, okay.

Nah, forget it.

I'm sorry, I'm willing to listen. I'm tired too. I just don't want you to feel like you have to tell me.

I don't feel like I have to do anything.

Well then.

So you wanna hear it or nah?

Yeah, sure, I want to know.

You sure?

Yes, Marcus. It better be a good story.

I haven't told anyone else this story.

So I'm the first person?

Yeah.

Why?

What do you mean?

Nothing. Tell me. I'm listening.

Aight, hold up, let me get one more drink. And just go toilet quickly.

Twenty-Five

So, my dad was dying again, that seemed to be what held together the message from my mum, what I'd seen of it so far, anyway. I was sitting in my dorm, flicking through unsaved numbers of family, friends who had fallen away, squeezing my phone as tightly as I could when I got to a number or series of messages I wanted to remove but needed for recall. I tapped my phone against my head, put it down. Put it in my mouth to bite down and then held it between my teeth for 8 seconds before spitting it onto my floor and replacing it with another pill. My family wanted me close to him, I knew, because they believed I could help change him, bring him back or push him forward, I'd never really known. But still, all voices seemed to converge to convey something solid, warm, a golden consistency they hoped to stay surrounding our selves, the richness of our origins closing in on us. But it wasn't true. I could see through the fabric and only one man sat on the stool: my dad. This was one reason for my distance, my coldness. But couldn't I listen to him talk, they asked, now that I'm okay myself? I know how it began, why they began to look for me, my aunt had told me, recalled it like a story, told me how my mum had returned home early from work, left when her students did, could plan her classes from home. She'd crept through the back gate, slowly stepped through the kitchen and then hesitated, paused, listening, imagining, a student, her favourite, finally reading aloud to themselves in the absence of an audience. My mum was home and he was awake, unaware, like child left alone babbling on its back, but heard from the other side, through a wall or breach, heard turning his words on himself, recalling and repeating something his mother had said to him when he was a boy maybe, in Twi, in Ga, in Fante, in Ewe, but without love, without narrative, without balance, silenced only when he emptied his glass, a clash from trembling hands just as it was refilled. Waiting behind the door, my mum considered consoling him by finding her own glass, sharing the escape on her early return, but she knew her limits, thought of mine and knew they were beyond hers, still young, still resilient, still strong enough to pull myself and others I loved away from a knife's edge, away from the bluff. But really, she had no idea. I needed to focus, focus if I wanted to graduate, needed to see death as the distraction, needed motion if I wanted to write, if I wanted to publish something one day, earn out my position, whichever route my turns of phrase would take me. I knew my dad would hold on until I could see him. And my mum would never think of taking his bottles, his medication, or his hope of both, so it was likely he'd outlive us all, if my dad was to be believed, anyway. And why not? Kweku, our very own descendant of Anansi, reincarnated, or the same life so long lived that fog enfolded everything but the last 60 years. I'd heard the slurred stories time and again, I could recall many without his body of lies or could embellish them myself, never hesitating over a word or emphasis or inflection or life lesson he'd failed to learn himself. Alone, like I was now, caught in a nostalgic loop and reciting his stories to myself in a whisper with my eyes closed, I often noticed I became someone else, someone I'd thought buried. But I tolerated him as he passed through now and again, regaling in hooded regalia, a griot of the estate in gilded garb. But not like him. Not like my dad. I would see him, I decided, before he died, a few weeks from now, and a few more times in the coming years, I was sure. So even with the obvious essence of storytelling in the text, there was a reason for it, some obscure candour in the deceit. I wouldn't call or respond, I'd just show up, expecting something between life and death. How can I die, Kwesi, eh, Kweku? he'd say, It can't touch me and you too, it can't touch you, I put my mouth on it. Imagine, my dad believed he could fend off something ephemeral and eternal but still I, inheriting so much from him, I was told by my mum, feared death to a point of anxiety grasping at psychosis, unable to even leave my house for fear of the delusion that a hand might reach out from the sky and crush me. My rational thoughts were of aneurysms or heart attacks, strokes and sudden death syndrome. I'd teased my own risks when I was younger, more reckless, desperately trying to distract myself. One way then, another now, though I guess less effective but more reflective at times.

I'd never even thought about dying until I was 8, I think, a year after I'd passed from one childhood in care to another without much control. I remember, North London, I had run outside to play, and without looking either way, crossed the road to the grassy roundabout, almost being hit by a car and only turning around when I heard the words *black cunt* being shouted into the air. My mum was stood on the doorstep watching me as if somewhere else her son's body had bounced off that car, turning not only his bones, but also her heart, to pieces. She didn't tell me off, not at the time, so I held onto that naive hope, that lie I became so familiar with in care, that our bond was one of love and trust and that no light could escape it. But we're all capable of despicable things, the danger is in how we hide it, so hours after my near death, as my dad sucked the soup from his fingers, sitting to the side of me, and together we watched *Terminator 2* or *Demolition Man*, my mum sitting silent in an adjacent chair, I feared nothing. Up until this point, my dad's tenderness, those bursts from his indifference, I measured by how closely he watched my mother as she moved around, searching, a school shoe or steel toe in her hand, how he'd recoil then rise at my mum's attempts to kill a spider. *This small spider and you're using such a shoe for it?* Even flies, as they flew around his meals, were just brushed away without much thought or force and ushered through an open window when his food had settled and he was ready to get onto his feet. If my dad noticed the insect first, he would put his hand beside or beneath it and wait for it to move, then scoop it into his free palm, closing his fist, leaving just enough space for life, and let it out onto the grass in our back garden, talking me through it, building to a story. Something so small in his grasp, all he'd have to do was close up completely, tighten his fist as he did when he approached me.

That evening, my mum didn't move. But I crawled backwards. *So you want to kill yourself running from this house?* His other hand was open and I could see his weight shifting from one leg to another: he was deciding how much he wanted to hurt me, not if he should. I knew it and waited. I could have run but I wanted to feel it. I had never been hurt before, no bumps or broken arms, though I sometimes wished I had, with that childish desire to be cared for in the way the injured or helpless are. The way I saw myself was not as the world did. Before my dad could follow through there was banging on the door. Whoever it was didn't use the knocker or post flap, they were using the flat side of their fist. My mum stayed still and my dad went to look through the peep hole. If you move, you'll see, he said to me, and closed the living room door. Muffled words, urgency and the front door closing. Next time you want to die, I'll kill you, you'll see, he said, and then went to the back door, put on his steel-toe boots and left the house. From then on, knowing I'd done something wrong, potentially wrong, I'd lay in bed, waiting for my dad to come in and kill me, counting the steps that were more him scraping himself forward, listening closely, waiting for an argument break out and to hear him beating my mother to death. What would come after? Could he beat me to near death, care for me, make me whole, only to do it again? Our circular narrative? How much could I survive? I wanted to know but never would, often thought to provoke him but couldn't. Death would happen one day, I knew it, and I would be carried through to eternity, a concept I eventually came to realise was more paralysing than the death itself. Eternal abandonment as the world receded from life. But it wouldn't be my dad, I knew, so what would it be, what couldn't I see? Death, it would find me eventually, fixed, unfortunate that some things had to happen, I thought, must happen, but they didn't have to happen at a time specified by the many hands of a blind watchmaker, no. I could control the variables, even though the outcome was inevitable. I could hide until the world became intangible, and then finally accept the approach, the fall, witnessed from any distance of the encroaching desert. Obsessive thoughts, questions such as these took hold for a while and kept me from conceding time and change until I moved out of my house and in with my cousins, where I no longer grasped at my spirit and split open a new aspect of my personality, the internality of home giving way to a protective animation, a phase I often forget I had.

Now I was pacing my room, 4 steps up and down the side of my bed, stopping at times to hold my hand in front of my face to watch for its weakness. It had been 30 minutes. I put the back of my hand against the radiator and tried to resettle its coolness to my forehead, wiping away the sweat as I did so. I took the envelope from my drawer again and reached in like my hand would come up with gold, and then I counted, adding things up. The benzos were slow. I was only a few hours late, waiting for one effect to withdraw while another slowly arrived, but the absence was making itself known and I'd heard stories of collapse or rapid onset of psychosis. Fuck. Usually I would clock watch, mark time when something perceptively small began to create change inside of me, but I'd been invited to a drink up at Gloria's, to celebrate the success of speed dating, though that was weeks ago, or days ago, I wasn't sure, but today time was creeping up noticeably. I did like Gloria, she was president of the University of Manchester's ACS, organiser of freshers' events, who'd also invited me to Thorpe Park, though I was still unsure if I'd go. ACS for her, as she'd told me once, was a way to develop the Pan-African Society, which was a lot smaller and whose events were taken less seriously. I'd soon make my way there, but for now I was walking up and down my room, waiting for something tranquil and trying to will myself to let things go. The thicker white pills from the night before were like a barrier, dissolving slowly, faster with anxiety or enough fibre but my diet wasn't what it used to be and the encroaching calming effect of everything else I'd taken moments ago meant for now disquiet was unlikely. I tried watching porn to stimulate things, felt something rumbling with my latent religious guilt, but not enough. Fuck. I couldn't risk going and then needing to find a bathroom. A group of people would most definitely turn my stomach, and what if San was there and saw me walk in, counted the minutes until I walked out? But why would she do that to me? Just to embarrass me? And what if . . . what . . . And there it was. I power walked to the shared toilet, sat down, up straight, heels off the floor and waited, relieved.

Nineteen

This was when I used to smoke weed, though. Obviously, I don't smoke no more, I'll have a cigarette now and then, but not really. First cigarette I smoked I was like 4 years old! Mad story. But yeah, when I used to bun, it'd be me, my cousins Stephen, Mensah, Victor and couple other man from the avenue. At the end of one of the lanes you could climb over the fence and there was this garden there that no one used. I think you used to be able to use it, probably before all us man moved in, but they blocked it off for some reason. Anyway, that's where we'd chill and smoke. I even think Stephen used to go there on his ones and bun all day without telling anyone. If you didn't know him, like if you'd never chilled with him before, you'd think he was always chatting to himself, having some deep convo and getting vex cah he was losing some argument, but nah, he was trying to remember lyrics. He spat a little bit. And had actually been on a couple all-star riddems so certain people knew who he was but I know say they thought he was a weirdo. One thing I didn't get about him was that he would spit the same 16 bars on radio but he was always writing and chatting new lyrics to himself. He was the tallest one in the family and everyone hated getting into beef with him. Not because he was the strongest, that was probably me, I won't lie, because of gym and that, but Stephen had some bony knuckles so when he punched you, that shit fucking hurt. When we were youts I was shook of him and if we were fighting, I'd be the one to run in the toilet and hide and he'd try kick the door in. But one time when he came to boot the door down I just opened it and stood there looking at him like what, come then? He didn't do nothing. After that I started chilling with him more than Renner, our other cousin, who was always in his room playing PlayStation or Xbox, basically any game that was online with his little headset. Renner was probably the calmest out of all of us and I know he was looking to move out after police buss through the door and handcuffed him and he couldn't play Xbox until they finished searching the crib for whatever. They never even found anything so Renner flipping out after they'd left didn't really make sense, but it's the first time I'd ever seen him vex like that, saying he knows say there was weed in the house even though feds didn't find anything. He wasn't on any of that stuff, shotting or smoking, but my man could drink, and I never saw him sick. Like ever, not just off alcohol, any typa sickness. But yeah, Stephen picked up and we were sitting in that garden in some circular seats like one canary cage with a side of it missing. I was lean. I must have been falling in and out of sleep when Stephen poked me. I hopped up like rah, who's touching me and they all started bussing up. I must have sat down again and the zoot came back to me and I took a draw and started dozing again. One thing them man said about me was that I inhaled too much. This was one reason they never let me spark it, they'll be nothing left after two draw. Stephen poked me again and this time when I stood up, the world looked different. Listen, it looked like I was in another universe, or felt like that, I don't even know how I felt it but I just knew something was off, like I was fading and fighting to stay in the world, or like I was in some invisible bubble and couldn't really touch anything, like man was being punished and cut off from existence or something. So I thought fuck this and started running home, jumped over the back fence and could hear the mandem laughing behind me except Stephen, he was calling my name. I sprinted up the street but all now I couldn't feel my body, I swear I was just looking at it while it was running up the road, like I didn't even care it was mine but then I'd be back into it and shaking like my body was trying to push my spirit out of it again. It was nuts. I could actually feel everything about my stomach as well. All the weed I'd smoked when I'd been with my cousins was in there floating about, like trying to hide something, something inside of me trying get out without being seen, like all the weed I'd smoked finally caught up with me and now I had to deal with it. Once I got to the house I ran into Renner's room and spun him around on his chair and I was like, bro, I'm dying, you gotta save me. This guy actually turned off his game and put his hands on my arms and sat me down on the bed.

Marcus, you're high.

I'm not, I'm not, I'm dying, Stephen put crack in the spliff.

Marcus, man, listen to what I'm saying.

Renner, I swear to God. Tell God I'm sorry, I didn't mean to.

Marcus, man! Relax. Lay down, try and sleep.

Are you sure?

Yes, man. This has happened to me before, it'll go away when you sleep.

I respected Renner a lot for that. Even though I weren't chilling with him like I used to when we were younger, he still had time for man. And trust me, that guy didn't have time for anyone when he was playing on Xbox. He'd even try tell his mum to shhh if she came in talking to him about anything and he was playing *Halo*. So I tried to sleep but couldn't, the world was spinning and I felt like something was creeping up behind me, bare slow, just pushing all the fear between us up into my body, one of them scary moments of clocking everything and knowing angels and demons were all around, that if they wanted they could heal or help man but they'd rather torment me instead. I was proper going mad. I got up and told Renner I'd sleep in my room and ran up the second set of stairs, opened my door and lay flat on the bed. Listen to this, and I promise you I'm not lying, the ceiling and the floor came up and dropped down to squash my waist and then next thing I know I needed to go toilet. When I got to the bowl and tried to piss, bro, cum started coming out. I wasn't even hard, how is that even possible?

Marcus, please don't call me bro.
Aight, my bad, sorry.

But yeah, so here I am standing in the bathroom letting all the cum out, shaking my dick like I was pissing. It didn't even feel good. This is when I knew I must be fucked. So I thought fuck it, I gotta tell my auntie. So I ran downstairs to her room and told her everything. Of course she started switching at my cousins, made them give her the rest of the weed and flushed it down the toilet. They were pissed and swore they were never gonna smoke with me again, like man cared, all I knew was something was hiding inside me, behind me, and that my mouth kept getting dry and even after like 4 glasses of water it was still like the moisture wouldn't come back. Anyway, so my auntie called an ambulance. I don't really remember anything more after that, like just flashes of moments where the ambulance people asked me what my phone number was, my next of kin, and, actually, one more thing, and I know you won't believe me, but I swear I saw them talking to someone, like some random guy inside the house, but then I clocked that this was the person who was following me inside my body and I started bugging out again and then they put me in the back of the ambulance and I was shouting at Renner to tell God I'm sorry. I thought I was finished. They gave me some pills and next thing now, my mum is in the hospital with me, crying, and Stephen is sitting near the end of the bed playing his little Nintendo and my dad is standing over me with this half smile on his face like say he couldn't keep it down. Then I closed my eyes and when I opened them again I was in this random house being walked up the stairs by nurses and when I turned around my mum was behind me with bags in her hands and my backpack on her back. Anyway, long story short, I stayed in that place for a few weeks, until the little bits I remembered became whole things again. I remember the day I started thinking straight, felt like myself again. I was sitting in one room with a nurse and she was asking me questions. I don't even know what she asked to make me wake up suddenly like that, but I remember saying, Why you asking me that? And then that was that. Things started going back to normal. A few more weeks now and they were ready to discharge me. First thing I was going to do was go to church. It was Friday and I can't lie, I was actually excited for Sunday, like I wanted to thank God for getting me through that. I needed to change my life, man, I couldn't go through that again. I don't even think I'm explaining properly because it was so weird. Like even when I think about it or I'm telling this story, I still get a bit dizzy. Not like I'm gonna go mad again or anything. I wasn't even mad, I don't know what it was, but I don't think it will happen again that serious. So I left the recovery house. Yeah! That's it. It was called a recovery house. So I left and my cousins were waiting for me, all of them had come to pick me up. That's love, man.

Yo, mad man, what you saying, you buss case, yeah?

Suck out, man.

Sam was driving and talking about one set he had at Flashes that night and how it would be live and we should roll. I wasn't on it. But they kept pushing it, saying gyal have been asking after me like, yo, what's happened to your lil cuz. I know they were chatting shit but I won't lie it gassed me. I wasn't planning to do anything, maybe it'd take my mind off things until Sunday, cut one, two shapes and then leave. Aight, cool, whatever, I said.

Oi, Marcus, you know what's so funny, Stephen said.

What?

Bro, that weed we were smoking.

It was crack?

No, man. Bro, man, low it, I beg you stop saying that. No one made you smoke crack.

Aight, whatever.

Anyway. But, yeah, that spliff, I don't even know where it came from.

What? What you mean, you don't know where it came from?

Listen. I picked up, and I was thinking I'll roll a spliff when I get home, but when I linked you man and before I could get in the yard, I put my hand in my pocket and the spliff was already rolled. I thought I was bugging.

Bro, you obviously already rolled it.

That's what I was thinking but nah, the ting just came out of nowhere. I was like nah, hold on a minute.

You rolled it, man.

Why you getting shook for?

Who's getting shook?

You're getting shook!

Whatever, man.

Ay, cheer up, Marcus, man. Gyal gonna be happy to see you buss case. Nah, on a real, though, I probably did roll it. Not picking up from my man again, though. First time as well and look it's turned Marcus into some madman. I'm joking, man. But foreal, though, there's bare skunk floating about.

Wait, so your cousin bought weed from a stranger and smoked something that he didn't recognise?

Nah, not a stranger like that. Just someone he hadn't picked up from before.

So he knew him, but hadn't tried his weed before?

I think so, yeah.

Hmmm.

What?

Nothing. Carry on.

Aight. You don't go clubbing, do you?

I've been to some places but I wouldn't say I go clubbing.

Okay, so you've heard of Flashes.

Yes, Marcus, I know what Flashes is. I have done my thing before, you know.

Oh, you've done your ting, yeah?

Shut up. I know you think I'm some good girl, and that's fine, but don't think I'm naïve or don't know how the world works.

Rah. Okay, bad gyal, sorry.

Whatever.

Can I finish what I was saying?

Go on.

So yeah, Flashes was ram. As soon as I stepped in, that was it, I felt like going home. Sam was already on the decks and hailing me up so I just thought I'd firm it with some drinks. Sam only does this so people know I'm with him and so it's easier to draw gyal for when he comes off and we'd end up staying there till the rave's done. But I wasn't checking for anyone. I don't even know why I went, because after like half an hour or something it felt like I had fallen back into that madness I'd just come out from, I couldn't hear the music any more or see people's faces, it was just like everyone had become plastic, or smoothed over like clay by one giant hand or whatever, moving around randomly but getting closer and closer to me every time they did. So I looked down and closed my eyes. I swear, I was gonna just drop on the floor and stay there, I didn't even care what people were gonna think because that's the only way how I thought I'd get away of that feeling: laying on the floor with my eyes closed and just waiting. But then someone put his hand under my arm and pulled me out into the garden. I'm still looking down, mind you, listening to the feet coming off the floor like worn-out Velcro on them primary school shoes, and focusing on colours you see sometimes when you shut your eyes really tight. I actually used to do that when I was a yout. It'd be like the world was trying to change colour. Or as well, I'd push the top corners of my eyes in, hold it like that until all these patterns came into my vision then I'd let go and run around the playground. Oi, I actually forgot about all those weird things I used to do as a kid. But anyway, when we reached the garden I could breathe better. It was full of smoke and that, yeah, but whatever was going on inside was choking man more than this. The guy let go of me and said, Yo. I stood up straight and opened my eyes. I must have looked like some lunatic when he finally saw man properly.

You alright?

Yeah, yeah, I'm cool.

You sure?

Yeah, was just feeling a little sick. Safe for that.

It's cool. You looked like you were gonna fall over so I thought lemme just take him outside.

Yeah, I hear you, safe.

It's alright. What happened?

What do you mean?

Why you having a panic attack in the middle of the dance?

Panic attack?

Or whatever. Outta body experience. Whatever happened.

Nah, I told you, I just feel a bit sick. Maybe I drank too much.

You don't smell like alcohol.

So?

Do you want a drink? Maybe it'll make you feel better?

Alright, cool.

What you want?

Gin and tonic.

Not Hennessy?

No.

Alright. Back in a bit.

The garden was usually as busy as inside but it was like everyone had made space for me so I could calm down. I say that, but no one was even looking at me. The people who were outside were either smoking on their ones or on the phone. I think someone was catching a whine in a corner but I weren't preeing like that. I could see faces properly now and my stomach was calmer but I needed to go toilet and let everything out. I looked up and started biting the skin from my lip. I could see the moon. It was close. Like, closer than I'd seen it before, not that I check for it like that, but it looked good. I felt better. Calmer. Sometimes you have those random moments where you realise we're all just living on a rock that's floating about in space. Actually, I think that's the first time I thought about it like that. And it felt good. Almost didn't notice my man back with my drink.

Deep in thought?

Oh, nah, just looking in the sky.

I can see. Here's your drink.

Thanks.

Counting the stars?

Not even.

You know, I feel like you do sometimes.

Feel like what?

Like, sick when I'm around a lot of people. It's almost like everyone starts looking the same, like the world has just switched up on me.

Yeah, yeah! That's kinda how I was feeling, actually.

I know. Okay, so can I tell one way to deal with it?

Yeah, sure.

Okay, so you open your hand like this. Then squeeze it into a fist as tight as you can. Then let it open slowly. And do that as many times as you need to. Or you can use your senses. You know what I'm talking about?

Yeah, smell, taste, hearing and all that.

Yeah. So you can close your eyes and listen to what's happening around you, smell the air, listen to the sounds, think about where you're sitting or standing, the ground beneath your feet. Trust me, it works.

Okay, cool. I'll try it, safe. Whenever I feel sick, yeah?

Whenever you feel sick. And one more thing works. Come.

What?

Come, I'll show you.

Come where?

You'll see. C'mon.

Bro?

C'mon, you'll love it.

Bro, listen, I won't lie, I appreciate your help, yeah, but I'm not on what you're on.

Huh? I'm not on anything. My girl is inside. Relax, man. Or don't come. I'm just trying to help you.

What's inside?

Come see. I promise it'll help.

We walked through the dance floor and I put my head down again, just in case, didn't want anyone else to see me start acting up. It's mad because I'd never even met this guy before but I appreciated what he'd done for man and he was chatting to me like he knew me so I actually didn't think he was on anything like that, like, these days no one really talks to you like that or helps you unless they trying to get something from you, and my man seemed like he was just trying to help me out for true and I rated it, so I thought let's see what else he was saying. There was a room that was basically behind the club and you'd only see the bouncer let certain man pass through there, even when I was with my cousin I couldn't get through and he'd just tell me to chill for a second while he went in and did his thing, leaving man standing outside like them guys who post up outside the toilet while their girl is inside so no man tries moves them when they come out. I always remembered where that back room was because it had some fire alarm light right above it, like some red signal that flashed sometimes when people walked underneath it. I'd never preed back there properly, but I knew it had no dance floor and the bar was bare small, but you didn't have to queue because there was hardly anyone in there, bare dark with some nice air con, like say the air was fresher than just standing outside. It was basically just a place to jam in peace and talk without having to shout in each other's faces, but yeah, only certain people could go back there. But listen, we walked right to the back and sat down, so far in to the point where I couldn't even see the bouncers any more, so obviously they couldn't pree us either, but you couldn't really see anyone, bare dark like you could be anywhere and not even clock. I can't lie, at this point I started feeling a bit shook because the way people were moving out this guy's way when we were walking back there, yeah, I was thinking, nah, who is this guy? And I needed to go toilet.

Okay, look, don't panic, he said. Then next thing man pulled out his wallet from his pocket, took out two cards and then a little bag from where you keep the notes. Obviously, I knew what it was, but I'd never seen anyone do all this in front of me before. He crushed up the coke with one card and then split it into lines. Then he pulled one piece of straw out of nowhere, them straws that have those lined patterns on them, out of nowhere man draws this straw and then does one line of coke like he didn't even inhale it. Then he offered it to me. Bruh.

Make sure you cover one nostril and then breathe in hard with the open one. Got it?

Nah, I'm good you know.

Are you, though?

Yeah, bro.

To be honest with you, Marcus, you didn't look fine 5 minutes ago.

Yeah, but this is all a bit mad for me. I aint trying to do any of this stuff any more.

What stuff?

I'm going church on Sunday, bro.

Church? Why?

Because I feel to.

Why, what happened?

Nothing happened.

So you've come to a club on Friday night, but going church on Sunday?

Yeah, and what?

Nothing wrong with that I guess. Then there's nothing wrong with doing this and then going church too. Trust me, it'll make you feel better.

I'm hearing you, but this is a bit too mad for me. I dunno, bro.

Yes you do.

Nah, bro, I dunno.

Why? Tell me what happened, then, and I'll understand.

Nah.

Then try it. Look, better now than any other time. It's safe here. Got people around you who know what they're doing, come on. You know how you felt earlier, like your reality didn't feel real or whatever, this is the complete opposite.

I dunno, bro. This is all a bit mad. Like, I hear you, I hear what you're saying, but I dunno.

Look, if you don't feel better, I'll buy you a bottle of something, whatever you want?

You know what, you see one thing about me, I can always tell when there's something mad going on in person's head, like, most people are shook because the way a person is moving means their thoughts must be even madder, and it's peak because we can't see those thoughts. I don't know why but it's different for me, like, when someone seems calm, I notice small things that show me what's going on in their head. People acting crazy never phased me, it's them quiet ones that are loud. I can see them trying to hide something and that's what starts making man nervous. And this guy was giving me those vibes. His finger was tapping his leg at the same time as he was blinking and man was blinking like say he was forcing it, not like it was just happening by itself. And even though my family was here, I really wasn't on anything like that, no energy, honestly. Obviously it was my fault for following my man through. I looked around again but I couldn't see anything, nowhere to quickly run or shout for someone. So I just thought, fuck it, lemme do this and man will probably go back to his girl thinking he got a new customer and then

I can finally go toilet. So I did it. Then sat down. He told me to chill, sit back, take a moment, let it hit. And, bro, listen, I'm not gonna lie to you, I actually felt better. Nah, a lot better, I was actually like rah, and I think I even said it out loud because the next thing man was like:

Yeah, exactly.

Oi, I'm not gonna lie, that's actually—

I told you.

At first I didn't feel anything, but, yeah, aight, I hear you.

Yup.

Lemme do one more.

Go ahead

Safe, bro.

Cool . . .

Shit tingles.

And so . . . bad begins and worse remains behind. Alright, calm down. Tek time.

Tek time?

Look, we can chill here and do the rest of the bag if you want, but just take it easy.

Wait, but what about the bouncer? Does he know wagwan?

Don't worry about the bouncer. I've got him.

Aight, cool. Yeah, cool, but lemme go toilet first.

When I come out the toilet cubicle I remember standing in front of the mirror trying to see my face, but someone left the hot tap on and there was too much steam, so I tried to wipe it but it was like it was dirty underneath as well, so I just thought, forget it, and went back out to my man. Listen, I don't even know how much coke we did but the night was live and couple girls joined us, I remember one of them, her name was Belina and she was the most on it. Not on me, on the coke. I think I went to bed at like 6 a.m. that day, or the next day, still with this Belina as well, but when I woke up she'd bounced, like, I know I could even ask myself was the night real, was she even real, but she left man her number and a note saying, *Come find me when you wake up*. I don't think we beat, though, just stayed up doing more of the coke my man gave us and drinking gin. She's cool people, actually, she musta said she was in care too and I was like swear down and we just vibed after that. But yeah, I took the guy's number and from then whenever I felt like I might be getting that feeling, I picked up a like a gram from one of his boys. Just to make sure. No one knows what it's like to feel like that, trust me, it's like you're mad but you know it, like, you know how they say people who are going mad don't know they're going mad? Yeah, exactly.

I see.

I know. I know. But you know what, I'm not gonna lie, while we've been talking, I aint felt like that.

Like what? I can't believe someone just gave you cocaine like that. And why did you take it?

Like having that feeling come over me. I feel calm. And nah, it's not even like that, he was just trying to help. And at the end of the day, not being rude or anything, but you don't know what it's like when you just suddenly feel like the world is not real. Or you're not real or whatever, like nothing makes sense, don't even know why you're alive, or how. It's hard to explain.

Trying to help, you know. I'm not sure that's trying to help, Marcus, but fair enough. Only you know, I guess. And so this happens often, then?

What does?

That way of seeing the world.

Oh, yeah, yeah. The thing is I think it's actually bare different feelings mixing together but it feels like they're the same. Something like that, anyway. But I'm saying, I don't feel like that now.

Isit?

Yes. You're actually calm so more time when I'm around you I don't feel like that.

Since when, though? Like when we first met?

Aight, not as soon as we met, I won't lie, but I knew quickly, still, clocked you had potential to make man feel normal, get me, make me feel like everything was real because you were chatting to me. I dunno, man, why you asking me this?

You're actually funny, Marcus.

Am I?

Yeah.

Nah, I'm just weird.

I'll work you out.

Oh, swear down? Okay. Not exactly sure what you're saying, but I hear it.

You're just different. Not in a bad way. You see the world in a unique way, that's all. I know you feel like it's like, what, an illness or something? But I just think you're unique.

Nah, not even, I think I'm just a bit weird. I'm not ill, though, not now.

Yeah, you are a bit weird, but so what? And the drugs?

Trust me, it's not that serious.

So you could stop?

Yeah, obviously, c'mon now. I know you're thinking I'm some kind of—

Interrupting because no. I'm just asking questions.

Alright, cool. Cool.

So have you and Anton ever done drugs together before?

No. Why you asking me that?

You two seem close, that's all.

Not that close. He's cool, though, like, I could chill with him outside gym but I don't really see him. I don't even know where man lives. And how you know he's even on that?

We talk a lot.

Dodging exercises you mean, I see you, you guys think you're bare smart.

So do personal trainers. I know I don't need 3 sessions a week.

You know what, fair. You know he's got a family, though, yeah?

Yes, Marcus, I know.

Aight.

I do find you interesting, though.

I find you interesting as well. So what we saying, then?

We'll see.

Twenty-Five

Gloria said she'd come down and get me, the way to her flat being complicated. I was sitting in the lobby area watching the numbers above the lift, waiting for them to change so I could figure out which floor she lived on, looking away whenever it stopped on numbers that unsettled me. Apparently these were the expensive flats and this seating area was supposed to be the first flash of cash, but Martlesham in Broadwater Farm had a similar foyer, only without the sofa to sit on and maybe a couple of Ghanaian girls huddled together getting licked off K cider. I tucked my jumper into my tracksuit bottoms and pulled the sleeves over my fingers as I sat down. I knew there were a lot of students who flew in and out of their dorms on a regular and no matter how much wealth you came from, you couldn't pay off the possibility of bed bugs, bites that could get infected. I also pulled my hood over my head and tightened the strings to close up my face. I felt like a child doing this, but also felt safe, as I did when I slept, with sheets pulled over my head and a small opening for me to breathe. Air felt more life-affirming when it was harder to obtain. I'd fall asleep in this way, but wake up on my back. I sometimes thought I would die like this, my face to the ceiling, an undiagnosed case of severe sleep apnoea. But then, I thought I would die every way. And maybe I did, or had. I wondered how my dad thought he would die, probably from some novel complication, a slow resistance to life that those caring for him had never seen before, bearing witness as he died with a tale on his stale tongue, ready to regale the adventure in the next life . . . Or maybe an overdose of his painkillers and sleeping pills, but I thought that unlikely, remembering the way he once stood over me, half smiling, with my mother's cries behind him, that sound and look on his face coming together as though he were failing to contain a laugh leaving through the faintest gap in the corner of his mouth. I know he saw suicide and cracked up, as if it were a folly for man to think they could leave this world on their own terms, as if he knew what none of us could ever understand, that the way you entered the world would be the way you left it, waiting on the blessing of someone whose hands touched you with their indifference. And then there was my foster mother, who had alluded to the thought of my death making her think about hers, and because of that, she decided to quit smoking. But I saw her as still in decline, still in pain, stumbling around her fading world, and for a time I watched her efforts to cry, the start and stalling in the folds of her aging face. Grief is by its nature incomplete, so her faltering tears were part of the process, I guessed.

A bell rang and the elevator doors opened. I looked at the numbers instinctively before noticing who was coming to get me. I'd missed the floor she'd come from and felt the heat beneath my skin, a part of me trying to step out to avoid the cataclysm I'd suffused with the digits of my thoughts. Quickly, I extended my hand down my leg and tapped my calf 4 times – the floor I guessed Gloria lived on – and then felt the equilibrium of an obsession appeased, with more placation if I was wrong, a number of taps easily multiplied to reach the correct floor.

Marcus?

Everything calculated, I stood up and said yeah. It was San. A part of me knew it would be, porcelain and polished, she didn't recognise me and before I said anything I counted her braids again, 4, thicker, meaning maybe she undid her fringe when she was home, going to bed, and didn't care for how it looked when she secured it again the next day as long as it covered her forehead. I felt sad thinking of it. I wished I could see her laying with those braids pulled back, or loose, down one side of her face, or stretched out from her roots to mine like a painless seam. I'd pull each one through my fingers like the feathers I plucked from the wind as a child.

Yeah?

Gloria is hosting so asked if I'd pick you up. Show you the way up, I mean.

Oh, cool.

She was standing with one foot inside the lift, and I wondered how long I'd been standing there just looking at her, with the concierge looking at us both, clearly irritated by our means of keeping the lift open. I walked over and into it, turning my shoulder to make sure nothing of me disrupted anything of her. She let the door close and pushed the number '8'.

★

It was a maze. Felt as if we passed through the same corridor several times. I started to think we were lost, that she'd got us lost, even though she never looked back, never saw me glimpse behind 4 times, feeling certain I saw the same sequence of numbers every time. But through a few more double doors I began to hear the voices, faint but finding footing. Finally, San said, and turned to walk through an entrance on our right. I closed my eyes so I couldn't see what number it was and was soon swallowed by the hopeful vocals of organised chaos.

Marcus!

Hey.

You made it. Aww, I'm so happy to see you. I thought you wouldn't come.

Almost.

It's because you love me, I know. Are you coming Thorpe Park? Come meet everyone.

We walked through a crowded hallway and into the living room. The first thing I saw was my boy Efe standing on a table, hunched a little and blowing smoke out a tiny top window like he was proud to be able to participate with the dying clouds, saw his smile as he turned to see me, a hand left halfway out into the twilight as he used the other to point at me over the disperse heads and then put his index and thumb to his lips. I shook my head as I always did and dropped my tongue to mouth the word, Nah. I rubbed my hand down my jeans pocket. San was already ahead of us, and as I turned away, just as I turned away, she fell into the lap of someone I hadn't seen before, fell in a way where the ground became an afterthought, I became an afterthought. I felt the impulse to look back, turn on the tiptoes of my worn-down soles. I blinked 4 times, then 8, as Gloria was telling people who I was, which uni I went to and how one day they should read my writing, if only for my imagination. But I wasn't there, read the room as formless external noise, but knew I said what was expected of me and smiled when a silence suggested it.

I think we met at a showing of *Hidden Colors*. You remember that, Marcus?

Yeah, I remember.

At the end everyone was like nah, they don't believe it. They thought everyone on the documentary was chatting shit and I'm sure you and I were the only ones defending it, right?

Yeah, I remember.

Then out of nowhere Marcus must have dropped some bar and that's when I knew, I thought, yeah, I fuck with this guy, this is my brother. What was it you said, again?

I said even if some . . . Wait, sorry, one second, 1, 2, 3, 4.

Marcus, are you counting?

Sorry, sorry, one sec, I'm just thinking, 5, 6, 7, 8. Yeah, erm, basically I said even if some, yeah, sorry, even if some of our past is fabricated that doesn't mean all of it is. When something is hidden you only find it by creating multiple routes, some lead nowhere but one will eventually get you where you need to be.

Man said it word for word, you know, someone else said.

Of course he did, Gloria replied. Probably had to school people like you so many times, with your flat headback.

It was rote, it was true, I'd probably read it somewhere and memorised it for moments like this. But right now, it didn't matter. None of this mattered. I was only thinking, or, abstractly feeling, one path, one recall, to a moment years ago, decades, a moment held with care, when we were all children. I felt the pull so intensely I had to sit down and focus on the thought and emotion so I could relive it a few times and then let it pass. I told Gloria I felt a bit dizzy and needed to sit down. She brought me some water and I leaned forward, put my head on my folded arms and replayed what I knew I needed to see.

Nineteen

You cracked it, mate, Anton said.

You think so?

She won't stop banging on about you.

Dun know.

Yeah, good for you, you cunt, not for me who's gotta listen to it. What did you fucking do to her?

Me? Bro, we just went on a couple dates.

Yeah, alright, mate. Don't fuck it up or you've just lost me a client.

Ah, shut up, man.

Fucking bell end.

After that second date, that was it. I was garn, wrapped, loved up like say you could drop me and I'd be floating not falling. We had to have couple agreements, though, before we could take it to the next level. And that was calm with me because more time when I was with her or thinking about her, I didn't really feel like doing them tings there. Obviously when I went out, or if for no reason things got too mad in my head and I felt like something terrible was coming, I'd do maybe one or two lines, but that's a minor, an emergency, because what could happen would be worse and I knew Adwoa weren't looking to come check me in that recovery place or see me on road like a nitty. Only thing I needed from her was to tell me whenever she was getting bored or I was becoming annoying and we'd take a break or something, but other than that, bless, bliss, even. Listen, I'm not really a phone guy but she'd have me chatting down the line to her for hours, even when I had to be up at like 4.30 a.m. for a 6 a.m. client. I never used to move like that, but watch me now coming into work and actually drinking coffee because I couldn't even see properly. Sometimes I'd shower the night before and just go straight to the gym in the morning, Lynx under my armpits and boom. Champions pour at 10 p.m. the night before and then one, two splashes on my face at 4 a.m. Imagine, some of my clients told me how good I smelled in the morning. They never knew I was turning all night so what they were actually smelling was man's stress sweating it out from held-back dreams. But true say them office types thrive on that kinda thing. One of my biggest issues, though, one of the most annoying things, was that for some reason when I knew I had to get up early it suddenly became impossible for me to sleep. No matter what. I tried them teas, promethazine tablets, even tried to get some sleeping pills from my GP but he wasn't having it. But if I was on the phone to Adwoa, I'd start dozing off. Not that she was boring. I think it was a comfort thing, still. So sometimes I'd call her on purpose just to get to sleep but she hated it because of course she wanted to chat bout stuff, tell me again how her dad was a wasteman or how much she hated working in marketing or loved going swimming and wanted to do more of it, or tell me something she'd suddenly deeped from her bible, a verse or chapter that suddenly made sense. But anyway, yeah, Adwoa would be chatting and I'd start falling asleep and this girl would start pressing buttons on the phone to get me to wake up or hang up and start calling again and then ask me about the last thing she said while I was trying to act like I wasn't sleeping. When you're about to drop sleep and someone is chatting to you, you start saying some random shit, bruv, chatting the most shit, like half in a dream, just random nonsense and I don't know why but Adwoa recorded me one time. I don't remember it but I know it was a time when I was proper tired from gym, one of them ones where my last client came through at like 9.15 when the gym supposed to close at 10, and I stepped into my room past Kane, who was sitting on the floor by my door waiting for me to get back from work so he could chill in my room with his headphones on doing his thing. No one was really checking for him like that because he didn't speak much and sometimes you'd catch him nodding his head even when he didn't have headphones on. But I rated him, still, so he'd be in the corner opposite my bed with the laptop glow on his face like say he was communing with some spirits or something, and then I'd get on the phone to Adwoa, ready for bed. It was defo one of these times that she recorded me because on my phone you could see I fell asleep like 10 minutes after I called her, and when you listened to the recording back it was like I was chatting to someone even though what I was saying wasn't making sense, but it's like the words had a target, get me, so Kane must have been in my room just watching me. I even thought I'd be saying something funny but nah, there was silence for like 15 seconds and then I said, basically mumbling, We have to turn the wheel, have you turned the wheel, we have to, and that was it. I didn't even try to analyse it, I was just like, swear down? And kept it moving. Apparently, though, there were other times when I'd mention my dad or some shit like that, but Adwoa never recorded those times so who even knows. But this is what started Adwoa going on about meeting my fam. Not as an introduction but just in passing, like a quick hello or something. But even that was a lot. So I just kept brushing it off like, yeah, soon, soon. Was I asking to meet her parents or people? I just wanted to enjoy these times rather than feel some pressure about moving forward. Why don't people like to just jam where they are? Every day we're moving forward and we don't even have a choice, just wake up and boom. So come we just chill for a bit? During these times my training was falling off because I was working out with her and she couldn't really spot man for what I needed to lift so I'd drop weight. I didn't lose too much muscle but I could tell I looked different whenever I'd watch myself in the mirror, but my eating was still decent and I kept my clients and P's up, I'd count it before each of our training sessions and then if I knew there was some extra P's that I needed to get rid of I'd tell her I'd booked somewhere for us to munch. I know Anton was a little pissed because he thought if she was training with me all the time, then why did she need him, but with me it was more of a spending time together ting rather than looking for progress, though her squat and deadlift went up and I know Anton was preeing when she was hugging me and saying thank you after she deadlift 150kg.

Oi, you cunt.

What, man? Oi, I beg you let me put my pants on before you start.

Was she in the shower with you as well?
What do you want, man?
Just remember who got you her number.
Yeah, yeah.

See Adwoa, she was one of those girls who didn't have to do much to look lean, to have abs, like they would basically just be sitting on her stomach no matter what, she could even back like 8 eclairs and bare of those cones with cream in them every day, or even sit there watching *Heroes* munching digestive biscuits with PG Tips like some auntie and still look like she never missed a class and buss cardio every day. But she was always wearing baggy clothes, more time they weren't even hers, so I was the only one who knew the body was banging like that. I know say if other women had her body they'd be showing it off all day because why not, but for some reason Adwoa moved shy. Nah, wait, actually, not really shy, but I think she thought, why am I showing off my body when I don't need to? I rated it, though, it's not like I told her that's how she should move, never really went into it like that, but probably something to do with her membership at KICC. Different with man, though, obviously. She hated my vests and any time she'd walk past me in the gym and we weren't training together she'd twist my nipple if it was out. She weren't thick from the waist down but she weren't slim either and I can't even say she was somewhere in the middle because that wouldn't make sense either because she was always switching up. Different light or day and the body would change up. It's a weird one. So sometimes she'd look like she could body man, like, when she'd get out the shower and lift the towel to throw over her shoulders her back semi-looked like mine, but then other times there'd be no definition, just soft skin like you could put your hand through it if you wanted to. When we slept downstairs, I'd be lying on her belly, turn around and blow into it. She had one of them laughs that would go on until you could only hear one tiny sound, like a light about to go out and then next thing you know, bare energy behind it again, them laughs that if it was at you you'd start getting heated. True she laughed at me all the time, but you know when guys just act dumb on purpose? That's how I moved sometimes, always trying to hear that laugh. *You're actually an idiot* – the words don't bun when you're trying to draw them out of someone. Her stomach used to dip so deep half my face would be inside her belly when I'd drop one dad joke or the TV made her laugh. I've never really laughed like that, like films and stand up don't really do it for me. I have to create the comedy in my head from something someone has told me. One time, Adwoa must have been walking down a long flight of steps at an underground station, she told me this, and then she slipped and started dropping down them one by one, like bumping up and down and then shouted, Help! Nah, I actually had tears in my eyes imagining that. So every time we went down some stairs I'd hold onto her like, careful now. I think we went to eat at almost every place round her area, as well. Like, every week she had a list of new things to do, some place new to visit, but we had couple places we'd go to on a regular. She lived alone for now because her mum had gone Ghana to do some business or build some house or look after some relative or something I can't even remember, and her dad was somewhere else doing his ting. Not my business really, but I spoke to her mum on the phone couple times because Adwoa was trying to get her to cut out rice, but the way our elders see it, if you aint got rice, you aint got a meal, so I'd give her a few other ways to eat. Not like she'd take my advice, but I knew it was just a way to chat to me and I was cool with that. Adwoa weren't chatting to my mum, though, nope, never that. Annoyingly though she spoke to my dad once. I think she clocked him one time before that, but I managed to style it out. Listen, my man was sleeping on a train platform we stepped onto after finishing one of Adwoa's activities. I know he works a lot and obviously he's tired most the day but he weren't even trying to hide the bottle, like, how can man be 45 and still lost like this? So I quickly switched with Adwoa so she was near the waiting train, nearly stepping on one woman's foot and positioning myself as if I was trying to stop someone pushing Adwoa back onto the carriage. This way I could talk to Adwoa in her face so she wouldn't notice him. But I think she did clock, actually, now I think about it, because she had this look on her face and kept eye contact with me when I was chatting shit to her. The funny thing is, I'm not even embarrassed by him when he's drinking like that, I've been around bare people who drink and throw up and act like the version of them I know is resting while this next version is having fun, so it's a minor. It's when he starts talking and getting into stories, immortality, spiders and death and how he's got venom inside him and all this other shit. And this is what almost happened when he clocked her and she spoke to him. We must have been near my mum's yard now and Adwoa needed to go toilet. We had walked for a bit after we left one restaurant and because I wasn't paying attention properly we ended up in Edmonton. It was like 11 p.m. so I knew my mum would be sleeping but I didn't really know about my dad because he's so unpredictable. But she needed it desperately so I couldn't even lie. It was like 5 mins from where we were. I went in first through the back door to check who was about. My dad was asleep on the sofa and my mum was in her room so I thought I could sneak Adwoa in and out. She listened to me and was quiet, tiptoeing and holding her breath, so it weren't even her fault, but when she flushed the toilet, my dad got up, sat up like someone had pulled a string on his head. I was shook. I was sitting opposite him on the floor with my head in my hands, my chin between my palms basically and my fingers up my face and rubbing my eyes when I heard him moving around. Nah, this was such an annoying situation, I'd been sitting there in the dark watching his movements in case this happened. Nothing I could even do. Adwoa walked out of the kitchen and of course this man stood up rubbing his own eyes, the light from the kitchen behind Adwoa like say it was spilling out of her, so I stood up too and tried to get between them, but hear this one now:

Uncle! You're up.
Ah? What's that? Yes, I'm up? Who is that?
Adwoa, come, man, let's go.
Wait.
Oh my days, man, Adwoa, please.
Hello, Uncle, nice to meet you, I'm Adwoa.
Eiiiiii, Adowa. Akwaaba. You have come.
I have! Thank you, Uncle. How are you?
Ei, Adwoa, makye yɛ me ya paa.
Dad, English.
Oh! Firi hɔ. Adwoa, wɔnte Twi?
I can't speak it but I understand it.
Oh, fine. Heh, Kweku, ente na wɔka nokwerɛ?

Oh my days.

Eh? I thought you were telling tales.

Nah, Dad, low it. We've got to go. Adwoa, come.

Where are you going? Wɔmpese me kasa anaa? Adowa, bra ha, come, sit, let me get you water. Or you like whisky?

No, she doesn't.

Excuse you, Marcus. No, thank you, Uncle, but water is fine.

Oh fine, fine. Ei, makye.

He walked into the kitchen and I didn't care how pissed off Adwoa was gonna to be, I pulled her to the front door, opened it, and we were gone. She took her hand out of mine as soon as we were outside the front gate, but listen, it could have been worse. My dad would probably just think we were part of one of his dreams or something, like, man's always telling us about things that never actually happened, anyway.

Twenty-Five

My earliest years were mostly happy. I had two dads, nowhere to fall without a soft toy to cushion my exhausted drop, lots of brothers and sisters who changed when the weather did, something I thought I was the cause of, because I noticed, when I was upset with one or more of them, a new season started to emerge and they would leave the house and never come back. There were only 3 of us who saw through all 4 shifting skies and went to the local school, practised katas at the community centre and begged our foster mum to let us outside to trick or treat. We watched from the inner curtain, sometimes manoeuvring our heads beneath to reveal our faces lined up in the window like Hallowe'en decorations for the village. My foster mum's hesitation wasn't religious, nor was it a distaste for sugar before bed, sugar that she knew would lie on our gums for days straight as some of us faked the brushes and ran the tap for 88 seconds instead. If my foster mum could shield me from hindsight, I knew she'd drag her favourite living room chair in front of me, torn, separated patterns on the cushions, a single thread in some places seeming to hold it all together, or waiting to be struck like a lone harp string to release the sound of years of her trying to get comfortable before dozing off and leaving us to tuck ourselves into bed. She tried her best. And not allowing us out at night was part of it. She knew smiles on the way to school could be something else under a full moon, maybe someone picking and prodding at our skin to see if we were actually real. To what end she fostered us, we didn't know. Private foster care meant she could charge as she pleased and with so many young black children's chubby palms patting her front door for respite from the threat of deportation, she could have been doing it to support her own children, 5 already now grown if I remember right, 3 working and 2 unable to, the youngest favouring my father with their thirst for chasing blackouts. These thoughts stayed with me as I grew up and began to question the whys of behaviour, the inception of seeing the world through the swaying light of deontology, unable to read what it illuminated but capable enough to draw my own intuitive conclusions. So for a long time, I thought she was wrong, not evil, but wrong, words I never spoke but thought and felt and let become the only way to see it, and so as I grew up without her, features began to change. Forced Christmas visits I saw as a reach for absolution, a gift stolen in the night given back in the presence of artificial light. She seemed older, thinner, where her skin had been delicate before it now seemed easily torn, blue veins atop her hands like living larvae beneath her skin, growing to eat her from the inside out. And what I noticed most was that her hair was no longer round and golden, her bouffant shrinking and fading to a weak hue that suited a life drained. She looked like she was decaying. But there was still life there, kindness, no dulling of the colour of her eyes, which still insinuated compassion. They followed my words when we spoke, looking for a phrase that would free her, something small enough to end the sentence and turn things around, a place where she could interject. But still she listened to all I had to say, gave advice, knew where to draw a line, but tried to relate to what she could sense were lies, or stories – but as my dad would say, Anansi wasn't a liar, he was a storyteller, whose fault was it if someone couldn't tell the difference?

I remember many of the stories my dad told me, about his past life, about me, about the spider himself, details not so distinct with the latter two, but their emotional resonance stayed with me, I guess only to remind me and intensify the moments they existed in, moments that held me like an embrace, but on the face of it the nostalgia kept me encased. One story he told me, on a day he and my mother came to visit me in care, one about Anansi the spider, is one I can recall verbatim, but I think that's because it's interwoven with something else that happened, spun in the same moment.

After I sat listening, rapt, I watched my mum telling a girl between her legs to sit still, her knees keeping the small body in place as her hands worked above her head, a thread in her teeth and another being curled around a puff of hair, turning it into a thin pillar among a few others. The girl was tightening her face then letting it go, with all tension falling from her reflection when another child held a mirror in front of her. She tilted her face upwards to get a better view of what had been woven above her, and from the mirror her eyes lifted to my mother's inverted image, who looked, pulled more thread through her lips and used her free hand to turn the girl's face forward. Round the columns of my mother's legs, the girl curled her arms and brought them closer to her as I bore witness to this biblical reversal of strength, a perversion of what I thought of as stability.

Marcus, are you okay?

It was over. I quickly opened my eyes before the memory could repeat itself and I'd have to go through it again and again. I lifted my head and the light fell over me like a rush of water to wake me from my scorched senses. I blinked only 8 times, soaking up the light and lustre like someone aching to be delivered. I told Gloria I was fine, picked up the water and took two pills from my pocket. Fuck San, and whoever she was with. I didn't look at her for the rest of the night, only drank and took pills until I walked along the walls with the string and sting of tinnitus keeping me up, drank until I had to be put in an Uber and then screamed at to get out of the car when I finally arrived home.

Nineteen

One place we always went when we were hungry but couldn't be bothered to travel too far was this hotel that had one of them proper nice restaurants inside it, like chandeliers and red leather sofas, dusty bookshelves with hench books on them, lifts with one level no one can get to and all that kinda thing, one of them where if you weren't wearing a blazer they look at you funny but even still anyone could just come through and eat or grab drinks and just chill. I always expected to see gym members in there but maybe it was too much P's for even them. They actually had computers in there too that you could come in and use like some old-school internet café. The first time we noticed it we were completely gone, like you know when you're trying to walk together but you're tripping one way and she's buckling a next and it comes like say you're trying to move on from each other but really you're just thinking about getting home and fucking so you find each other again. Like we were actually all over the place, coming from some bar where every time Adwoa and I went to a corner and started licking off each other's necks, you'd see the bouncer appear like from smoke and just be standing there screwing. Anyway, we were both pissed and in one of those moods where every 10 minutes you're telling each other how much you love them and reh reh reh, as if the words were made of gas or something and after 10 minutes the proof of what you said was gone so you gotta hit them with the reminder one more time. In between all that we must have been chatting about the best place to go for our first holiday, can you imagine, last place I'd been was Ghana when I was like 11 years old and I don't even remember the flight so it had to be somewhere close with short flight time, and while we were chatting I must have dropped the same country she was thinking or something, or actually it might have been that my middle finger tickled the right nerve on her palm while we were holding hands, because the way she stopped me in this doorway and kissed me like say we were saying goodbye before I reached my hotel room, penthouse suite before a flight and she wanted to convince man to invite her up. It was a lot. Nah, man, you see that kiss, yeah, only matched by the one she gave me while I was sleeping and I must have woken up looking at her closed eyes above me like say she was going to fall into my body, and I swear it felt like that, like our lips finally found a way through for a moment, like we finally broke the rules and touched. It was mad. But anyway, yeah, this hotel, I didn't know what the rooms were saying but if they were on the same level as the food then I wouldn't even mind paying for a couple nights. So yeah, we must have gone there to munch one day straight after my last gym session, and my client had just paid me in cash and I must have forgotten to pile it up in my locker because I was running late, and so I had all these 20-pound notes floating about in my bag and I didn't even wanna take it off when we sat down at the table. I told Adwoa wagwan and she took the bag from me, put it between her legs, bit her bottom lip and raised her eyebrows at me. I semi smiled and looked away and then heard her push the bag off her chair onto the floor and say, Boo, to herself, I think, in some voice she probably thought wasn't loud enough for me to hear. Listen, I know I'm a bit weird sometimes but so is everyone. What did you say, I asked after. Nothing, she said. Imagine. This was a minor but I swear, sometimes people only act normal when no one is looking. The way I see it is like, who cares, man, do what you feel, be yourself, get me, because when life is done I promise you, people won't remember how normal you were, I swear I've clocked it, it's only the weird things about you that will bring anyone any comfort or whatever because that's how they'll know you aint just some any person, some carboard cut-out of someone who might be sitting next to you one day. Anyway, so I was sitting opposite Adwoa now, feeling semi self-conscious because obviously I looked a bit mash up even though she wasn't dressed up either, and she looked a little sad but that just made me think how much I proper loved this girl and how I wished I could just take her home and just chill and drink Grey Goose cocktails in front of her big-back TV watching *Heroes* or *Mean Girls* or whatever, but I didn't say anything because I knew she loved being out and around people and I think she was starting to think I just wanted to lips and beat all the time but it wasn't even that, I just wanted to be touching her all the time. Man, you see Adwoa, I'm always saying it, but that was my girl foreal. She even knew how to match whatever vibe I was on, because obviously after work I'm not gonna be looking fly or flexing or anything, so why would she, that's how I imagined her thinking, even if we were going to a semi-posh place to eat. I wouldn't mind if she did, though, like I'm not insecure like that, but still I wouldn't wanna be all up on her with my work clothes smelling of other people's intervals and failures on the days when showers were ram and I was running late, my underarm bare sweaty with no Lynx and she's there sparkling, clean, looking like one Diana Ross lookalike or something. Don't get it twisted though, even when she was casual, she still looked fine, sexy even, and in the restaurant I had couple of those moments where I'd pree her and then look around like say I was making sure everyone else had clocked the ting, how banging she looks even without trying. Anyway, we already knew what we wanted to eat and so we gave the waiter our orders as he was bringing us to our table, but this man actually ignored us, gave us the menus, went to chat to some other customers and then came back, like what was the point? Okay, cool, sometimes there are ways you have to do things, but nah, my man took the piss even if he was doing all this because it was part of his ritual. We were just sitting there hungry, like.

How was your day?

It was fine, calm. Nothing really going on. Wagwan for this waiter, though?

Which one? Our one?

Yeah, man. Didn't you see what he done?

We've ordered anyway so it doesn't really matter.

Yeah, but still.

Any new clients?

How you mean, I've always got new clients.

Okay, Mr Motivator.

Mr Motivator you know, fucking hell, what throwback. Shit.

You used to watch him? Was he your inspiration?

No, are you mad? Mr T, maybe, yeah. Remember him?

I do, indeed. He had that haircut. He looks like your dad a little bit.

Yeah. A real G. And no he doesn't, what are you on?

He does! Just maybe a little bit.

If you say so.

Can I ask you something?

Yeah, go on?

I've wanted to ask you this for a little while, actually.

Yeah?

What happened?

What do you mean what happened?

Why don't you like your dad?

Who said I don't like him?

Okay, let me rephrase. How come he gets on your nerves so much?

I'm baffled, because when did I say this?

Okay, let's leave it.

No, I'm not angry or anything. It's just random. He is annoying, yeah, I won't lie, but nothing major happened. Like, he hasn't done anything mad to me.

Right, okay.

Yeah. I think I just grew out of the way he moves, his stories and always wanting to chat or whatever. Plus man drinks too much.

Yeah. African dads.

I mean, yeah, I guess so. But anyway, what about you? What's your day been saying? Sorry, is that all you wanted to ask me?

Yeah, just that. Thanks for answering.

It's cool.

And my day, err, you know, same boring stuff. Same shit, different day. I think I need a new job because I've realised I'm not really happy, not really.

Yeah, I feel you. I'm sorry. You want me to help you look? Should we look when we get back to yours?

Maybe. I'm just thinking about it for now. Nothing serious, but we'll see. How's your mum by the way?

She's cool.

And your cousins?

Just there, init. They seem bless.

Excuse me. Yeah, hi, can you put some more ice in this, please? Thank you. Sorry, your cousins, just there. I get that. I was thinking today, you know so much about me. I've told you more than I tell anyone and I don't regret it or anything like that, but I don't really know much about you.

What do you mean? How? Adwoa, are you serious, you know bare about me. I even told you about certain things on our first date.

Yeah, but it's only surface stuff. I feel like it's stuff you could tell anyone.

Yeah, but I don't say it in the same way I say it to you.

I get that. I'm just saying.

Nah, it's not a big deal. I hear what you're saying. You can ask me anything you want.

Anything?

Yeah, come, I aint really got anything to hide at this point.

I don't think you're hiding anything. I just don't think you offer yourself up to people? And I get it.

Like some sacrifice, you know.

You're so silly. You know what I mean.

Yeah, okay, well ask me, then. Anything.

You sure?

Of course. Go on.

Okay. Well, do you have two people you see as your dad?

Huh. Okay, that's really random. Why?

Because when we talk, you slip up sometimes like you're talking about two different people.

Yeah.

Yeah?

Yeah, I have. Had. I guess that's true.

That's really cool. How come?

Foster care.

You were in foster care?

Yeah, bare people were.

That's not me saying that in a negative way. I just didn't know. Wow.

What's wow?

I mean I just didn't know.

Oh right, yeah. Yeah, foster care. Maybe like 8 years, from when I was like a few months old. It was only supposed to be a few years but my mum left at some point and it was just my dad so I was there longer.

Wow. Are you two still in contact?

Stop saying wow, man. It's not that deep. And my foster dad is dead and I don't really see my foster mum a lot. And obviously you know my mum comes and goes. But me and my foster mum talk now and then. She lives in some village in Norfolk.

Are you satisfied with that?

Yeah, why not?

I'm just asking.

Okay, I hear you.

Aww, Marcus. I love you.

Adwoa, you're actually moving mad, I swear. I didn't live in some basement you know, my life was bless.

Oh my god, you're so dumb. I love you for sharing that.

Okay. I love you too.

Do you?

Yes.

Really?

Yes, man.

In another life would you love me?

Sure.

What if I wasn't human, what about then?

Ah, allow it, man.

I'm just asking!

I'm telling you now this is the most annoying question.

Is it? So you've been asked this before?

All of you ask this same kind of question.

All of us?

You know what I mean, man.

Whatever. Can I continue?

Yes, what?

Don't say *what* like that to me.

Okay, sorry. Go on, I mean.

Thank you, dearest.

Yeah, you're welcome.

Okay, so in another life. Like, imagine I was an insect. No, a beetle or a mantis or an ant! A red ant, the ones who bite. Or wait, a praying mantis.

Yes, I'd still love you. You want another drink?

What if I were a spider? And we couldn't reproduce. Still?

Oh my days, man, seriously?

Answer this last question.

Yes, man, still, I'd love you still. Praying mantis or whatever. Are you finished?

Okay, okay, calm down.

I am calm. It's just annoying sometimes. And I meant are you finished with your drink?

Stop lying, no you didn't.

Nah, honestly.

Anyway, I just wanted to know you love me, that's all. It's nice to be loved in all variations of life.

When we got back to Adwoa's all I wanted to do was sleep, but it was too early for my body and my mind was even racing so I turned on the TV and flicked through Sky movies looking for something boring that might help man drift off before I started getting shook about only getting 4 hours' sleep and having clients in the morning. It weren't the same when me and Adwoa were together like it was on the phone. Sometimes Adwoa would be snoring and I'd be just there laying behind her with my eyes wide-open staring, trying to imagine I could see through her bonnet. Anyway, when we got in, Adwoa went straight to the kitchen, making her food for the next day, trying to chat to me through the wall between us, asking what's on and if I wanted another drink. Fuck it, yeah, I said, and I swear I heard her drop one excited, Yes! and clap her little hands in the kitchen because I know say she only liked drinking when someone else was drinking with her. More time when we got home after a meal she'd make some green or rue tea and I would be drinking alone, but sometimes her mood shifted the same way mine did and so we'd get licked together. She walked into the living room with two glasses now and I asked her what food she made and could I have some. She put the drinks down and just looked at me and was like, seriously, Marcus. And you know what, I actually felt bad so I said, nah, actually, I'm not that hungry. She said she'd go and make me a sandwich but when I told her I just wanted margarine in it she said she aint doing it. I know she thought I was taking the piss but at night all my body wants is sugar and salt. She was still standing over me after this, just watching me, and then leaned in closer to my face. I knew what she was coming, what she was coming to say.

Have you been washing your face?

Yes, Adwoa.

Liar.

How?

I can see your pores are full of that gunk.

How can you see from there? Why you trying it? You just want to squeeze my face.

Can I?

Yeah, sure, whatever, man. Lemme just find something to watch first.

Yes! Okay, let me get my face scrub bag.

Cool.

She ran upstairs and I quickly started squeezing my nose myself, flicking through the channels as well, but faster because I knew when she came back she weren't going to be looking to wait. I looked at my fingers but there weren't any of that white stuff on them so I knew this girl was coming to hurt me, trying to push shit through that might not even be there. Just as I could hear her running down the stairs like say she was falling, I landed on a film I must have watched about 15 times, lucky it was on this late and only just starting as well, one film I remembered bare of the words of, and I remember saying a couple of them quickly before Adwoa came back and clocked me. Watch me saying in time now, *that with devotions visage and pious action we do sugar over the devil himself.*

Are you ready?

Yeah, come.

I sat on the floor and Adwoa sat behind me, opened her legs and I moved between them. She pulled my head back and I swear I got a bit heated because she was just handling me anyhow, but I caught myself, counted to 16. I was calm. Making progress.

Oi, take time, man.

Sorry! It's just hard to do when you're looking straight.

Don't do it too hard.

I won't. But, Marcus, you really need to start scrubbing your face.

Twenty-Five

During the second week of uni I decided to give my body to science. I'd met a lecturer in the sports science building one morning while I was looking around for a gym I could sit and think about using. Since my early 20s, I hadn't spent much time on my body and now for some reason the thought of working out reminded me of children obsessed with presenting as adults, a flash of recognition for me, sure, but I think I was the reverse, a perspective to absolve myself of responsibility? Or that's what a nurse said to me once. Her name was Arella, or it could have been Laila, and she'd cared and given her hands over to me when she was supposed to be taking time for herself. This was during my crack up, a time when I sat watching my reflection rippling in the sea of tranquillity or skipped stones across its surface, supposed to be resting after I'd been compelled to turn away from the world and endure the horns I had thought summoned the reformers of belief, auditory hallucinations more frightening than visual because there was nothing to stop the sounds. Arella would sit and talk to me in the garden of the hospital I was staying in, sit in an uneasy plastic chair so glossed she could slide out of it and lie above the cracked and ashy concrete waiting to embrace the day as it descended. She'd smoke two cigarettes like this, one after the other, always biting the butt before letting it rest between her lips and inhaling, blowing out the smoke through one side of her mouth even without anyone being close to her. She'd listen to me talk to her about what had happened me, missing out what she later told me were the healing intersections of my story. Later, when I'd cross my chest to reach for my shoulder, trembling, gently tapping the hand of the bracing angel or demon, things she'd said would surface and I'd forget who I was, forget who they were, saw who I could be, holding only her words, dismayed that insight so kind and revealing could be buried so deep in a river called time. On days I knew it would be her, days I knew she'd be checking on me, I resisted, kept my room locked, but she'd come in anyway, through the door like a gust of wind, that downstroke of the divine, a pinion lifting and waking me from my breathless sleep, no strain from her keys when opening up or when contained in her loose pocket, as if she and everything she touched were immaterial but me. The afternoon I left, I brought flowers and chocolates to the office and after a faint wave goodbye, she stood and shook my hand, rubbing her thumb over the top of my finger and said she hoped to never see me again. So the cycle was complete and I slowly walked away from the moment I had fallen in love.

In the sports building, I didn't meet a nurse, but a doctor. I'd asked him about a gym and he told me he wouldn't know, he was better suited to helping others than himself. So I asked him about the lumps under my chin, about the ones that slipped away when I touched them, gathering around the corner where my thigh met my hip, about the single stone like something thrown and lodged in the back of my head, and what would it be like if I abruptly stopped taking muscle relaxers.

Are you taking muscle relaxers?

No.

Who is?

My dad.

So he's prescribed muscle relaxers? Which ones?

I think it's called alprazolam.

How long and how many has he been taking? What's he taking them for?

I don't really know but he's been taking them for a couple of years, I think.

Then he'd need to taper if he was going to come off them. Not just stop. He shouldn't just stop. Not even for a day.

Why? What could happen?

Quite a few things.

Like what?

Is your dad planning to come off them any time soon?

I don't know. Don't think so.

You sure it's your dad?

Yeah, it's him.

Then it's fine. His doctor will give him all the information and support he needs. You shouldn't be worrying about that.

Yeah, fair enough.

He took me upstairs to one of his teaching rooms and told me strip down to my boxers and lie on the bed in the corner. There were open plastic bodies around the room, one with half a face and the skin peeled to expose the skull beneath, another with its chest open and organs missing, the heart in pieces on a metal tray to the side of it. Some skeletons hung from the walls, one with a leg missing and the other contorted into a raised arm salute cut off at the wrist. In the centre of the room there was a long glass table that when you stepped close enough revealed a touch screen that displayed the human body, every part open to explore, and had been, the prints of the previous classes smudged all over. I lay down and the doctor, lecturer, Chris, warned me his hands were cold and then began pressing my neck, putting his hands under my jaw, felt around my groin, asking me if I felt any pain any time there was pressure. I said no.

They're just lymph nodes.

I know. But there's a lot.

Yeah, you have a lot of them, which is unusual, but they're soft and movable so it's nothing to worry about.

Are you sure? Sometimes it's like they're swollen.

Probably just an infection. Doesn't seem to be any issues.

You sure?

I'm pretty sure, yes.

Alright. That's good, then.

Yes, it is. Anything else you'd like me to check?

There was but I said no and walked over to the skeleton with no leg and started trying to put it into a pose to match the other. Chris asked me how comfortable I was with his examination, and I told him it was fine. And from then, a few times every month I would walk over to the sports building and let anatomy and physiology students press and prod my body, looking for abnormalities, checking my breathing and heart rate, testing my reflexes and looking into the backs of my eyes and ears. Some of them, speechless, quickly lifted their hands from inside my boxers, stepped back from the table, went over to Chris and whispered while he looked at me and smiled. Then they'd come back and continue, ignoring what they thought they'd found. Sometimes I would find myself falling asleep while all of this was happening and the feeling peaked if I took some benzos before laying down. It was a few hours each time, and afterwards I would always stroll back to my dorm and nap as if closing my eyes for the first time.

Nineteen

Adwoa weren't the first Christian I dated. Back in the day I used to be onto this girl called Hannah and she used to bring me to her church every Sunday and Tuesday and sometimes you'd even catch me in bible study listening to the gospel tryna get closer to her, asking her to share her bible so basically man's face was touching hers, so if I turned around quickly enough my lips would brush her cheek with those tiny hairs I could sometimes see when she was sitting in the light. It was never enough, though, and so I'd try putting my knee next to hers as well but she'd move away, vex, cussing me when we walked out those massive doors at the end of the service. Listen, the church used to be a casino, a casino you know. Like I know it sounds mad, but trust me I aint making this shit up, the place used to be the devil's playground but now come and see conversion. Honestly, though, at first I was just there because I was feeling Hannah and wanted to wife it, but after a while I was asking questions about certain passages and even picked up my mum's bible one, two times before I got my own. Obviously couldn't read it because it was in Twi, but like, it actually got to the point where I'd be looking forward to certain things, like when random people from the church would call me up about whatever was going on with youth service or bible study, or hearing and listening to what the pastor was actually saying, counting how many times he stopped mid-speech, watched the congregation, bouncing the mic off his thigh after he dropped something deep and then walked back to the spot on stage he'd started preaching from. See me there taking notes when that section of the sermon began again, pastor hoping and knowing we'd catch it this time, feeling like say the holy spirit was on repeat, teaching spiritual growth and alla that and knowing this time it'd be appreciated. And fair enough because he did have some bars, like one thing I will always remember him saying one time, when I was pretending to look down our aisles to see who was getting up, but really I was watching the side of Hannah's face, trying to make her turn to me instead of following pastor, is that: God will not have his works made manifest by cowards. Yeah, after he dropped that I remember turning back to the pulpit, listening hard and hoping he'd say it again, and when he did I got this mad tingly feeling all over my body. I know say some of the PTs would have loved what the pastor was on, I even should have tried to bring some of them through because the way they used to chat to their clients was on the same level and I'd preed couple of their books lying about or in their lockers, all that Tony Robbins motivational stuff and I know say he came like a preacher too. Imagine, they might even have found a ting to wife like I did. Hannah weren't no ting, though, sorry. But yeah, even couple of the songs they'd sing would be stuck in man's head all through the week and the only way to get them out was to hear them again on Sunday. I'd been on and off with this church thing for time but when I met Han, that's when I really started to go hard for Christianity, on fire for Christ and all that, you'd even catch me handing out leaflets in ends, taking man's numbers, belling them and asking if they thought they'd go heaven if they died right now? Crazy. I even got baptised in one swimming pool in her community centre, I'm sure my certificate is still somewhere in my mum's yard. When I came out the water, dripping, she kissed me on my mouth and the pastor didn't even say anything. Mad. Listen, I used to think all church was suspect. I used to think like, if the devil is the biggest liar, how you know he aint the one you're praying to? Actually, not all church. For some reason I had this soft spot for Catholic Church, I don't even know why, but it called to me, telling me to come through and sit down and just chat to God. I didn't think you could do that with them other typsa Christianity, I just thought they were all about the P's. The idea of confession made sense to me as well. In fact, you know what, I think that's what it is, that's what I liked about them Catholic churches, that you could just sit in that cubicle or whatever and just say what's on your mind or show dem what's heavy on your heart. But yeah, just being able to walk in and it's just you and God, get me, or maybe someone else, who even knows, the devil is a liar, but honestly, before I met Hannah the only time you'd see my faith start sliding up on man is when that feeling would start coming over me again, like, that's when I'd start to proper believe in God, like I could actually talk directly to him, like it's just us in an empty room that used to be my life, you know them ones, and I needed to grab his attention quickly or something permanent was gonna happen to me. I can't even explain it, the feeling was like nothing made sense any more, like I'd clocked the game of the world and because I'd deeped it, it weren't working no more, like everything just shut down and God was the only answer to all that. I don't even like thinking about it, but that feeling of feeling close to God would only last for a bit, but with Hannah now, it felt permanent and like I could chat to God when I was praying. But yeah, so now the only thing was, well, nah, not the only thing, but one of the maddest things was that the pastor was on me to marry Hannah, like proper putting pressure on man and can you believe I almost said yeah, fuck it, but luckily Hannah had a dream and said she saw my future and it weren't with her because we were unequally yoked or some shit I can't remember, and so we'd have to end it and just be friends. Obviously we didn't become friends, but I carried on going to the church for a bit until she started chatting shit about how it was her space and I couldn't be coming up in it anymore. Christianity won't see me again. I aint chatted to her since. But every now and then I do miss them typa churches where everyone is on their feet during praise and worship, to the point where even if you're tired and need to sit down, you can't because you'll look like you're trying to disrespect the ting. It's kinda like tryna walk into a mosque with your trainers on or something. Actually, not that extreme, but it's a disrespect either way. One girl I used to date, honestly, she was actually my girlfriend but we didn't show no one, but yeah, she taught me about Islam and mosque and I'm not even joking, I nearly did my Shahada. I wasn't even checking for it like that, it was just that I respected what she was doing, like trying to pray 5 times a day and all that, I respected her religion, get me. But then we'd be chilling at her yard and she'd show me all these videos about how similar the bible and the Qur'an are and how the differences basically came down to if you're burning or floating in the afterlife because how can you be worshipping a man and I was like yeah, I hear it, it made too much sense to me at the time, like how the devil used to be a djinn and how this isn't the first universe that Allah has created, that he's destroyed many and we're not the only civilisation, and she even showed me evidence of how Muslims back in the day knew things that science only realised recently and how the prophet Muhammad (PBUH) received the Qur'an and how it's meant to be sung and easy to remember and you can recite the whole ting if you work hard. But also how the angels cannot disobey God so how can the devil be a fallen angel, how that's putting them man on a level with us, alie? It just felt right, get me, I liked the way they prayed and how much respect they had for the mosque and the Qur'an and just the whole vibe really, like, you could never disrespect it. One time someone must have left a Qur'an on the floor after mosque and we were just chilling and chatting and the way one of the imams switched on us and explained why we can't be doing them things. Yeah, that's how I think it should be if you're dealing with something like God or something close to him. Obviously I don't really believe in all that stuff now. But that's how I see Catholic Church as well, though obviously I know them man get up to some mad stuff. The thing is, Layal wasn't even strict with it when it came to Islam, like sometimes she wouldn't even wear her hijab and her dad was calm with me coming to their yard, though I never went to her room, we'd just be in the kitchen more time and if her dad went out then we'd lips or whatever. Yeah, she weren't strict but she still weren't trying to beat either. And the body was crazy, like, you see them Somali gyal, I'm not even joking when I say if I married Layal and she wanted to wear full niqab, I wouldn't even be against it. But yeah, no trainers in mosque, and you know what else they were proper nice to man, not like church, it was different, though, yeah, they're nice to you too, but you can just tell who is being real and who is moving like they think God is dumb and can't see how they really are and why they're doing what they're doing. If me and Layal never locked it off, well I locked it off because I could tell she wanted to but wouldn't, I thought I was even being considerate, but yeah, if we were still together, I'd be out here rocking beard and chewing khat with them man till like 4 a.m. I still used to text her and check on her because I like knowing my past is still there, get me, and I'd also ask for passages from the Qur'an to read, but she said I was moving stalkerish and harassing her so of course after that I had to delete the number, but I can't lie, that bun me. All girls bun me in the end, even when man's just trying to show love, but yeah, in one way or another, they bun me, but I always still have love for them, usually after a couple weeks of stress. Anyway, I remember the last time I went to pray on a Friday and one yout was outside and when I took off my trainers, he asked me if he could try them on. The kid had like size 5 feet and I'm a 10. Layal warned me that sometimes people would take your crep outside mosque but she didn't know if it was on purpose but it did happen sometimes. I didn't wanna think this kid was trying to rob man so I thought fuck it, I'd give him one and it would probably be funny, but nah, it weren't, because after like 8 steps, his next one dropped him in a puddle and he fell on his face. I helped him up, said sorry or whatever, but I was pissed inside because those crep were exclusives and cost too much, I don't even think the shop I got them from is around any more, one place called the Locker Room, where Eve moved to me and brought me in on her bedrin's discount on Jordans and all them exclusives that no one really knows about. She was older than man by like 15 years and I swear when I met her the only trainers you'd see me wearing were white Air Force ones – low me because I was only 16 – but by the time she said she can't deal with man any more because of my age or whatever, and so I locked it myself, I had like 23 pairs of trainers, like it was actually too much, like one day I just opened my eyes and someone had left all these boxes in my room, Jordan 1s, Jordan 7s, Jordan 8s, Bordeaux Jordan Spizikes, Raging Bull Jordan 4s, Hyper Blue TNs, Lightning Bolt TNs, these sexy Tide TNs, Adidas shell toes in bare different colours and some high-end brand trainers like Margiela Replicas and Dolce, but I weren't really on them like that. So yeah, I had to give bare of them away and only kept maybe like 4 pairs for myself, but back then you'd catch me waiting in line early in the morning, wind trying to blow man's braids out, rain that's broken through my clothes now trying to get under my skin, or I'd drop one of the employees £100 to hide one pair of Jordans in the back for me until everyone thought they were sold out. I can't even remember what she looked like, I mean Eve, but I know even now you'd catch her booking flights to America just so she can try grab some trainers no one in the UK ever gonna have, or aint gonna have any time soon. I never went that far but it was a lot and I didn't even have P's like that at the time but I'd still save from my supermarket job or Eve would drop me some P's after we beat, but only after we'd beat. She'd draw man into having sex and then only after that she'd be like let's go shopping, get some trainers or garms or some other shit, probably just so we could both walk out them shops holding boxes for both of us, like it was a flex for her that we went shopping like that. I think at one point I was even signing on as well after telling them man was homeless so thank God I managed to find my way into the gym even though I've always been on and off with lifting weights. But it was Anna who brought me in properly, probably one of the sexiest white girls I've ever seen. The body wasn't banging, like I know man would see it and think, yeah, they want to beat, but it was one of them where you'd want to see her naked just so you can see how far the muscle and definition goes. Well, not completely naked, but you get me. Obviously we don't chat any more because she cheated and now she's loved up with her rugby husband and they've got a yout, but I'm happy for them, still. Listen, sometimes you only meet people so you can learn something from them, like, losing someone you love and slowly dying are the only two things I can promise you you'll experience in this life, so I guess you gotta keep practising so you can firm it at the worst time. And that's calm for me.

Twenty-Five

The 4-hour coach to Thorpe Park was quiet, with whispers sailing on intoxicating breath, siren calls to turn someone's throbbing head, though most gaped out the window to keep themselves distracted, pining for the fresh air that could heal a hangover, but the sight of the passing greenery was enough to keep their insides from rolling around too much. Everything slows with a hangover as you try to sense the minute changes in your belly so you can get to the bowl or sink in time. I wasn't yet seeing in slow motion but was aware of those who passed me to find comfort in the back or collect themselves, chill with a friend or queue for the toilet with their hand tightening atop my headrest. I couldn't remember the night before and didn't want to. The most I knew was how many and which medications I'd popped from their blisters. Although I always ignored and went beyond recommendations – online, on packs, suggested in doctors' offices – I still made sure I knew my dosage, how many pills, when and with what, though I did sometimes forget to take however many I might need for whatever occasion and could end up either overdoing it or wanting to squeeze myself into a ball as my skinless sensitivity returned. Last night, stupidly, I'd mixed with alcohol, excessively, and this was why every speed bump made me feel like my stomach was the only organ in my body, liquid spilling and swirling around inside it like a chemistry beaker, enough force beneath it and out it would come through my mouth. I took another pill to settle myself, knew I would not be drinking today so the most that would happen if I continued at this pace was that I'd become a slight tremor in the air, seeing things that maybe weren't there with my attention held to the past, and my hangover would be tempered, submitting to the alchemy of benzodiazepines and codeine.

My dad, though, he could conjure effects more effectively than I could, descendant of the lesser gods having an intimate understanding of which medication affected the others in ways that wouldn't kill you but get you close enough in your sleep. The sweet spot was the in-between. Not life, but living, where my dad lodged himself, swore was nowhere but could be reached everywhere, the closest to where he'd come from and where he'd likely return. With a morning cup, coffee reaching over its edges with his swaying speech, he'd tell me there was no present, no point grasping anything, the future was waiting to come past, he'd say. Refusing to let go, trying to enjoy, why? Just be, now. Because once held, where was it? It was nowhere now, ah. The past is gone, you can't find it again. Look at tomorrow and yesterday, when you think of it, it comes, when you think of it again, your memory don fail you. Trickster on the tongue, my dad was Anansi before and Anansi after, a remnant for now, dormant, nothing substantial for anyone while in-between a life, nothing gleaned, and seemed I didn't make sense either, nothing fitting, ill-shaped to find space, he wouldn't reach for me, but he'd stay, he said, more or less, put into the mouth of the spinning spider. For him, life waited before birth and rejoiced after death, and so with many eyes all you can do is hone in and divide the detour, split open the present, needing as many legs as can carry you to the place where time stops and you can watch life drift, attached to nothing, and you wake the next day, hanging, the world upside-down again until once more you search for the eyes that recognise the middle ground. He'd wash down zopiclone, tramadol, diazepam, trazodone and everything else with whisky, Jim Beam or Johnnie Walker, Dalmore or Macallan when I used to sit with him, watching old action movies and listening to him tell me which actor was a champion or legend. But it stopped the day my mum walked into my room one morning and dropped to her knees, asking for forgiveness for putting me into care, and understanding she was responsible for my earlier collapse, and knew that I drank because of it. But she was wrong. I was grateful for care and though I couldn't see or experience the cause, I assumed I was just unlucky rather than a victim. So, I drank because I liked to drink, and took medication to calm me down, only a few really knowing what the alternative was like. But as my mum knelt, the cracks became clear, and so I listened and I left my dad to sleep alone, sofa or floor, sometimes the cold kitchen tiles, sometimes thinking maybe he'd sent my mum to warn me away, saddened by my visits, wanting me to remain at home. And so I passed through the phases of bright daze and drunken darkness alone, metaphysically assisted by my dad's monthly prescriptions. At least we shared that. And there were some days when I did understand him, days when I matched his magic with medication and Macallan. Understood that creation was dilution so whatever I was feeling, my dad had confronted worse, and won, always, a success story every day. Made in his image, pity him, pity Him, wondering how multiplied must be the melancholy of God?

We pulled into the car park and rushing past me back to her seat was San, just out from the toilet, wiping her mouth with her sleeve.

Thorpe Park. The group I was with would walk to rides, queue, and then turn back when it was time to get on. Hours into the day and we'd only risked being sick on one, Tidal Wave, but my own nausea was passing and so I walked back and lined up a second time on most of the ones we'd walked out on. Once I'd been on them all and was only a little shaken, I decided on another go round and searched for the group to drag someone along with me. I found no one, but no matter, I was having fun. It was so simple. I fought for words to describe it but it was useless, pointless, even. I remembered my dad's words, knew for the moment he was a liar, a dying man seeing profundity in everything, even his own thoughts, and trying to match what left his mouth with what he thought, so to be fair to him how could he not have lied? I felt good, in the present, the butterflies in my stomach vague but familiar, a distinction between their emergence and the moths of anxiety now so clear, the chrysalis no longer subdued by self-medicating. I couldn't find my friends but was fine with that, saw an arcade and walked inside, searching my pocket for loose change.

Nineteen

You see the gym I worked in, basically it was completely different to the ones I used to train in, and I swear because where I worked was like a 'soft' gym, there was limits to how much growth you could achieve. Like, the ones I used to train in were proper old school, them gyms where the seating had sponge splitting out of it like clothes that couldn't contain its growth or something and more stretch marks than the people using them, like, one of those gyms where you could actually smell that one gym member you were cool with even when they weren't there, like everything you could smell was mixed up with the tears in plastic upholstery and burning rubber weights and you could hear chips coming off each cast-iron plate as it was dropped by some dickhead who thought they'd get stronger by releasing the tension instead of controlling it. Yeah, I missed them typa gyms but I know say I'd never meet someone like Adwoa up in there and no way I'd be making the money I was making either, but it weren't just that. Like, aside from the one, two things that were annoying or whatever, there was something about my gym that made me nostalgic for it when I weren't there, like, it had personality, quirks that were the actual people or things that never worked properly like the fourth shower, and there was always something mad going on or at least something that was semi-interesting. As a personal trainer, though, I couldn't really be up in the mix like that because I needed to make sure I presented myself a certain way, get me, but I always wanted to get involved, sometimes even thinking maybe it would be better if I just dropped back down to a fitness instructor again. Sometimes staying in the same place is calm, it's not always about moving forward, especially if you're already happy, like what's the point? But even as a PT, even though realistically you were self-employed, there were always some fuckrees you couldn't escape. Hear this, yeah, once, maybe like a few months after I met Adwoa or whatever, Yaa, who actually started working at the gym around the same time as me, she was on reception and must have asked me to get her some products to clean up one of those fat glass protein shakes that had smashed on the floor. She couldn't go get it herself because her bedrin was on a break and no one else could watch reception so I thought, aight, cool, whatever, and I knew where everything was as well so I walked through the changing room, stopped at the pool, put on my overshoes, thumbs up to reception through the glass window that looked onto the pool because we had no life guards, and then walked through to the cleaning cupboard which was just out of view. I was putting in the code now and it wasn't working so I just thought okay, been a while and they've changed it. Most gyms use these dead padlocks where if you pull down hard enough and move the digits, every time you hit the right one, the padlock drops just a liickle piece and that's how you know it's onto the next number. So I cracked the lock now and opened the door. See the thing about the cleaning room was that the latch that had the lock on it was too long for the door, so even though you couldn't completely open it, when you pulled it, there was a gap where you could get your arm through. So while I'm seeing what I'm seeing, I'm thinking rah, this guy must have stretched out his arm and put a padlock on the door while he was inside with this cleaner. Cleaner, bro, it was even his employee. I opened the door and man had one of her breasts in his mouth and then when they both turned to look at me, it fell out, like he didn't even stop, the situation did that for him. I closed the door and then put the padlock back on. All this happened in like 4 seconds you know but as soon as I saw them, time was like nah, let's process this and slowed everything down like we were in one drama or Nollywood film that dropped one of them loud keyboard noises when they turned to look at me. Anyway, I went back to reception and told Yaa what happened and at first she was just bussing up, but then I think she deeped the situation and how that guy was supposed to be the supervisor, giving extra hours to the cleaners who were mostly from Spanish-speaking countries and yeah, I was deeping it too. Yaa said she was going to report him and at first I was like nah, low it, because then I have to get involved, but when she asked me if I'd like it if I was taken advantage of like that, something didn't feel right and I started to think maybe I'm asleep or having some intense daydream and I knew Yaa was staring at me but I couldn't remember what she said, so I said, Huh, but the words coming out of her mouth didn't make sense and it was like she was moving her mouth trying to find the right language so I'd understand her, but it was all getting weird and then I started feeling like something was creeping up on me so I just said, yeah, cool, like I understood and walked away. I was telling this story to Adwoa, just on a casual one, like it was part of my day or whatever and she just looked at me and said:

Have you thought about going to therapy?

For what?

To talk to someone?

What's the point in going to therapy when I can just chat to you?

I will always be here for you, Marcus, and I like listening to you as well, your stories, but I'm not a therapist, and you do worry me sometimes.

Why are you worried?

I'm not worried all the time, just sometimes.

But why? I'm good. Honestly, and I'm not even trying to gas you, but I think it's because of you as well.

What is because of me?

The reason I'm good. Like, I feel calm most the time these days.

Well, that's good. I'm glad I can do that for you.

Yeah, you make me feel like I'm never gonna die or something.

Okay . . . Marcus, I'm not going to lie to you, that's a bit of a weird thing to say?

Why?

Because we're all going to die.

Why you gotta bring the mood down?

I'm not. I'm sorry, I'm not, I don't mean to. It's just that it's important.

I'm saying you stop me from wanting to die and you're here saying I will?

No! No, Marcus, don't do that, that's not what I meant.

So what then?

See, this is why therapy would be good.

Because you can't be bothered to listen to me?

Let's just forget it.

Crazy. Man gives you a compliment and you start moving like I'm trying to marry you.

What? Excuse me?

Nothing. You said, let's leave it. So let's leave it.

Marcus . . .

Adwoa?

Okay. I'm sorry. Let's leave it. Maybe I am being negative.

Nah, nah, I am. I'm sorry. Seriously, sorry, you're not being negative.

It's okay, you know I'm always here for you, but please try not to be so defensive.

She grabbed my cheeks and pulled them wide like say I was a baby who wasn't tryna smile at the situation, kissed my lips and then she started walking out the living room and asked me what I wanted to eat. I can't even lie, she must have read my mind because I was proper hungry.

Twenty-Five

I've only stepped into a few arcades that offered up gifts, and I've always been wary of winning. And in none of them did I trust the strength of the grappling hook to follow through, but with the confidence of not being crippled by anxiety, I willed it and filled the hook with the strength of my own fingers, a few inches from my face and the glass casing, curled into the shape of the clasp, closing them as it closed, lifting as I raised my bent wrist up above my head, watching the claw stubbornly open and drop the stuffed toy into the box beneath. I pulled it out, held it in front of me and said, Finally, as if I knew all paths would lead here, as if I'd been struggling since the Mega Drive to have my own character who could white knuckle it with me. I put him under my arm and looked around. I was alone. So I held him in front of me again and bumped my head with his, plush, pausing for a few seconds to let my smile find its curve. I walked in and out of the machines, sizing them up, found a way to make change, picked up the coins spilling into the metal tray, the sound filling me with excitement but no one even caring to look. So we started our run, me and wide-eyed Knuckles, wired Knuckles. I shot 42 balls into shuddering hoops, tearing off the raffle tickets the dispenser spat out with disdain. I was getting it, beginning to sweat by the end, but I was beating my own system, learning the system of the arcade. I played again, challenging for the top score. Not even close. But I kept going, always pulling out an extra ticket like I was snatching something illicit, crooks in a casino getting the better of chance, optimism over fate, a silenced audience with their money on me as Knuckles blew on the dice. I rolled wheels for grand prizes, dropped mallets to reach the top, bowled into open holes and smashed the heads of rising moles. I dashed balls at glowing clowns, missing only a few, weak throws as I calmed down, watching people pass and tossing the ball as if throwing to someone who would struggle to catch it. They caught on and as soon as I thought I was alone again, I picked up 4 balls and threw them all at once, knocking down two more targets before my time ran out. More raffles, and so much more to do. Knuckles sat by my feet as I lifted a sniper rifle, feeding the machine more and more pounds as my aim increased with each round. I partnered up with a little girl wearing a fisherman's hat, bobbles attached to two braids that seemed to fall out of it. I looked at her, trying to remember the last time I saw bobbles, or the last time I had seen a child and taken notice. As you grew, without them in your family, you only clocked them as shapes and sounds from the past, abstractions adjacent to your reality, a temporary phase before life began, or began to end. Her mum or carer was a few feet away with her arms crossed, watching. I smiled at her and she smiled back, rolling her eyes to say, What is she like? I said to the girl,

You ready? She said, Yeah! And we went in, dropping our guns to reload, shouting at the other to get whatever was hurting us that we couldn't see. We played again and again, but only got to level 4 before she said she had to go. Onto the next game, jumping from one illuminated square to another, losing at a game I thought I would smash, rhythm actually having nothing to do with the directionless dance moves. I tried another hook, another hand in imitation, but this time Sonic slipped through my fingers, his rival sitting upright against the booth with a perfect grin across his cheek. I liked things to be right, to be level, for things to look comfortable. I felt anything inanimate I touched must have some internal life, so Knuckles had to be sitting straight and his balled hands by his flimsy legs. A splash of 10 pences dropped above his head, then another wave with a 5-pound note caught in its swell. That soon became change that I used to beat Balrog, Vega and M Bison, relishing the repetition used to high kick and sweep my way from country to country, from victory to victory. There was pleasure in every extremity, and I suddenly thought of my dad, blinked away as a hand shot into a cold chest and pulled out a beating heart. At the trade-in booth all my tickets could get me was another teddy, so I walked around, looking for a boy who looked like me to give all of my winnings to. No luck, but I saw the little girl again, her hat on the floor, her braids flailing as she played the basketball game, stopping to aim every shot, jumping, missing, and losing time. I walked over and gave her my tickets. She didn't thank me; her face went red. I lifted my hand to spud her so she didn't have to search through the unease of gratitude and find something to say. We bumped fists and I quickly turned away. I started walking towards the exit, but before I touched daylight again I looked back at the girl and with the bunch of raffle tickets by her feet she was shooting more freely, making one basket after another.

Nineteen

Sometimes I wish I could remember the first time we kissed but I can't picture it, it's just like it was always happening. Anywhere we felt it. On a high road, train platform, while we were waiting for takeaway. Adwoa's lips were like ice that never completely melted. I always had bare saliva around my mouth when we came apart and she'd wipe it with the back of her hand and say sorry. We spent tiiime on her living room floor lipsing and hugging up and rubbing up, feeling all over our bodies trying to catch these bits of static electricity like excitement, like pleasure running through our fingers. You know when you're feeling something so intensely you just know they're feeling the same? Because the more I moved around, the more she did, it just felt like we were both searching for the same feeling and only getting samples of it, but we knew we could have it all. It was mad, things with Adwoa were just different, like I didn't have to force it and all she really offered me was herself and that's all I really wanted, I was good with just that. We slept downstairs most the time because there was no TV in her room and the one downstairs was one of them big-back TVs from back in the day. Sometimes

I'd have my last PT session at 9 p.m. and be back at hers for 10.30, drinking Grey Goose and cranberry, getting waved on the floor, lips, sex, search our bodies then fall asleep. When we weren't pressing on her living room floor, we'd be trying a ting in the bathroom of random bars or restaurants we went to. One of us would go toilet and then soon come the other like say the Charlie was lined up but really she'd be up against a door and I'd be trying to find her clit with my tongue or sitting on the seat with her riding me. Proper reckless, but when you're loved up, like who even cares? Everything is just there for you to have fun with it, like love turns the world into a playground or something, like you'll even be doing stuff you know is gonna be embarrassing when time comes and you look back, but in the moment it's just like yeah, come den. See us pissing off couple people with our antics too, like Anton, obviously, but he was wrong for that, and sometimes Gym Manager Rafiq would walk round the gym like man was on a loop checking for me, picking up balls of tissue found round the back of chairs during his spot checks, knowing I was in the building, the other PTs telling me he looked vex because all now I'm in the pump room with towels spread out on the floor. I think the maddest was when me and my cuz Stephen drove to Adwoa's yard at like 2 a.m. to pick her up and her aunt must have been staying over for a few days, checking in on her, and she was one of them strict Ghanaians who couldn't understand why you'd be trying to leave the house after 12 a.m. so she'd locked the door, but watch Adwoa now, jumping over her back gate and then diving into Stephen's open car window like she's coming to attack man.

Oi, stop fucking around, man. Oi, Marc, I swear down if she buss my window I'm gonna buss your head.

We drove to get some Krispy Kreme and when Stephen got out the car that was it, jeans and boxers round my ankles like a layer of skin just dropped and she was pulling off her panties over her purple Kickers. I think I must have just slipped it in when Stephen come out switching, telling us to respect his whip. Fair enough. Next day he bust in my room with a stick and some Ann Summers on it like, why the fuck am I finding this shit in my car, you fucking wasteman?

Oi, Marcus, if you love this girl so much why the fuck you fucking her in my whip?

Why you always chatting like you don't get gyal?

What does that even mean, you prick? Ay, Marcus, you're actually tapped, you know that?

I can't even tell you how long we did all this madness for, the moment was just stretching like it would never snap, but now I look back, even if something won't break when you pull it, it still becomes thin. That's how I saw it and that's when I started to become paro like she was checking for next man. And then little things she would do would annoy me, like I'd be proper vex sometimes and have to go sit in the toilet. I was tryna chill with the Charlie as well but at those moments it was like I had no choice, so I'd pick the bag out my pocket and just watch it, flicking it in front of my face. Adwoa knew that sometimes I'd just tune out, like, I can't hear nothing and it's just bare thoughts going round in my head and it's like man's dizzy and I can't even lock on to anything in my head, so trust me, because I'd be in another world, I know Adwoa would try and take me for an idiot, like, we'd be talking and she'd just drop a man's name in the convo like we been chatting about him from day. Or she'd tell man where she was gonna be and with who, like say she was just making sure that if I clocked her out with a next man it don't look sus. I remember she tried to get me to buy some expensive perfume, Black Ortid or something like that and I won't lie, it smelt good, like, I would have rocked it, even over Chanel Blue and Black XS, yeah, Black Ortid, that ting smelt crazy, like sex in a bottle or something, but you know why I couldn't rock it, because hear this, when I asked her how she knows about it, she tells me, oh her friend Kay wears it all the time. How can you want me to smell like a next man? So all this is why, and I promise you I've never gone through anyone's phone before, but this is why it all started, because she kept moving bookey and thought I wouldn't notice. My instincts are good, like, I'm usually right, if not, then just wait a bit and you'll see. So many times I've thought I was wrong then see gyal coming back months later like, yeah, you were right, I was moving mad, sorry, let's try again. So I trust myself when it comes to things like that now. It even got to the point where any time I'd get close to her, she'd move away just a little bit, turn her head, screwing up her face and nose like I couldn't see it, sneezing to style it out (yarhamuk allah). Or she'd be in the toilet with her phone, but with the speakers in there too so all I could hear was Tank or Tyrese or Ginuwine, sometimes even Joe! And I'd be sitting outside like one idiot. It all got a bit mad one day when I came back to hers and she was in the shower. I didn't have a key to her yard but you could just open the door if it wasn't locked and she was cool with me doing that. I clocked her phone on the arm of the chair and lemme tell you, the way my heart started beating. Usually when she heard me come in the house she'd shout me, but nothing this time. I held my breath and started tiptoeing, counting each step I took, spreading them out as well so when I reached her phone on the fourth step, I knew I had to look. She didn't have a PIN so I went straight into her messages and looked for any guy's name she aint told me about before. I found some but the messages were minor, so I went into her Facebook app and there was one recent chat open and I was like hold on, who is this Michael guy, you miss him, yeah, link up, yeah? Okay, say nothing. My hands were even shaking when I put the phone down, picked it up again and read him saying he misses her 7 more times, then I think I blinked 42 times before I started walking up and down the living room, 4 steps each way, my hand tapping my thigh 8 times, my head feeling like someone was gripping my thoughts and pulling them up, stretching like say the heat from my anger had melted everything inside me. I think I was even starting to sweat, I didn't know how I was gonna react. I aint violent, I'll never hit a woman but I'll tell you about yourself and I swear sometimes I think that's worse than if I licked someone in their face. I heard her coming down the stairs, started clenching my fist, then opening it, she was humming and then stopped on the last step, eleventh, looking at the front door.

Babe?

Yeah.

She walked into the living room, one hand holding and twisting her towel under her arm, over her breast. I was fucking pissed.

Oh my God, Marcus, you scared me. I thought the door was locked. I was gonna run back upstairs.

Adwoa, we need to chat. Right now. I'm not gonna pretend I'm not fucking pissed.

Straight away, no hesitation, she looked at the arm of the chair then back at me. Then at my hand gripping her phone. She breathed out like she was disappointed in me. In me, you know. I thought, are you mad!?

You went through my phone, didn't you, she said.

Twenty-Five

Marcus, said Gloria.

Yooo!

Yo?

Yeah, what you saying?

What am I saying? Heh, Marcus, gyae saa ruffian language. Mempɛ saa deɛ.

You're so dumb, man. Where is everyone?

Heh! What do you think I'm trying to tell you and you're here doing me rough? C'mon, yɛ ntɛm nyɛ saa bus no bɛ gyai yɛn wɔ ha.

Yes, Mum.

Wo nim sɛ apɔnkye.

The coach had come alive. People were still deciding where to sit, having made new friends in the park, voices and phrases traded, pitches amplified, hangovers digested with McDonald's or thrown from their bodies as they finally hurled through the air. Packets of all sorts rustled and cracked, large lollies and rocks sweetened tongues, giant teddies watching their new environment with apprehension while the giant white eyes of mine were still full of the flashing lights of the arcade. Again, I sat near the back and positioned my dreaded echidna in the seat next to me, stopping short of ensuring him a safe journey back to Manchester. I realised I hadn't been to the toilet all day and had only taken a few benzos this morning so it was possible my stomach would start responding, digestion geared up through the fluttering motion of the present moment passing. The driver announced that we would be starting for Manchester in the next few minutes. I shuffled in my seat to get more comfortable, so I could lean my head back and try to sleep the journey home, when someone leaned over the headrest to my left and asked if they could sit down. It was San. She was about to throw my Knuckles to the floor but I took him by one of his locks and put him between myself and the window, a pillow if I needed it. I counted and waited for her to feel settled enough to start talking, but before I could acknowledge the sixth braid hanging just above her brow, it had developed a sheen, everything began to develop a sheen, a lustrous finish, as though each object or person was made from something transient, like if you reached for them your hand wouldn't stop, just slide through them, warmed by their immateriality. I felt as though I could get up and walk into the centre of the coach, look around and see so many in the midst of moving but preserved, a softness caught by a camera. San would be slowly turning to face me, her light skin streaked on the moment of swirling, and begin talking, never catching up with my dissolution and absence. I put my hand in my pocket, popped, then rolled it up my face with my palm, sliding it between my lips, my palm on my chin as I swallowed deeply and waited. She must be here for a reason, I thought. It was an odd thing, how someone I could have collapsed into less than 24 hours ago, who had stirred only tender curiosity moments before, then, sitting next to me, had the power to force such an acute stress response that my mind fabricated flight while I fought the feeling, blinking, 15 times, 16 times, 23 times until finally she spoke.

Hey, she said.

Hey, I said.

Have fun?

Yeah, it was alright. You?

Yeah, a bit. I felt sick most the day but I'm alright now, now we're leaving. Not because we're leaving, just that it's now we're leaving that I'm feeling better. Anyway, what you telling me?

Nothing. Just here—

I heard you at Gloria's place.

Heard what?

Talking about history and Pan-Africanism and all that. Well, I didn't hear you but someone told me what you said and I thought, hmm, okay.

Yeah?

Yeah. I thought, hmm. This guy seems interesting. Not you as a person, I mean what you said sounds interesting.

Thanks.

Are you Pan-African?

Sometimes. I don't really know enough to be honest and—

So what about today? Like, right now, how do you feel about Pan-Africanism? Would you say you're down for the cause?

Erm, yeah, I think. I dunno, I guess. Are you?

Alright, good. That's good. I wanted to invite you to this event we're doing. We, is me, Gloria and a few other people. We're gonna watch *Avatar* then have a discussion.

What's the discussion about?

Colonialism, imperialism, fascism, socialism, every ism, we're about it. Just the good isms, though, feel me?

Yeah. I feel you.

Good, good. So you're down, yeah? San, by the way.

I'm Marcus.

I know. Speed dating.

You remember?

Obviously. Anyway, just wanted to invite you. We need more people supporting the ting. Can you come help us set it all up in a couple of days?

Hmm. Maybe. Depends, I guess. Which day and time?

I'm not sure yet either, to be honest.

You don't know when your event is?

No, I mean when we're setting up, getting things ready and that. Erm, hmm, okay, gimme your number and I'll text you the time.

Okay, cool. Or you could just message me on Facebook or—

I could, but I might not be at home when I find out what time we're gonna be organising everything.

Fair enough. Give me your number and I'll drop call you.

Aight, say nothing.

Nineteen

I felt like I was the one in the wrong even though I'd caught her letting another man try move her up. I weren't walking around any more, I was just sitting there opposite her on that busted sofa I'd told her to dash away, with my leg twitching or going up and down when I put my hand on top of it to stop it moving. She hadn't even changed into clothes, just had her towel up around her chest. I couldn't think about what she was saying and hear the numbers in my head at the same time so I stretched my legs out and put one foot over the over. That seemed to work and the first thing I heard her saying to me was that she was sorry.

Sorry for what?

I'm sorry I was hiding stuff from you. But Marcus, why did you go through my phone?

Something told me you were hiding shit from me.

Something told you?

Yeah?

Like what?

I don't fucking know, I just know when someone is doing me dirty, something just tells me.

Really? Something like what? Anansi?

Are you fucking dumb? Why you chatting shit? What the fuck, man?

You can't go through my phone and then get upset when I ask you why you did it.

Don't chat shit about my dad again. Adwoa, I'm not joking.

Okay, whatever. Sorry. Does that make you happy? But answer my question.

What question?

How can you go through my phone then get angry when I ask you why you did it?

At this point, does it even matter why I went through your phone?

I guess not.

Nah, how could you do this? I've been nice to you, man aint chatted to no one. Do you know how many gyal try holla at man and I just tell them to move? Do you know how many numbers I've deleted? Nah, you take the piss.

Yeah, I'm so lucky.

What?

Nothing. At the end of the day, it's happened now. And it was up to me. I understand why you're upset and I'm happy to give you space so you can cool down but—

Give me space?

Yeah, it feels like that's what you need.

Adwoa, are you actually dumb?

Can you stop calling me dumb, please? I get you're upset, but stop insulting me.

I could feel my hand opening and closing. I heard one van go over a speed bump outside and whatever was inside it bounced around and probably bruk and there were still people playing in the park opposite the house. The way I wanted to cuss her out. Like, I've been in this situation before but it was different because the girl would usually be screaming in my face trying to blame me for her cheating or begging man not to leave so I'd just be caught up in the chaos and it wouldn't matter what I said. But Adwoa was just sitting there, calm, so whatever I said it was like it was amplified and there was no reason for me to say it, like, I'd feel like the bad guy. So man had to act sensible even though my girl was cheating on me! Opening and closing, listening, smelling. She'd made food, I hadn't even clocked it until now because I'd been on a mad one as soon as I came in the yard but I'm not gonna lie, it smelled good, so I thought lemme try a ting.

What are you cooking?

Oxtail. With plantain and rice.

Just for you, yeah?

Marcus, when have I ever cooked *just for me*?

Oh, so for you and Michael, then?

Michael?

Yes, Michael.

Michael?

Yes, man, don't try act dumb now. I swear, just cos man aint out here like my cousins don't think I'm some prick.

Michael. You're pissed off because I've been talking to Michael?

Adwoa, I swear I'm gonna start—

Marcus, Michael is my family.

Stop chatting shit, man.

If you keep talking to me like that, I'm just going to leave. I'm not having it.

Family how?

He is my half-brother. Michael, the guy you're sitting there clenching your fists about. What, you're gonna hit me now?

No. Don't try it. That's not what I'm doing. You know that's not what I'm doing,

you know why I'm doing this, don't try it. And don't try switch the subject, I'm not stupid. Stop lying. Michael aint your brother. How come I've never heard about him? Why do gyal think they're so slick?

The reason I haven't spoken about him, and my name is Adwoa, not *gyal*, is because I wasn't talking to him. He has some issues and his mum don't like me and makes it known. I don't talk about people I'm not in contact with.

Like your dad, yeah?

Wow, okay. Is that what we're doing now, Marcus?

So you can chat shit and take the piss about *Anansi* but I can't speak the truth about your dad?

Look, whatever, just take it or leave it. Michael is my brother. We haven't spoken for a bit and he contacted me recently.

And you miss him.

Of course I fucking miss him, Marcus, he's my brother. You're so fucking immature. What's this really about, Marcus? Are you just trying to get me to say something?

To say what?

So there were more secrets she was hiding from man. Cool. I'd have to run game and move like I knew what it was, to get her to say it, and if she didn't say it then I was out. Garn. Bro, the way I just wanted to do one fucking line right about now. I had some in my wallet but I couldn't leave the room. Not because she'd clock what I was on, but because I was so close to getting her to tell me the truth and if I left it for a bit I knew when I come back she might have thought of another lie or a way out of it. I had to keep applying pressure.

So what, we're just gonna sit here until you tell me the truth, yeah?

There's nothing else to say. You've come into my house, cussed me, shouted at me, invaded my privacy.

Because I knew there was something going on. Forget Michael, I just wanted to know who he was, I don't care if you chat to other man. I'm not insecure. But when it comes to the proper truth, I want to hear it from you.

Hear what?

You know what, Adwoa. You know what, I don't even know why I'm still here. Like, I'm giving you bare chances to tell the truth but you just keep lying. I really thought this was something different.

Did you?

Yes, you know I did. Look how I've changed. No drugs, I don't chat to gyal in the gym like that any more. Just focused on stacking my P's, eating good, going gym then coming home to you. Like some little family. I weren't like that before.

You don't do coke any more?

No. When was the last time you seen me doing that?

Marcus, I've never seen you doing it, but I know you were doing it.

Okay, yeah, but do you get the feeling like I'm doing it now? Am I still hype all the time?

Yes.

Okay, but I told you man's just like that. Look, what I'm saying is things are so bless between us. Why let the trust go now? Just tell me the truth. I already know but I need to know you can talk to me about these things.

Marcus . . .

Adwoa, please. Just say it. I can handle it. I'm handling it right now, see, I'm calm, you saying it aint gonna make it more painful.

Marcus . . .

Why do you keep saying my name like that? Just go on.

Look, can we just leave it for now? I need to get dressed.

But why long it out? Adwoa please, all I'm asking for is the truth and you're doing man dirty.

How am I doing you dirty? I just want to put clothes on and think about things.

But think about what? How you're gonna create a next lie?

Stop saying I lied. I haven't lied about anything.

Okay. Okay. Sorry. But listen, please, just talk to me. Let's keep things honest between us.

Marcus.

Adwoa, come, man. Let's just sort this out now.

Okay, fine.

Thank you.

Bro, I couldn't even believe it. She looked down between her knees and just said it like it was nothing. Listen, the way my body went hot, like I had humidity under my skin, like man was back in the steam room, like say there was steam blowing into man's skull trying to push everything up outta my head. I stood up, then sat down, stood up again now and sat down again. I opened and closed my fists 4 times, then 8 times, then 15 times, then I stood up again and walked around the room.

Marcus?

I heard her but it was like trying to read words on a page, like I was trying to put everything together but nothing made sense. Numbers, though, bro, I couldn't stop counting, couldn't stop the countdown. That feeling was lurking somewhere, I could sense it, and it was like the numbers were holding it back in a way. I took 23 steps around the room, then just stopped and stood there, looking in her face. Pregnant you know.

Yo, this is a lot, this is a lot, man. I need to walk. Can I just walk? I'll be back, I just need to take it all in.

Okay, Marcus, that's fine. Please come back so we can talk about this.

Yeah, I'll be back, I swear.

And then I walked out the door.

Twenty-Five

I'd tried not to hold San to what she'd asked me on the coach, but we'd bumped into each other again while I was trying to get into the uni library. Without saying anything else, she reminded me of the date. Not *a* date, but the day and time she'd already texted me and possibly forgotten. I tried to leave before she noticed my loitering was to sneak into a place I didn't belong, but as I turned, with the receptionist tapping her pen on the desk beside us, San opened the gates for herself and reached for my forearm, grabbed and pulled me through behind her, squeezing my wrist gently before she let go on the other side. In her grip, I remember feeling my heartbeat in my hand.

And so here I was, early. I walked up to the locked door and peered through the window. There were people inside, but when I gestured to them to let me in, one of them wagged their finger at me like a metronome. I sat on one of the steps and waited, watched the people coming towards me and the backs of those walking away. I could have walked further down the street and found the book stall I sometimes visited, or passed into a social space behind someone who actually attended the university, but I didn't want to move. Pushing up through my back pocket against the concrete step were the two books I'd been reading, *Heart of Darkness* and *Self-Reliance*. This was the second time I was going through Conrad. The first time had been a struggle. There are some sentences that stop you, some words that feel so out of place you can't read past them the first time around. You have to go over a sentence again and again until your mind adjusts to this new texture and you can move on. I had adjusted and was now enjoying the read-through, the narrative distance and decline, finding myself disagreeing with what I believed to be the best work of prose our grand-uncle Achebe had written. *An Image of Africa*, San was now walking towards me after jogging through a traffic light. It was one of those jogs that a walk could outpace, a jog to appease the waiting cars rather than put wind behind her stride. She walked with her head down and moved like she was trying to break away from someone she'd noticed close to her but wanted to avoid. She was wearing a hat, so I had to quickly find something else to tally and was looking away from her when she took her final step – her seventh, and jumped in front of me, 8.

You came!

I did.

Sorry, I think it might be just us. As in, just us organising. Everyone else pulled out. It's cold, but you're still here! I appreciate you. The struggle continues.

So what we doing then?

Here.

What are these?

Leaflets. Gotta let the masses know about the event. Planning and preparation. And everything in-between.

Right, okay.

Don't worry, if we finish before 6 I'll buy you some wine. Any later, though, and we'll have to do it another day. The glass of wine, I mean.

Alright, cool.

We stood about 100 metres apart and began handing out the flyers. I watched her as she smiled when she offered them up, giggling a little with her thank yous when a black person took the handout. Our people, for some reason, are more likely to take what they're handed, put it in their pocket, finding it later in the day or sometimes days later, scanning it and taking note or tossing it away, but at least they take it. White people avoid eye contact, sometimes even taking the leaflet out of your hand just to throw it on the floor. When we were finished I asked San what she thought about it and she said it was a mentality of scarcity for black people, and overabundance for the mzungus.

Remember that bit in *Coming to America*, she said, when Eddie Murphy is all like, look at this country so free it can throw glass on the street! That's what I'm saying. The last time I went Ghana we had to return our Coke bottle to the shop!

But aren't they standing around Queens?

Proper Queens. Every black woman in that movie is buff.

I didn't know San well enough yet to distinguish her sarcasm from sincerity, but did hear her faint intake of breath through teeth that never finished biting down whenever she said something odd. We finished the work after 6 so she left me to go pre-drink where she'd be getting ready for the night, just easier, she said, and we'd have our drink another time. No problem, I said, forgetting what I was feeling, sliding my feet home to assisted sleep with a glass of Dalmore and a handful of diazepam. That night, I texted ex-partners and friends in a daze, an indistinct haze, asking what they honestly thought of me and how I made them feel when we were together. When I woke up there were 5 replies on my phone, but I deleted them all without reading them, knowing the words from past expressions of my weakness to recognise myself in any reflective shard of memory. I tossed my phone away and picked up something to read, a book I was taking 15 pages at a time . . .

Neither of the two languages available to black Londoners appears adequate for the expression of their complex cultural experience by itself. Both are needed and the partial and inadequate versions of inner city culture for which . . .

I didn't know much about Pan-Africanism in practice, only what I'd read or watched, so I still didn't have an opinion one way or another, but found myself veering towards shallow premises when it was attached to something, someone, I found appealing. The closer we became the more acutely the ideology and politics unfolded in my mind without threatening to drown me. For now, of course, I only found San interesting. The intensity of feeling when I first saw her, the time dilation, the dissolution of myself when she sat by me, the cold that could have cracked me open when she fell into the lap and arms of that random fucking guy at Gloria's, all those feelings were gone. Poetry had left me for a vague conceptual curiosity, I saw only her outline again. And this seemed to work for us both. Instead of going home, instead of giving in to my mother's terminal blackmail as I'd planned to, with large pills or small, I followed San around Manchester, at times ending up in Liverpool or Birmingham. We made our way through uni panel discussions about neo-colonialism, black Marxism and black love, debates about the place of indigenous religions, European philosophy's place on the continent and America's disruption of the progression of Africa, lectures on counter-intelligence and the fall of the Black Power Movement, minor protests outside the uni and screenings of obscure films like *Besouro*, *The Epic of Sundiata Keita* and *Hidden Colors 2: The Triumph of Melanin*. Non-committal discussions always trailed our walks home, to bars or to other events on the same night. To San, Blackness was more than an identity or currency, it had transcended its roots, cut through the legs of its origins in enslavement and resistance, and become soul, an essence now deified, rarefied to most melanated peoples. So there was no awakening like black love, devotional consciousness embracing to see the world for what it really was – theirs, the universe flowering into a black cosmos held under the noses of gods. Imagine two gods fucking, she said. Something elemental in every stroke, I replied and she laughed. With understanding and learning there came belief, faith, and though I winced at the mention of pineal glands and communion with creation, I saw gods and goddesses born to be remade with every word, every movement and every gesture San made. She was teaching me to love her, and through her I could love myself.

She questioned me always, and watched as I struggled to find answers to please her, a silhouette to meet hers. One evening she asked me about my favourite books and words, and I wanted to lie to her. I told her *Pale Fire* without mentioning the author, and she told me *Kindred*, asked me what I would do with such a power, what would I do with my life? I wanted to say I already had such power, that my fingers twitched with awareness above every key, but there was something more honest to express, so I told her, that I wouldn't relive anything, I would change things, would reshape my younger self in someone else's image. So would she, she said, but whatever is supposed to happen, probably will happen. And my favourite word is inamorata, she said, and then, without thinking, I asked her if she'd ever loved a woman. She looked at me and bit her lip and told me, in her way, that the night was over and I shouldn't be so interested in other people's lives.

I texted her when I got home, got into bed and put my phone on the floor face down. It buzzed as soon as I'd flattened my pillow and turned to face the window, blinds up so I could see a tiny slice of the moon peeking round the side of the opposite building, like the eye of a child waiting to see what I'd do. There was an empty glass on the ledge. I reached for it and held it in my hand, squeezing till my palm was drained, suffocating and shaking with the force and thought of breaking. I closed my eyes and heard it fracture, felt it slice through, blood running down my wrist, but still I couldn't let go, not until my fist was closed and a shard had cut through the back of my hand, causing more agony if I opened up again. I lifted my eyes to the window and implored the witness to my lies, the voyeur of the sky. The glass was unbroken, nothing ruptured, but my grasp still shaking to make it so. No, but *there was a time in my demented youth*. I put the glass back on the ledge, turned around and picked up my phone. *It's fine*, the text read, *but don't let it happen again*. There was a wink emoji at the end of the sentence. Then another text before I could let everything go. *Sorry if I was rude. Goodnight King x*.

Nineteen

I slid my finger over my bank card and rubbed the rest of it on my gums. Pregnant, you know. I got up and sat back in the stall, sat on the closed lid, flushed, my stomach killing me. Nah, what, pregnant. I couldn't even remember us not using a condom so how could she be telling me she's pregnant? Fuck, man. I put the vial back in my pocket with my cards and wallet and walked out of the toilet. I didn't even know where I was, some bar, I'd just started walking and hadn't stopped until I'd needed to go toilet then remembered I had half a gram in my pocket. Fuck it. I needed a drink. Double something. Nah, nah, triple, actually. I ordered 3 double Hennessys no ice, no mixer. I poured them all into each other and the bar man just watched me do it and then took the two glasses back. I walked away from the bar and out onto the street. The security put his hand on my chest when I stepped out but I showed him I was just standing in front to drink. Too crowded in there, man.

What you expect on a Friday?

I hear it.

Don't leave that out here when you're done, mate

Obviously.

I walked away but kept myself close to the building as if it was raining. One thing I've noticed is that when it's raining, even if the building aint got no roof over you, the rain won't be heavy like it would be if you moved away from it, so I could control how much rain was falling on me. Anyway, I was basically rubbing up against the side of the wall so man knew I wasn't going anywhere with my drink, like I could probably walk around the whole place, like out of sight, but if I kept myself right next to it while I was walking, man would be satisfied. I backed my drink at the corner and sat down on the floor. I took the coke out and put it through my hoodie pocket, licked one finger, opened the vial, put my finger over the top of it and turned it over, then rubbed whatever had come out onto on my gums. I didn't even care if the bouncer clocked what I was doing. After couple minutes, I started to get that humming all over, that feeling like my whole body was trying to vibrate to one tune it'd forgot, trying to shake it out of me until the rhythm made sense. Fuck, man, everything was always so mad. But wait, I was thinking, even if she had the yout, how was I gonna look after it? Could I even look after myself? That was one thing I needed to tell her because I weren't not trying to be like my dad. Yeah, the P's was there, but so what? I didn't have time, man. Time! All now I wasn't thinking about time. Not even 20 yet and my life would be done. Over. I didn't care what anyone said, from when you have a yout, you're done. Imagine I was trying to look after it and I started losing my mind again, so this kid was gonna end up looking after me, yeah? Nah, there was too many risks. Imagine my yout was that one kid in school whose dad is on the street, walking around like no one knows what's going on in his head, chatting to himself, no trim, mash-up clothes, them ones where if he goes near the school they're locking the kids in the classroom. Nah, nah. Even though I wasn't like that now, I knew the stress of a yout could bring it out of me. Even this relationship stressed man out. Nah, what, so man's gonna be doing coke in the toilet while the baby is crying because I don't know what I'm doing, can't even feed it or change it, so I'll be trying my best but all I can do is try keep it company doing lines on my knee next to the Moses basket? Then I've fucked my life and the baby's. He aint never gonna be the same again. Even me now, my dad wasn't on the street like that, but when I saw him, like, I wasn't even angry or anything like that, my body just felt like the only place it could recover was on the floor. Like I'd clocked him sometimes, like them little moments when everyone stops laughing, I'd seen him backing his whisky or Skol with his mates and for just one moment, a proper small one, I'd seen him lower his head, like, sad or whatever, and the way something would just bang me in me chest, like, I couldn't even look at him for long after stuff like that, and later on I'd realise that all up inside my mouth would be bleeding, like, not bare but just like gashes here and there from trying to chew out my face. Nah, all now I couldn't bring anyone around him. Nah, this was crazy. Imagine watching your dad kill himself, or even, imagine you couldn't even help him because he'd just bring you down too. This was the guy who gave me my first drink, you know? Man put Castle Bridge on my tongue when I was crying. Imagine I made my yout feel like that? Imagine I gave them whatever it was that I'd got and they went on a mad one too or had a breakdown because of me? Nah, it was better they aint even born, just stay in the dark, because from when you're born, going back is scary. What's even the point of this life, like, why we even need this detour? Just to make man shook? Listen, I swear when I was a yout deep down I knew this, because for some reason I started crawling backwards instead of forwards, like, it wasn't even a crawl, I'd just lift up my bum and then slide myself back as if I didn't have any legs, trying to go back to before someone dropped man in this body I don't even know how to use properly, swear it feel like man's malfunctioning most the time. I only started crawling forwards because my dad would put me down in front of a wall or in front of his feet like some oak tree so man had no choice but to try move forward because where else was I gonna go? Nah, man, there were just too many ways I could ruin this kid's life and Adwoa wasn't even trying to see it. She was just thinking about herself. Nah, I needed to show her that I aint on it. Even if she left man, I gotta do it because no way were people coming to call me 'bra Nancy', fuck that.

One more drink and it was time to do this.

Back in the bar there were way more people than I remembered, everyone talking shit to each other and not even seeing or looking out for man. I knew I was about to start bugging because next thing now all the people in the bar started moving slowly like the world's clock just started lagging again and for some split second I forgot where I was. Actually, nah, you know what, I actually forgot who or what I was, like I was just empty and suddenly realised it and so next thing whatever was left of me was trying to find who I was again, like, the feeling was so fucking nuts but it was gone quickly, but even that little bit of what I remember made me feel a certain way and that's all it took to bring that shit back again.

I went into the toilet and locked myself in and after a few minutes some prick was banging on the door saying he's gonna call the police. I must have done two lines and thought I'd do one more and then actually go to chat to Adwoa. I picked up the Henny near the toilet brush that I must have left there from before and backed it. I couldn't find my fiver so I just put my nose over the line on my card and then was ready to let Adwoa know wagwan.

Marcus, you're drunk?
  So?
  So, I'm sorry but I can't have this conversation with you while you're like this.
  What?
  Goodnight, Marcus, I'm going to bed.
  No. No, you're not. Let's chat now, fuck it, if I sleep I'll forget what I wanna say.
  Why are you doing this?
  I'm not doing anything, you're the one who started this madness. Oi, listen, do you love me?
  Oh my God.
  Do you?
  How is this relevant?
  What do you mean, how is it relevant?
  God. Okay, yes, I do. Now what?
  Adwoa. I got bare love for you too, you know that, init? Like, obviously, man loves you, it's obvious. But looked how fucked I am. A yout? I don't even think I can do that, you know.
  Marcus.
  It's actually crazy because I know I'm gonna be like my dad.

Can we please just leave it, you're just going to make yourself even more upset.

Oi, Adwoa, why did you lie, though?

What did I lie about, Marcus?

You know what.

God. I didn't tell you because I knew you'd be like this. It was my decision.

To tell me? Yeah, I get that but—

To tell you; to do whatever. It's up to me. It's my body.

Yeah, obviously, I know that, I'm not stupid, but we did this together.

Did what?

Fucked. Or you saying this baby is for a next man?

You know what, fuck you, Marcus.

Fuck me, yeah?

Yeah, fuck you.

Nah, fuck you for lying to man and now you're tryna force me to have a yout.

How am I trying to force you!?

So you're not?

No!

So you're not gonna have the baby?

Marcus, there is no baby.

What?

Yes?

Bro, what are you telling me?

Don't call me bro.

Bro! What are you saying to me right now?

Marcus, I'm saying you don't have to be a dad. Don't stress yourself, okay, there is no baby.

Huh? So you lied?

How did I lie? You're not understanding.

Understanding what, though!?

Marcus, you stink of alcohol, can you go home please?

You're trying to fuck with my head.

No, sorry, I'm not doing this with you.

Yes you are, just like everybody.

You're not even making sense.

Everyone just wants me to die.

Marcus!

What, man. What?

Let me call you a cab.

No. I'll walk home.

You can't walk home. Can you please stop this?

How can I have a baby? I can't even look after myself. Am I even alive?

Marcus, you're not having a baby. Please, you're scaring me.

Adowa, man, why have you done this? What did I do?

Marcus, can we chat about this tomorrow, please? I'm calling a cab.

Adowa.

Stop saying my name like that!

Where's the baby?

What baby, Marcus!?

Our baby.

There is no 'our' baby. Marcus, please, let's not do this now.

So what you are telling me then?

Oh my god.

Go on, talk.

About what?

Go, I'm listening to you.

You haven't been listening.

I am now.

Oh my god, this is crazy.

Adwoa, did you get rid of our baby?

Marcus.

Adwoa, I swear down.

What!

So you're actually telling me you had an abortion? And you didn't even chat to man about it?

And say what?

Anything, Adwoa, for fuck sake!

Marcus, you need to go. Seriously.

Fuck, I feel sick.

No one sent you to go drink.

And you had an abortion. I'm actually fucked. I know I'm fucked.

Marcus, how are you fucked? Please stop saying this, it's really not fair.

I knew you were like this. When I go crazy it's gonna be on you.

What?

I should have known, init. I'm so dumb, man.

Marcus, fuck you, yeah, fuck you, you prick.

Yeah, fuck me. Fuck Marcus.

Yes, fuck you. Now can you get out my house, please, or I'm gonna call your mum. Or your dad.

Twenty-Five

People walked out of the building through different exits as if each represented their position on the film we'd just watched: *Robert Mugabe: Villain or Hero?* I had no opinion and hadn't really been able to muster the presence of mind to think it through, not with San sat next to me, leaning forward as if to listen past the dialogue from the second row, exposing her neck and the scent of Roja Dove's Enigma, a fragrance that took me back to nights sitting alone in my dorm with an expensive bottle of whisky and a can of cherry Coke at the centre of my crossed legs, trying to decide if I should open it or not, sometimes ending with bending a hanger out of shape and coupling it with a belt I'd taken and kept from my dad's room. San didn't like the pairing with liquor at her expense and said I was lying, only interested in comparing her to something I had between my legs every night. I thought that was fair but I told her I didn't want to have sex with her. After I said it, I watched her and thought the evening was done once again because of my imprecision of speech, but she smiled and changed the subject. Once the film was over, San, with no mirrors before her but still leaning forward with an open eye bulging as if trying to see through the braided head in front of her, reapplied her mascara, then her lip gloss and perfume, one spray, jasmine and cognac subduing the lighter notes of cocoa butter, S-Curl, Dark and Lovely filling the air. She took my hand as the credits reached midway and we shouldered our way through a crowd, voices that sounded as if by a switch they could be silenced, their collective reflection borrowed, I felt, coming from the speakers or notes of their most recent lecture. The audience was majority black and a few times during the viewing there had been claps that had silenced the next cast member, even shouts of agreement, ones that had taken me by surprise as a Zimbabwean politician had expressed his belief that many activists had done more and been forgotten just because they had not been allowed to languish in prison for 27 years. Someone involved with the film who had refused to take questions before we left but preluded the opening scenes with pride and clarity for the undertaking, had explained that after years of doing as the white establishment required, lying prone while it extracted what it needed, he had now reached a point of acquaintance with vertigo and was able to pull the people and ideas he thought needed more exposure up to his platform. As he talked about the games of the white world, he pointed to his wife and said she knew why he'd married her. At this, I counted 4 clicks from San's fingers hidden in the dimness between her knees.

When we got to the foyer, where there was a small bar being tended by a student who was actually outside smoking and watching the thrum of black sentience developing as people left the building with the enthusiasm to change the world through discourse, San stopped me walking out with them and said we should sit down for a bit and let the film marinate and then we could discuss it if I wanted to. I honestly couldn't be bothered, I don't think I cared enough, but still, I reached for lines severed from different sources, quotes quoting a quote, words coerced or wound into coherence, drawing from book chapters and interviews, monologues and Q and As, overheard chatter as well as a small sample of my own thinking, and as I organised all these potential responses as answers to everything, I counted each person who left through both doors and then combined that number with the strays left around us and arrived at 42 without much additional effort. I felt safe. And prepared. San was wearing a beret I'd never seen before, sitting on her 8-braided fringe more than it did the rest of her head. She had on tight jeans that just about dented where her bum should have fallen, and a tucked-in oversized white shirt with sweat patches like liquid bruises all over where she had leaned forwards and backwards in her seat, contorting herself as she tried to understand a point in the film or disagreed with a conclusion. She was drinking a white wine, and I had a glass of apple juice, taking it easy because I had already taken two 10mg of diazepam before I left my student village and another 20mg while we were watching. These were blackout levels of benzo if mixed with alcohol, no matter the brand, and I wanted to remember everything about the evening and remain aware of where things might go. Maybe San would be the proof that my medication was useless, that she would be right after all, not about mine specifically, but in general, and maybe I could shape how I felt without the pills into a means of appreciating what I had, what we had, because if nothing felt real then how was San able to take my wrist and pull me through so many people and sit me down, angelic or obedient, staring at me now like she could have convinced our modern thinkers that demons had no hold, no doubt about who she was, could close her eyes and having already laid eyes on the world, it carried on existing.

You're doing too much.

What?

Apple juice. Really?

Yeah, just taking it easy today.

Do you want a drink-drink, Marcus?

Nah, I'm alright, you know, honestly.

You sure? I think they have whisky here.

Nah, it's not very good whisky, though. Seriously, I'm fine.

Sure sure?

Sure sure.

Okay, cool. So?

I like your hat.

Of course you do.

So, what did *you* think?

Hmmm. I'm still digesting it. The film, I mean. Or documentary, really, I'm still digesting it. What did you think?

I think it was interesting. There were a lot of things I wasn't aware of, like the promises that were made and never kept and how people were treated and stuff like that.

That's what I'm saying!

And also interesting how the way people see you changes depending on their interests.

Speak on it.

So basically, I think the curse is, you either die a hero or live long enough to see yourself become the villain if that makes sense?

Marcus?

What?

No way you're out here quoting Batman! Well, not Batman, the guy who wrote the movie. But my guy, c'mon, seriously? Why you always got bare shit like this in your head?

I didn't even realise that was from a film.

So you've never seen *Batman*?

I have, but I can't remember every line of it.

If you say so. Well, that's a line from the movie, sir.

Okay?

Yes?

Okay, but does it not still apply?

Let me think. Does it apply? Maybe it does.

Why does it feel like you're always trying to start shit with me? Do you think I'm stupid or something?

Erm, what are you on about?

You know what, man, nothing.

No, go on, tell me how I'm making you feel dumb. Or like I'm starting shit. Tell me, sir?

I just feel like—

Yes, go on, all-knowing, all-knowledgeable Dutty Boukman. Go on. I'm listening.

It's nothing.

Don't be shook now.

I'm not shook.

So?

Nah, sorry, seriously, sorry. I'm tired. And I think maybe I do need a drink.

So you're done?

Yes, sorry.

Crazy. Not you, but damn, I need another drink now as well.

Sorry.

It's cool.

So what did you think?

About the film?

Yeah.

I said I'm still processing. Maybe I'll tell you in the morning.

Am I staying at yours?

Huh? What's going on with you tonight?

Nah, I thought you meant, like, nah, I thought you meant something else. Sorry, my bad.

Marcus kills the vibe once again.

Ah, you know it's not like that.

Not trying to have sex with me, he says.

I'm not, though.

Well then, what's the problem with you going home alone?

There is no problem. I just thought you meant something else.

If you say so. But I do have to go. I just wanted everyone else to leave first.

Why?

Mind your business.

San saw me off at the station, was stood frozen on the platform moving only her hand on its pivot, waving goodbye. I think she wanted to come across creepy, but it was just annoying and for a moment I wondered why I went to these things with her, always tired on my way home and never really feeling like I'd learnt anything about this person I was trying so hard to understand. This might be my last event, I thought to myself. There were more, we had planned many more, but I was beginning to feel maybe San only brought me to these events because she saw me as a 'soldier' for the cause, a weak mind to be indoctrinated, maybe, and without the idea of a unified Africa, would she even talk to me?

So it is you.

Huh?

I turned around. At the end of the carriage, standing in front of another set of doors was Ama. The ends of her hair were tinged with purple dye and I could tell that her curls were only just retuning after being straightened. Guilt can take you like grief and as I looked at her the world seemed to split, the past tearing itself violently from the present. I wanted to bend forward and hold my stomach like I could fall out of myself as escape, watch from farther down the carriage, or cover my eyes with my fingers opening at intervals to assess the danger. But seeing me lean forward, as though embracing the child, a victim in perpetuity, I knew she'd call it out, call me out, as she'd done so many times, and remind me that I was manipulative and didn't know it, made worse because blame then became untethered, and needed someone to attach itself to so as to balance the relationship. In her favour, of course, but I never said the words. Fuck it, I thought, and bent forward, popping another pill into my mouth, prepared for the potential of pulling one heavy leg after another if the effects arrived too quickly, then stood up, blinked 4 times and walked towards her.

Stop. No, sorry, what are you doing? No, stay over there. I'm sorry, but who said I wanted to talk to you?

You just spoke to me, though?

And so? I was making an observation, not trying to make conversation. You can stay over there with your little girlfriend.

She's not my girlfriend?

Yeah? Good. If she was I'd tell her all about you.

Why do you love being like that?

Being like what? Marcus, am I lying?

I don't even know what you're saying.

Don't even fucking try that with me. You know exactly what I'm saying. In fact, why am I even chatting to you?

Ama, listen, I'm—

You think you can say anything that matters to me?

No. But that doesn't mean I'm not being honest. I'm sorry.

Sorry for what?

For shouting? Getting angry at you when you took my medication. And trauma dumping. I know you said I—

Stop saying medication, it makes me feel sick.

So what then?

Drugs, Marcus, your drugs.

Yeah, technically they're drugs, but—

Whatever, Marcus, Whatever. Look, I hear your apology. I don't particularly want it. But I hear it. Thanks? Now leave me alone, please.

Alright, cool. I am sorry, though.

I walked further back into the carriage, sat down and rested my head on the window, looking into the sky and all the stars that were visible. I looked for my own cluster but now they all looked the same, all mine and all so worthless. I pinched the top of my hand, squeezed tight, rolled my fingers, wanting the nails to eventually meet through the skin, but just when I was going to break through, Ama appeared again, above me, and spoke:

I'm sorry I was rude.

It's okay. I understand why.

No, I don't think so. You never get it. But I think you believe you do and so your apology is sincere. I think.

. . .

I don't know why you're looking at me like that because I already said sorry for being rude, aint no parts of me sorry for that relationship.

Yeah, I hear you. I don't blame you.

Fuck off, Marcus. Stop doing that thing, it's so annoying.

Sorry.

Stop saying sorry, man.

So what should I say?

I dunno, just keep quiet? Grow up? In fact, let me even sit down.

When our stop arrived and we made it through the gate, Ama turned towards her road, arms crossed and waiting, but I was still, silently facing her. She began walking away, then pivoted on her heel when she reached a traffic light and shouted back, asking me why I'm just standing there. I'm not sure why I hadn't moved. Maybe I was waiting for someone to turn me around, change my route, maybe San, with one hand round my wrist and the other in my palm, pulling me back, whispering she didn't mean it, I could stay with her, but no sex; or maybe I just wanted to see Ama leave me, leave me again, wiping clean dated memories for something new, something real, something easily attached to reflections I was at times forced to replay of how she left me the first time. But for now, she would stay, we both knew, both moved, and we would take the same route we'd taken many times, open the same door, kiss at the same spots, climb into the same bed, and find the same playlist.

Petey Pablo played on as she pulled away from me and looked from my lips to my eyes.

You're not fucking me.

Okay?

Yeah, we're not having sex.

So what's happening, then?

Suck my breasts.

Take this off properly, then.

Okay, bite my nipple.

Shit. Okay, now put your fingers inside me.

The zip is stuck.

Fuck, okay, wait. Okay. Try 3 fingers. Uh. Suck my nipple again. Okay, now suck my clit.

What?

Marcus, please, don't stop, I'll give you head after.

. . .Whatever.

. . .

. . .

Okay, okay, yes, yeah, stay there. Shit.

I didn't picture San, but I thought of her, wondered where her reasoning took her once she'd processed the film, how long I'd have to wait to hear her views because of how we left things, wondered how complicated she found the Lancaster House Agreement, and was it naive to believe the promises of freedom whispered by those who fought to keep it from you, was the heroism of our countries' leaders always edging towards dictatorship, how much of your past was needed to absolve you of your future, or future intentions, did you bank good deeds, only to cash them in for necessary evil? Could a hero truly become a villain if the people whose lives had been changed, or saved, were still willing to give testimony of your courage, valour, before any gathering of the middle ground, or opposition, and did we create gods in our own image, when we needed them most, when we were at our worst, and so what should we expect, when their voices fell from the sky? And should we, as comrades, as Africans, as pan-Africans, share our opinions no matter what, no matter our home, or locale, our distance from the issue, our lack of depth, depth, deep, deeper . . . A part of me didn't even want this, not even with San. Not yet. Ama came, trying to pull my entire face into her vulva, and then crossed her legs around my head as she moaned and tried to squeeze out the dying thrill of her orgasm. I couldn't breathe, but firmed it. When she let me go, I picked up my shirt from the floor and wiped my chin, goatee and moustache, then threw it back and lay facing the ceiling, waiting, listening to track 4 from *See.SZA.Run* which had begun playing mid arch, a song I'd only just managed to disentangle from my short time with Ama.

I know I said I'd give you head, but I'm really tired now. You made me cum so hard.

I knew you were going to do this.

Do what?

Nothing. Let me just get my stuff.

You don't have to go, you know. We can just chill.

So basically you just wanted me to eat you out?

No. I thought we might have sex, but then I was just like okay no, I'll give him head, but now I'm just so tired. Don't be angry, please.

Trust me, I'm not angry. I don't even care about the head. Just why lie?

I'm sorry. I accepted your apology. Now can you accept mine?

Whatever.

Come, don't go. Come here. Let's just lay with each other.

Yeah, sure, whatever. Move over.

Enough? Is that better?

Not really.

Okay, sorry, hold on. Now?

Yeah, fine.

Come closer, please.

Cool.

I can't lie, I have missed you. You're always so warm when you're not being a dickhead.

Yeah, whatever.

Honestly. I don't hate you, Marcus.

Thanks?

So what's your girlfriend's name?

San.

I thought she wasn't your girl?

I'm being patient, I guess.

Sounds boring.

I think it's supposed to be.

How is your hand? Do you have a scar?

No.

Marcus.

Yes?

Can I ask you something?

Yeah . . .

Don't get angry.

I won't.

Swear?

I won't. I'm tired. What is it?

Was it really an accident?

If I answer, can we just leave it here and go to sleep?

Okay.

No follow-up questions?

That's fine. So? Was it an accident?
No.
Alright. I understand. Marcus.
Yeah?
Come closer.
Okay.

Nineteen

That's nearly 600 a month done. Cheers, mate.
　She's coming back, Anton.
　How have you fucked this up for both of us?
　I can't be bothered to chat about this right now, seriously.
　I knew you'd fuck it up.
　Bro, seriously, stop.
　Yeah, alright, you fucking bell end, I'll see you later.

Now I had time to train properly. I wasn't happy Adwoa was gone, but at the same time I did feel like we needed some space. Bruh, lifting 50kg dumbbells again was not easy. I probably should have gone up slowly or even warmed up a little bit, some dynamic stretching because my shoulder was fucked, but I just wanted to go in and get back to where I was before, get me? Anton spotted me. I hit about 5 and half reps, depth too. But one thing about me is that if I set my mind to 8 reps but I only manage to buss 4, it's gonna be stressing me all day, picturing the lift over and over again till I start to feel sick. Gym is serious for me. My rest periods were from 2 minutes to 3 minutes, but if I remembered my pre-workout creatine and nitric oxide, I'd cut it to a minute and a half to 2 minutes. Most PTs will tell you if you're only doing up to 5 reps, then you're only training for strength, but it's never been like that for me. I put on size with any rep range, as long as I'm failing on my final set. That's what it's about: failure. None of those calm 12 reps and then you're chilling, bussing jokes, on your phone, nah, if you're doing your ting properly, then that last rep gonna feel like God himself pushing his two fingers down on them dumbbells becah you aint getting them up. Everything to failure: flat dumbbell press, incline dumbbell flies, decline barbell on Smith machine, weight dips, bent-over rows, one-arm rows, seated rows, weighted pull ups, bicep curls, reverse bicep curls, cable curls, tricep extensions, skull crushers, close-grip bench press, squats, lunges, walking lunges, hack squats, Romanian deadlifts, normal deadlifts, incline leg press, leg extensions, leg curls, calf raises, shoulder press, lateral raises, upright rows – every ting haffi fail. Then intervals on the treadmill, 20 seconds on, 20 seconds off. Trust me, after that, you're finished, slumped when you get home. Couple times I even forgot to go check Belina, bare missed calls on my phone when I woke up. I trained twice a day on the days when Adwoa would message me from Ghana, though, some long-arse text explaining shit to me like I don't already know. I can accept an apology but that don't mean I'm checking for you like I was before. I tried explain to her how she done me, how this is how everyone ends up moving with me when I let them into my life or start to think they're cool. Like, I'd even been picking up my bible again and thinking about the future when more time I didn't even bother to think about next month, and that was all because of her, like, man felt like living was finally calm, like nothing was waiting to remind me that I'm gonna die one day. She said she hears me, she's sorry and the reason she done it and lied was because of whatever but I weren't even trying to hear all that. Just let me focus. She done what she did, now she had to deal with it. And yet, was she even doing that!? She was gone after a week, about her mum needs her. To do what? But cool, I didn't say anything, just left it, she'll come back, 4 weeks aint that long and I'd be waiting. Where she gonna go again? I told her ask her mum who's in the wrong. All now I was even saving as well. Anyway, yeah, gym was banging and my food was on point too. I'd buy 23 chicken thighs, get my Cajun seasoning, dash the chicken in one Tesco bag and pour it all over. Then I'd shake that shit up and that's my protein for 4 days. For carbs I'd either have some sweet potato, cut up and boiled for half an hour, or this grain ting called fonio. Ay, don't no one know about fonio, you know. Less carbs than rice, more nutrients. A superfood, trust me. My clients hate it but that shit is calm for me. To be honest, most food is calm for me as long as I've got the right seasoning so it tastes familiar. I don't eat food because it's nice, oi listen, if I wouldn't die or lose muscle, I probably would eat like once a week. But annoyingly, it aint like that so I'm backing like 3 meals a day, sometimes 4 if I feel like my body needs it. But not a proper meal, maybe couple slices of sourdough bread with strawberry jam. You know what, tell a lie, I actually like eating that. Okay, yeah, bread and jam man would eat on a regular but that's probably it. Been eating that since I was a yout. I remember once on the playground, one kid, can't even remember his name, but yeah, one kid, and you know what, that yout actually had muscle on his body from early. Like when we'd go swimming he was the only man who had pecs and abs. Anyway, his hair was never combed, peps, man had bare peps, and someone must have told him I said when he goes home he eats his peps instead of rice. He walked up to me like, is it true? These times I was the only kid in school who wore white shirts and black school trousers, my mum tryna tell me that it's because I had to look smart but I know she was lying because see my collar and my cuffs with streaks of brown. I didn't even know it was dirt and my mum didn't really care, though one day my dad must have clocked and started chatting to my mum about disgracing us and how we were welcoming bullies or some shit like that so he started hand washing them in the bath and drying them hanging over our hench TV. And by bullies I know he meant one of his friends must have chat shit to him about me. But yeah, that's how I preed I was dirty. So now this guy had come up to me and I didn't even know what to say when he asked me, I think I was just surprised he was chatting to me because I didn't have friends like that, more time when I tried talking to people on the playground they made one face and walked off or closed their group up like they were all trying hide something in the middle of them. Sometimes some random student would run past me and slap the back of my head. I remember when I first recalled them kind things and actually laughed, like, kids actually move mad for no reason. Anyway, he grabbed my lunch box and opened it up. All now I'm just watching him. He took out my sandwich, opened the plastic bag and whatever he was coming to do to me, he wasn't feeling to do it no more. He peeled back one slice of bread and then couldn't even look at me, but because he wasn't looking, I knew he was, if you get me. I thought he was gonna try run some jokes but then he ate one of the sandwiches, like proper chewed it up, like man was more hungry than I was, but I'd always see him in the lunch hall eating school dinners. Anyway, he gave me back the rest of my food and walked off with his crowd. I think they were as baffled as me, like, I knew they wanted to see me get beaten up or something like that. But from then, whenever that guy saw me again about playground, he never troubled me, just flicked up his head at me like wagwan. But I never did anything back. Just sat and ate my sandwiches.

Twenty-Five

I left Ama's and took out my phone to message San. I hesitated, thought maybe I should get home, shower and at least cleanse my palate before opening up to conceal the truth, my truth, or was it now ours? I tried to call her, but no answer, so with fingers struggling to find each letter, I eventually sent her a message asking her to come and see me at my halls. I turned off my phone. She had never been anywhere near Bolton before and I knew she felt no interest even though I called it home, for now, but it was where I felt safest to explain how I was feeling and where I would like things to go. Bolton was a place existing almost outside of time by the force of the world's collective indifference to it. The students on my floor would be in lectures, hopefully, so I wouldn't have to explain who San was, why she was there, intuit them thinking she was a loose link who'd found her way back to the thread, or just a friend, posing as something more. I hoped for something more. Across the road from me was a little girl with her mother. Though she was about 4, she walked like she was only just learning, and I remembered the fun of Thorpe Park, how good it had felt to be around children again. Why grow up, why not choose to freeze yourself in time, not even a fracture when put to fire? I blinked hard as I turned away, to push out the intrusive thoughts, and didn't look back at the girl. Up towards my halls the sun was slowly rising behind the red-brick buildings. Some of us students could see the dorms for what they were, reworked homes for disobedient thoughts never nurtured or broken enough to create their own prison. I saw some students ahead of me. I knew their faces, that our relationships remained in gestures like daps and spuds, nods and lifted brows. As they walked past me, two on each side, I held out my hand and they each gave me theirs in passing, as if bestowing their respect for what had happened the night before. But once past them, I remembered why I kept my distance, slighted by the thought that one of them had slapped my palm with more force and haste than the others. At Ama's, I had woken up in a daze, reached for my medication but found only the side of her face, one of my fingers slipping into her mouth and sliding around the peeled skin on the inside of her cheek. She closed her lips around it but I pulled it out before she could bite down. You're cute sometimes, you know, she said. I opened my eyes and she was just there watching me, propped up on her elbow. Then I realised where I was. She said good morning and I rolled away from her, out of the bed and sat on the floor with my palms to the ground like I could push off and break away through the ceiling. I couldn't shower or brush my teeth, I almost felt like I couldn't leave, opening and closing my palm over the carpeted floor like gathering snow that had fallen during the chill of night. I felt guilt, but I wasn't sure why. San wasn't my girlfriend and I owed Ama a debt for how things had ended.

Walking, I stopped at the local coffee shop and picked up a medium vanilla latte, added cold water to it and drank it down in 4 gulps, enough to pick me up for 10 minutes then allow me to sleep until the late afternoon when I hoped to see San. Opposite the coffee shop was Bolton One, where I'd met the doctor, Chris, and where Sports Science students had their practical lectures, and also where you could rent part of their squash court or go climbing on their wall. I'd been climbing a few times and made it to the top, looked out the window at eye level and watched the people and cars and life that carried on no matter my point of view. Aside from climbing, I didn't do much exercise, but often tired myself out at night through overindulgence or overstimulation of my nervous system through various means in spite of my habits. Those were the best sleeps I had, when my body raged against the dying diazepam and Xanax and lit up my central nervous system to slow time or heat me up or make me faint or dry my mouth or make me freeze, moisten my palms, make me dizzy, make me doubt, make me cry, make me split, make me excited, elated, overzealous, unbearable, make me weak, make me strong, make me laugh at the pain or court it, make me run once, twice, maybe 3 times to the toilet, making me worry at the frequency or make me hear it all approaching me or make me hear nothing but the single solid note of tinnitus, the chord of anxiety . . . or make me soft, make me hard, make me roast, make me see it all from above like a spectre, or make me kneel, make me wheeze, make me fear, make me panic, make me touch the floor to know it was there, or make me wait, make me still or make me approach those skinless fingers that could shatter our will. Anxiety made me and so much more, so I slept when I was consumed and left a pillow by my door. I got to my room and was ready to fall face first onto my mattress and scattered books when San messaged me back and said she was going to visit her family in Bristol. I was suddenly depleted on my feet so fell to the ground, faced upward and began to feel around for something, glass bottle, pages of A4, plastic bottle, nail clippers, charger, room keys, lone fork escaping the knife, and then I felt and picked up a comb I used for my beard sometimes. The end of it was like a needle, there to separate swirling hair and then comb the curls into submission. I put the needle into my ear and began scratching, trying to clear out the wax I was certain only in that moment was the cause of my tinnitus. I pulled it out and looked at what I'd collected, wiped it on my shirt and went back to work, trying to ease the string of ringing, more slowly this time, going deeper. And then I shuddered and with just a small movement of my wrist the needle pierced the inside, missing anything deeper, but cutting the soft tissue. Blood dripped from my ear, into my ear. Then I stopped the trickle with my finger, stopped up and plugged my ear with some used tissue I took out of the plastic bag that hung from my door handle as a bin. The tinnitus had never been louder and I knew I was going to struggle to get sleep.

Nineteen

There's levels to this when it comes to running and I wasn't really on any of them. True, if man's got good music in and I've had at least one litre of water, I can go on for a bit, but otherwise I'll just end up walking after like two miles, I don't know what it is, I think I just get bored really easily or something. To tell the truth, even if the playlist is popping, I think about stopping after every tune. Anyway, I don't really believe all the hype about running is gonna burn bare fat off my body, I could just stick to intervals and be fine. These times I was only really jogging because it was something to do to take my mind off everything that was going on. Some of my clients had dipped as well so more time had been freed up. The way it happened was my fault, though, like, I wasn't focused, and they could tell. When people are paying 45 pounds for an hour of your time, they want it all, even if you're not getting them the results they say they're looking for, they at least want you to listen to them tell you how much they wanna switch up their career or slap up their co-worker. But I couldn't even do that. So like 4 of them didn't renew after their sessions finished. Usually I would be stressed, but I didn't really give a shit, I could get more, I'd be back to my old self soon, I just needed to push through this, get me. On my jogs I'd go past my old school, changed up, finally got some money, the playground smaller now and there was one square building where us man used to play football, just there looking out of place. Where it used to say girls' and boys' entrance, and don't forget this was one of them old-time schools, I think it was set up by a missionary or something, but yeah, well, now instead of that, it said Year 7 entrance and Year 8, like they'd split them up for some reason, like I swear I remember when Year 7 to Year 9 was basically the same thing, I think we even had our own playground separated from the olders. It's crazy how fast time moves. Back in the day, whenever I would be excited about something coming up, I'd say to myself, 'In no time I'll be doing reh reh reh', because I thought that would make things go faster. Last time I said it I was in one of them changing rooms in one of them shops where they sell your school uniform. Now look? Nuts. And these days I don't really get excited about anything. Across the road from the school was a tiny theatre with a library on the side of it. I've actually never been there, can you imagine, a school next to a theatre and we never even went in there for a school trip, not even to check for the library. Mostly if anyone from school was anywhere near it, it was round the back sparking a zoot. So yeah, running, I'd pass the red-brick buildings and them betting shops and Turkish barber's where one Year 10 dashed a brick at a PE teacher's head after he just got a trim as well, and then past the chicken shop, King Rooster. Nah, King Rooster, that chicken was too addictive, too nice, them fat and juicy pieces had man trying to sneak out for lunch at like 11 a.m. Probably why people from my year were so wam. I remember one of my boys dashing a leg at one guy's head during lunch time, I think he must have been trying to talk like he was bad and ended up collecting one lick of chicken on the side of his head. The thing about them days, maybe even now, is that you didn't have to be on road to be on something. Anyone would back them self so you didn't really know who you could chief up and get away with it, like one minute you could be talking shit to some random guy in ends who looks like he's not on anything, next thing you're wiping chicken grease from your cheek or you've taken couple gun shots to your back. Anyway, I'd usually stop just outside the second park on my run, back some water and then walk in, trying to catch my breath. Yeah, that and boredom were the only barriers, my legs never got tired or cramped or anything like that, maybe once or twice I'd keep going, jogging under the trees, past flowers, bare flowers, if you proper look, there's so many different flowers in ends, even the trees are different when you deep it properly, but everyone is always in their own world where everything is probably dead. Then it was past the swings and a climbing frame and a zip line with kids all over them like bugs and that, and then I'd be sprinting, the noise of them kids screaming never catching up, then I'd hail couple guys playing football who I knew, then back out onto the street, through couple blocks and then around the outside, next to the high road, back on my way home. By the time I got in I had to start getting ready to go check Belina, one thing onto the next, I had to keep it moving otherwise I'd just be sitting there getting angry and that feeling would start to wake up and I'd feel like any minute I could slip and my thinking would never be the same and I just needed to escape somehow, like climb out my own body or leave the world in ways I don't even wanna chat about. Adwoa knew all this as well and I told her to keep it in mind because I'm not trying to blame her for something that happens to me so let's see what she's saying when she gets back. I shouted my dealer before I got in the shower, picked up like a gram and a half, then called a cab and just sat in the back seat with the window all the way down, watching people out and about enjoying their day.

Me and Belina spoke now and then, dropped each other a line just to keep in touch, but when Adwoa bounced I'd shouted her to link up and she'd told me just come to her yard. Aint even like Adwoa didn't know because when she texted me asking what I was doing I'd tell her I was with Belina. I wasn't even trying to be a prick, Belina and me were just cool. Her foster dad was this famous television host for like *Gladiators and other shit like that and at first I found it weird like say a cartoon suddenly come to life because I used to watch that show every weekend with my dad and in my head I couldn't bring the two things together, like everything about Belina actually looked unreal sometimes because I didn't even know people like her lived in ends. Her house was small, though, looking like one of those trendy coffee shops, one of them carefree places that I reckon black hippies used to jam in back in the day, cats running about, some of them not even hers, but her own sculptures all around the house just about hanging on walls. The was one giant mirror she said her foster dad gave her when they had to move out their mansion, mansion you know, she dropped it like it was normal,* like we all had P's like that or something, like, trust me, only P's my foster mum gave me, actually, only thing I was allowed to take, that my biological mum allowed me to take from foster care, was my small

DeLorean toy car, but a next kid stole it from me when I reached primary school in Tottenham. But yeah, I had P's in a bank somewhere but I lost the book for it and I know say there weren't a lot in it because no one had P's like that when I was young. Belina also had a rocking chair I think she said she found on one road corner and the chair actually had this gold metal square attached that was dedicated to someone's grandma! I remember how she used to sit on the edge of it, swinging and rolling a spliff, then sit back and spark it with her legs crossed like she was waiting for something that she knew weren't never gonna come. You'd also see incense ash in places I don't even know how, books looking fresh and others looking like they been splashed with her morning coffee and just bare other random things scattered about. Even though there was incense always burning, the first thing that got you when you walked into the living room was the smell of weed. The first time I went over there, I had to stand outside for a minute because that smell hit me hard and I swear it felt like I was back with my cousins smoking, like everything that had happened after that moment was a dream and I was still sitting in that cage ting falling asleep. Belina was calm about it, though, and sat on the floor in the corridor with me until I was ready to go in. In front of her sofa bed, she had this 3 table set, one under another, and on the lowest table there were stacks of books and a mirror and we'd either do coke off whatever she'd been reading or off the mirror if she could get all the dirt and dust off it with the sleeve of her jumper. She could get her own stuff of course, but the one time I listened to her and did a line of her coke the next thing I knew my nostrils were burning and the day after all I could smell was gasoline and when I sneezed I could see bits of blood so I told her next time I come I'll bring my own. Fam, we'd be doing lines and chatting shit till like 4 a.m., looking at each other happy to lie like one more bottle and we're done. And next morning I'd always think we must have done alright, couldn't remember much but not too hungover so couldn't have drunk too much, but come see the living room now and there'd be like 8 empty bottles of rosé around the sofa like it was some fortification. But anyway, yeah, what was I saying, yeah, so Belina could sculpt, and she loved to sing too. That's usually how I knew it was time to go bed, when she started singing and it was like say I wasn't even there. One thing about me is that cocaine never made me hype like you'd see other people, I've always had bare energy since I moved in with my cousins so to me coke was more like a distraction, like I could focus on one thing at a time instead of my mind just being all over the place. It was never something to make me vibe. But my body felt it, though, sometimes in a way where I'd get a bit shook. Like my heart would start beating funny or it felt like I had a stitch in my chest instead of my stomach. Belina said it was normal, but whenever it happened I'd just sit there and wait to see if man was gonna die or not. I'm one of those people that if someone pulled out a strap and aimed it at me, I'd just stand there. Not because I wasn't shook but because I was. I don't know why, but when it comes to death or dying or things like that, I'm lost, like I can't function properly unless I'm in one of those weird moods and then I'm thinking it might even be more peaceful than this, but I don't really think like that, just now and then, more time I'm positive and try keep the vibe lively but thinking about death really shuts man down.

*

Belina, are you even listening?

I am. I'm listening. You're annoyed that your ex had an abortion with someone else. You wanna watch porn?

No, man! I mean, yeah, fine, but no, not that. I mean I am angry, but I'm talking about when I was a kid. And what are you even talking about? It was with me, not someone else.

But you said you found the message in her phone and she'd gone to do it with someone else? I thought that's what this was all about.

No, she went by herself. I think she did. But I never went through her phone. She just dropped it on me out of nowhere, can you imagine?

I can, Marcus, it's her body. You didn't even want the baby.

Yeah, but don't do it behind my back, though, like, I should have an opinion, you should ask me or at least tell me wagwan.

Poor Marcus.

Fuck you.

So dying and death. I don't want to talk about your ex's body and what she does with it, you know.

Bro, these lines are way too big, man.

Yeah, I've got it. So you were a scared kid?

Not of everything.

Then what?

Like I was saying. The end of the world. How I was always thinking about the end of the world. I'd be in class and suddenly I'd remember the world was gonna end in 1999 and then all of a sudden I can't do no work.

Who told you the world was gonna end in 1999?

One of my teachers. Fucking nuts, man. She said a philosopher predicted it.

Nostradamus was a philosopher?

Who is Nostradamus? Nah, not this. We've watched this one bare times.

But it's so hot, though!

Yeah, but I'm not in the mood for this gay shit today. Let's find something else. Maybe later.

Fine.

The acting is so bad, as well.

Everyone's acting is bad.

So let me think, 1999, 2000. Oh my days, yes, 2000 as well, I thought the world was gonna end.

Because of that computer bug?

Yeah! And then there was some Jehovah's Witness who told me the world was ending while I was sitting on a bus. I swear I looked out the window after she said it and the sky was red! And then a guy in my class brought in this book called *The Bible Code* with bare predictions in it, proper scary. And the 6th of June 2006. Oh, and then there was that machine in Switzerland that was gonna end the world. Yeah, man, there was bare of them. And every time I'd think about these kinda things my head would be gone, in another world.

The Large Hadron Collider, I remember that one. So you're scared to die? You know the world's going to end in 2012 as well?

Wait, what, who said that?

Does it matter? It won't happen, anyway. So you're scared to die?

Yeah, cool, okay, it probably won't, I know that, but I still wanna know.

Marcus, answer my question.

Yes, man, most the time. Everyone is. I know you're gonna say you're not?

I'm not. I'm honestly surprised I've lived this long. I always thought I'd die as a teenager.

Why?

BPD. Thought I'd kill myself.

What's BPD?

Borderline Personality Disorder.

Like you have different personalities?

No.

Then what? Can I do this line or you want it?

Yeah, it's fine, you can do it. And, Marcus, you know I love you so take this with love, but I don't want to talk about mental illness stuff right now. Because I know if we start talking about it then we're going to be here all night talking about it, you know? Let's not bring the mood down, okay, so enough burying the world in rubble for today.

Fine.

But I do want to know what it is that scares you about death?

I don't really know, you know.

Are you sure, Marcus?

Yeah?

Does death feel like the world is abandoning you when you think you need it most?

Rah, okay.

Deep, init. Think on it, maybe?

Nah, I'm good you know. How are you still scrolling?

There's nothing good!

Go to your Pornhub favourites.

No.

Why not?

Because you'll think I'm gross.

Come, man, let me see, I won't judge.

Yes you will, trust me.

Nah, I won't, I swear. I already think you're weird, anyway.

Fuck off.

Seriously?

You promise you won't judge me?

Belina, you've pretty much told me your life story.

Yeah, but this is different. That's just oversharing.

How, though? How is it different?

It just is.

C'mon, I swear I won't judge.

You swear?

I swear?

Actually no, I can't.

Fine fine. Let's listen to music instead then.

Oh my god, yes, what do you want to listen to?

Does it even matter because you're just gonna put on what *you* want to listen to, anyway.

Okay, Amy? First album?

Yeah, that's fine, actually. You gonna sing?

You want me to?

Yeah.

Okay, exciting! Are you going to write your lyrics as well? While you sing?

Yes! I'll sing over an instrumental and you write your rap lyrics.

Grime.

Rap, grime, whatever, let's just do it. Yeah?

Your beats are too slow, man.

But I've listened to you rap over them before and I liked it.

MC'ing. I'm not rapping. And, yeah, nah, I hear that but it's too fast, man.

You said it's too slow.

It's both.

So let's do that then?

Nah, I'm not in the mood.

Ergh. Boring. Fine. I can still sing, though?

Yeah, do your thing. Maybe you'll inspire me.

Okay, one sec.

Cool.

Wait, what's the time?

Like 11.

Should we get some more coke?

Don't we have enough? Actually, yeah, let me holla at my guy.

Yes!

Only half a gram, though. I think I've got a client in the morning.

So what? Just do more in the morning.

Nah, G, I can't do that.

Why not? And stop calling me—

Yeah, yeah, but nah, not before a client, not in the morning. Like can you imagine drinking in the morning? That's when you know.

When you know what?

When you know, init.

Marcus, can I ask you something?

What?

Don't be offended or anything, it's just a question.

Yeah, go on.

Actually, never mind.

No, go on, seriously, I won't be offended. What's it about?

The way you talk to me.

How do I talk to you?

Calling me 'bro' and 'G' and everything else.

Yeah, and?

And?

Yeah, and? I don't even know what you're asking me. Aight, he'll be here in 30 mins.

Boring!

So what are you saying?

Nothing.

No, seriously, Belina, c'mon, what is it?

Sometimes you sound like someone else is what I mean, you know.

What? What does that mean?

You don't know what anything means, do you, Marcus, darling?

Oi, come, man, foreal, what are you saying? Someone else?

I'm bored. Spliffy?

Nah, I don't smoke.

Oh yeah. Boring.

I think I get what you're saying but at the same time I'm trying to understand it. It's such a weird question. You think I'm like, so basically you think I'm acting or something?

No, not exactly acting. Maybe performing? Like when you rap with me. But I do think it's a little bit pretentious. Just a tiny bit. I'm bored.

Pretentious?

Okay, this is boring me now.

Bruh, you're the one who brought it up. Do you have more wine?

Yeah, in the fridge.

Cool.

You want me to get it?

It's your house.

Ergh. Fine. Ice?

Nah, I'm good. Just bring the bottle.

Is your dealer coming?

Yeah, actually, lemme check.

Adwoa had sent me bare messages but I didn't like chatting to her when I was too gone. I knew she could sense it too, some evil eye reaching man from Ghana. She was back in 23 hours, though, and I knew she'd wanna talk as soon as she landed, even asked me to meet her at the airport but I said nah. Four weeks gone too fast, man, I wasn't ready and plus I was gonna have a hangover and probably wanna stay in bed. But also, I just wanted to get it all over and done with. I didn't know if I was gonna lock it off but I needed her to understand that what she done wasn't right. She said she did but I wanted to get my point across then see what she was saying after that. And I weren't trying to hear just sorry.

God hath given you one face, and you make yourself another! I brought ice in case you changed your mind. Are you messaging him?

Hold on, I'm just thinking.

Painful?

One sec.

Marcus, are you counting?

Wait, hold on, what did you just say before that? Are you trying to say that's me? So you think I'm fake basically?

Is that what I said? I shouldn't have brought it up.

Nah, I'm not annoyed or anything, I'm just asking.

I used to do it as well, that's why I noticed.

Do what?

I used to see someone I liked and then tried to take on their personality, a celebrity or a character in a novel, the way they spoke, everything. I thought it made me more interesting and that maybe that was really who I was and that's why I connected with them, you know. But really I didn't really know who I was at the time or what I was doing. Sometimes too I didn't know *what* I was. So scary. Or fun. Depends.

And then? So you're pretending now? This aint you?

No. I grew out of it. Had therapy. Decided I like being Belina, you know.

I hear you.

Where is this guy?

He's coming. When are you gonna sing?

Is it the same guy from Flashes?

Yeah, it is.

I fucked him you know.

Did he give you some more coke?

Fuck you.

Twenty-Five

When I finally made it back to Edmonton, the first thing I noticed was the smell. The sun was shining and when you looked up to avoid the odour you were forced to wink at the sky. But it was obvious, if not believed, that a sewer ran so close to the surface of the ground, a cesspool polluted with what fell from the residents' sour bodies and tumbled through trenches, blending with what we discarded ourselves as too tainted even for us, so that if you looked down a grate, something looked back at you. I decided to walk from the station and see if I could notice any signs of change, vanguards of renovation, likely a welcome sight under the sun, resentful when it rained. But nothing. And I honestly understood it. It seemed the same people walked out of the same buildings, the same shouts came from the same boats, those excited or angry calls to the distance to unseen mates or boys or even girlfriends who were stood right beside them. The same glass crunched under your feet, chewed black circles with trainer prints, and I honestly recognised some of the same people with bad luck trying theirs for some change, feeling relieved recalling that I'd been given a 5-pound note inside an off licence that refused to take my card. I handed it to one of them and turned away before they could thank me, embarrassed by the act, like passing scraps under a table weak from being stacked. The only cafes open were the Turkish owned and I was a little surprised not to see any quirky food shops offering cereal for dinner, cocktails for breakfast, or authentic African food – jollof rice in paper bowls, or wrapped like a doner roll with pieces of beef poking out the top. There were no bars proud of their bare bones, their USP splintering wooden seats, or bakeries that promised 4-ingredient sourdough. Pubs held onto corners, broken from chains but still their charm remaining, locals stood outside waiting with lagers, stretching to see a mate coming past to divert them to the bar for a half pint soon to double in size and the next round on them. Edmonton was still owned by the wrong'uns and stressed, man who might hail you or watch you, T-shirts under their stab-proof vest, those who saw sunshine and thought they'd suffocate under anything that put weight on their chest. Change was laughed off with a drink and a tap on the nose, discouraging outsiders from peeking in to pick up the pieces and claim them as something eccentric to be sold. I was home. Tottenham was almost lost but Edmonton dragged its feet, expecting its allowance without looking for ways to work off the week. I took a turn onto my road and saw the back of a delivery moped leaving its driver behind. There was a new tree planted in the middle of the roundabout with wire circling its trunk. A half-full skip was outside a house and Christmas lights stretched through an overgrown bush next door. I walked around the side of my house and tried to open the gate, getting a splinter in my knuckle after pounding the latch, that annoying latch, trying get it open. I took 8 steps back and looked at the house, squinted through the inner curtain to see if the window handle was up, then took a bottle of water out of my backpack and swallowed one and a half alprazolam. Something was blocking the gate. I put my bag in front of my shoulder and pushed against it, dragging the garbage bags behind across the floor, fraying and splitting them open. Empty bottles of whisky and rum hit the ground but didn't shatter and I put my finger to my ear to dampen the sound, then sliding it out with the loose plaster from the day before that was beginning to irritate, thinking how fucking insane my family were, what if I decided to come home, how was I supposed to get into the house? If the back door was locked then I'd have to fly through a window so I pushed down on the handle a little too hard and it gave way and more and hung limp when I let go of it. From the kitchen, behind the living room door, you could smell the alcohol and I walked in intending to ignore it all and go upstairs to my room, but my dad wasn't up, he was on his stomach on the sofa, an arm hanging, his wrist bent on contact with the floor. It was only 5 past 4 and already he'd lost. A bottle of Jim Beam stood beside a glass three-quarters empty. I put the back of my hand in front of his mouth and then stood in the middle of the room and just looked at him. One day, someone would look at me the same way, maybe San, maybe my mum, maybe someone already had. I shook my head 4 times, sat on the floor and crossed my legs, one finger looped through the loose material at the back of my Timbs, one side of my face in the palm of a hand.

My dad could be a good man if he let himself feel something, feel sadness. Instead, he was somewhere in the middle. Once, he stepped onto the same bus as me and I shuffled to a window seat at the back so I couldn't be seen, but I watched him, saw him look into a bottle, sad in that moment he knew he'd wasted another day to it, that it was this or a living death, an unwanted death, and I understood he'd given his all, that poison on the tongue was, to him, a step towards freedom, that he felt he had nowhere else to look, a dying man who I'm sure believed life was an unending, unravelling of painful stories that he did his best to revise or resist, rewrite, and so he began to speak without following the rules of his life sentences, turned his back on pages of grief and wrote his own odes to immortality, and here I am, a griot to remind us then blind us by the divinity of his belief. There were times, I remember, when love came upon us both like something descending from the sky, times when he'd speak and I'd listen, and I felt the glory of life's unfolding narratives reminding me I was his son, that I could take what he had and be proud of it. But now we were too scared or sedated to talk to each other any more, to see beyond the surface of what each of us presented. My dad, with a few drinks, he could fool anyone into thinking that how he made them feel was proof of his misunderstood morality, divinity, even, or that there was virtue deep within him that could be realised only with some help. But only family remained, obliged, no one else, no sacrifice at the altar of bra Nancy, no one caring to listen to him the way that I used to. And with the stories my dad told me there came fictions he hoped to make gospel as well.

As a boy, on Tottenham High Road, my dad pulled me through a doorway, turning so suddenly with my arm I thought we were passing through a wall where I could be frozen between the building forever waving to the street. The place was invisible when you were looking for it, but inside, the shop was adorned with what my mum called kente cloths, hanging like flags, a gentle breeze from air conditioners undulating them like their sights were set on the sky for escape: black and gold, black and white, blue and gold, purple and red. Clashing hues, symbols touching. A woman sat at a sewing machine, her foot rising and falling out of time with the cacophony of colours. Eiii, bra Nancy, she said. Named, a satisfying lie will catch on. Oheme, my dad replied, as we walked towards the back room. My dad told me we were there to collect his money. We passed through billowing curtains with a widening mouth seeming unsated by whatever passed through it and soon, we were on the other side, to a back room with a lighted path ending in a corner set apart from the rest of the room by its luminescence. On a table was a bottle of Castle Bridge, a stack of pink notes and a game, the game, a broken bough split in half, 6 depressions either side to hold the stones they carried. My dad reached for the gin, pretending to pour some in my mouth like libation, the lid still fastened tight. Then came voices like they were once whole but now split into unequal parts: Hey hey, he's too small, came on, mfa mano. Eiii, he has come! Who has come? Bra Nancy! Whan? Obarina wei? Wɔ ferɛ, ana? Heh, gyae saa, wo nkanfo no too much. Kojo, find space, let him sit. C'mon, my dad said, let me correct my money and go. Around the table were Uncle Dave, Uncle K, Uncle Charlie, Uncle Kojo, Uncle Sam, Uncle Kwabena, Uncle Kofi, Uncle Tito, Uncle Ata one, Uncle Brobby and Uncle Wofaa. Uncle Dave and Uncle K sat opposite each other, heads down, watching the beads of the game. They looked up to greet and click with my dad – I saw so many hands reaching for him at the same time that day, and somehow he managed to satisfy them all. I was put into a corner, sat upon a stool, climbed and stood and stretched to see him over the lives, the bodies that crowded around him. But he shouted for me to sit, and so I watched the backs of the men, forgetting their faces so imagined them to be as my dad's was, unaged, smooth dark skin like a mask, beneath which there was something someone was always searching for. I tried to pick up words I'd heard before and draw new ones from their proximity to the ones I knew. The last time we had come here I picked up the word koromfou. This was the day I'd learn its meaning. My dad used to tell stories like crafting the fabric that was sold here, intricate, easy to mistake one thread for another, but then years passed and prescriptions slowed his speech, whisky shrivelled his reach, and he began to speak as if reciting from pages composed by someone beneath him, the monotone strumming the truth without the animation of honesty, the three-part structure collapsing when it was time to conclude and so his friends having to interrupt to get him to abandon his story or they'd be locked in the lies with him. So, now, among his friends, his voice soon drifted and fell, his voice a whisper among cries in pidgin and peacocking crows and I wanted to walk into the middle of the swell and take hold of it, elevate myself with the language, look at my father and tell him I could continue where he left off. But from his weakness spun some strength, and he was the first one supine when the game demanded silence, a silence that seemed to diminish those unaware of it but dignified my father as if he were saying an internal prayer for the others. With a raised hand and then a closed fist, he held their voices, deified still, and the passage of time was marked by the drops of seeds into grooves as the game progressed and my father flourished. And then it was over. He stood and the room turned, and I knew it was time for us to go. Disquiet held the air. My dad took my hand and helped me from my numb seat, lifted me and held me to one side of his body as we gently made our way, everything so suddenly delicate. Outside, he put me down and removed a thread, or silk, from where I'd pressed against his body. He appeared satisfied with himself and in one of his pockets I knew he was counting the money he'd made, his mouth parting slightly with each multiple between his fingers. Before we got to our bus stop, he stopped counting and looked down to me, one cheek full and the side of his teeth beginning to show, and asked me which I'd prefer: this chicken shop here, or Kentucky Fried Chicken?

At home, he'd lie watching the world spin, cocooned, awaiting his life before birth to return without death. Watching me from the sofa, he waited for my mum to leave the room after refusing to give me money for a Pot Noodle or Cornetto, the difference in meals being whatever my friends sat in their gardens eating, then he called me over, spun into a seated position and told me to stand back, he was going to bring money for me. He'd push his hand into the corner of the sofa and bring up pennies, some silver, a 50p he lifted into the air and appraised, said it's not enough, then plunged his hand back in and the 50p would then become a pound. See how your mum is always praying, he said, can she pull money from somewhere or is it me who can do it? She should ask God for lottery numbers. He swung around and fell back into his idle, middle ground. Much later, I sat in that seat only once and decided to reach through the torn fabric, finding first only pennies and receipts, but desperate for something to answer the ice cream call, I kept searching, and finally pulled something meaningful out of solid material, a flask full of whisky. My dad was a storyteller, took his words from the sky, I could believe it all sitting here watching him twitching in his sleep, all lies believable when the speaker stops speaking them, finally pinned down to a real time and place. But a story, like deceit, or myth, is never finished. Each retelling or recalling is embellished by what came before, adorned by what could come after, fortified within the present iteration. My dad spoke himself into immortality so he could pass on the narrative to me. He was a story incomplete, resisting any possible conclusion, so solidifying his own fate.

I thought about what lay beneath him now. I walked up close to him and kneeled again, watching his face, puffed and ready to burst, his lips being slowly swallowed by the almost connecting thickets of his surrounding goatee. His nose, like mine, was as if he'd been rushed into the world, as if the nostrils had fallen from higher up on his face, pulling the skin down with it as it dropped, sinking, and the skin, the only sign of aging, I imagined putting my hands beneath his mandible and pulling away the mask he wore so lightly. Watching him, I tried to match his breathing, stopped when he did, my body resisting so I put a hand on his shoulder to startle the apnoea into letting him go. Letting me go. And I knew then, I thought then, that once you get close enough to a thing you participate in its decay, watch it recede from time, slowly abandoning its flesh, slowly abandoning you, my dad, I thought, slowly abandoning me. I stood and walked to the foot of the sofa and took off his boots, put them against the back door, downed a glass of his favourite whisky and then opened up his medicine cabinet and pocketed 4 blister packs of co-codamol, the off-brand stuff that I hated, that my mum had suddenly started getting, but it was better than nothing. Apparently, the more belief you have in painkillers, the more they work, and people had faith in brands more than they did the alchemy that they stood for. Already in London I decided I would visit my foster mum as well, stretching my social spirit to encompass everyone who might need to see I was still around and doing okay. It had been a while.

In my room, I pulled out all the books from my bag and set them in a line in front of me, closed my eyes and tried to recognise my mood. It was always in motion, so I needed possibilities, like each book was a path to follow to influence the scribes who may write tomorrow. My mood wasn't right for Huey, had put it down a few days before because I was unsure about the truth of his words, especially if he was influenced and enamoured with *The Republic* and the linguistic manoeuvres of Plato. *The New Jim Crow* was the next to go and I flicked through a few pages of *Keeping Faith* before I let it sit atop the other two beside my bed. So I was left with Assata and her journey, one I had read before but was happy to return to again and again. I held the book up in front of me, put it to my ear as if to listen to what was beyond the words on the page, as if it could answer me and my questions of impulse. I remembered the chills I felt seeing that raised fist from her hospital bed and wondered how San reacted to reading blackness staying strong even in the face of death. I would ask her when I saw her. I put down Assata and picked up Huey again, suddenly drawn back to that *Revolutionary Suicide*. I hoped sleep would take me quickly and my eyes would open as if from slowly blinking, and I would be back to San, back to Manchester and what might be, what I could see, and what I hoped she could believe. In that moment I wanted to text her and tell her I loved her, that I would love her in any life, but other thoughts prevailed, and I decided to sleep on it and wait for the common sense of the morning.

Nineteen

You're not saying anything, Marcus.

Yeah?

I thought you wanted to talk.

Yeah, but obviously not now. You're the one who even said I should come here.

Because I want it over and done with.

What, us?

No, Marcus, not us. The pregnancy stuff, you being so angry with me. I wish you could just get over it.

Get over it!?

I mean forgive me. I'm sorry. You know I am.

Yeah, but it's not that simple.

Because you're making it complicated.

How?

You're not talking to me.

I'm talking to you now.

Marcus, please.

Adwoa, you can't just force me to talk.

I'm not forcing you, I'm asking you.

Yeah, and I'm saying can we not today.

What else are you doing?

Why?

So I know why you won't talk.

It's not about what I'm doing.

So what then?

Adwoa.

So you want to end things?

Did I say that?

You're acting like you want to.

I don't even know what that means.

Is this because of that Belina girl?

What?

Belina. You know who I'm talking about.

Yeah?

So is it because of her? Is something going on?

Why you trying to flip it?

I'm not. I'm trying to understand.

Belina is just my bedrin. She hasn't done anything.

And I have?

Belina is just my friend.

Are you sure?

Is this what you really wanted to chat about? This why you brought me here?

No, you know it's not. But—

But what?

You were with her a lot.

Yeah. Just chilling.

And doing?

What are you even asking me, Adwoa?

Did you guys have fun together?

Yes, we did, actually.

Right. Okay, okay. Okay, I understand.
Understand what?
You fucked her?
Adwoa, are you fucking high!?
Don't swear at me, please.
I'm not swearing at you. I'm just swearing.
Well, then please don't.
But you just did!
When?
You said did I fuck her.
Well? Did you?
No.
Why not?
Nah, Adwoa, I'm not on this, I'm not doing this right now.
Swear on my life.
Swear on your life what?
That you didn't fuck her.
Adwoa, this is dumb.
Marcus, swear on my life, and I'll leave it.
Adwoa, man.
Swear.
Yeah, whatever, I swear I didn't fuck her.
On my life.
Yes, on your life, for fuck sake, do you know how dumb this is?
Okay, good. I believe you.
My days, what are you on?
You're asking me?
Excuse me?
Nothing.
S'what I thought. Okay, so what now?

We're not finished talking.

Aren't we?

No, Marcus, we're not.

Adwoa, seriously, my boy's coming to get me. Look, can we just talk another time? I'm going out, I'll shout you tomorrow.

Out where? So you're just gonna leave me like this?

Leave you like what? I aint done nothing to you.

Marcus, please just talk to me. You've been guilting me.

How?

Saying how I snaked you and you thought I was the one and all that kind of stuff. Saying you'll come church with me. It hurts, you know.

Yeah, because I did think that.

So I'm not any more?

Did I say that?

Then let me come with you?

What?

Let me come with you.

Come where?

Wherever you're going. Raving, to a club. Let me come.

Nah.

Why not?

You won't like it, Adwoa.

I'm not a child, you know. I have been out to clubs before.

Yeah?

Yes, Marcus. So can I come?

But why?

Because I love you, that's why.

Okay?

If you don't want to talk, let's at least spend the evening together.

But what's the point?

We can have fun before everything becomes sad.

But I can't just bring you.

Why not?

Because obviously my boys don't know you're coming and they might not be on it.

So?

So no one else is bringing their girl.

It can still be you guys' night. I'm just coming along to take my mind off things. You haven't even asked if I'm okay.

I always ask if you're okay. Even when I'm pissed off, don't try it.

You haven't asked me today.

Adwoa . . .

Marcus, please, let's just go out and enjoy ourselves.

I dunno.

Your boys will understand.

Oh isit? You think so, yeah?

Or you've been talking behind my back to them?

I don't chat about you to no one.

So I can come then?

You just want to spy on me.

Why would I need to?

You don't.

Marcus, I just want to be with you.

Fucking hell, man.

Marcus, can you please stop swearing at me?

Alright whatever, man.

So I can come?

Yes, sure, whatever.

What time is your friend coming?

I'll tell him to chill, don't worry.

Okay, okay. I'll be quick. Yes. Oh my god, I'm actually excited!

You just wanted to buss my head a minute ago.

She ran upstairs quick, was proper on it and I won't lie I thought it was funny but in a good way, like, to be honest, I didn't actually mind her coming with me. True, I was still vex and wanted to tell her about herself and see what she'd say but I just needed my mind to be somewhere else for a while, get me. I missed her as well, her lips were a bit darker but still every time I saw them I wanted to slide them across mine a couple times, not kissing, just like trying to understand how we feel where it's most sensitive. She looked more ripped as well. Maybe she was banging gym in Ghana the way I was over here, getting ready to confront man or chief me up. Anyway, she didn't even take as long as I expected and when she ran back downstairs and I saw her, listen, all I was thinking was I must be dumb to want to lock it off. She was rocking these shiny black bottoms that made her back look crazy, and one top that I swear was just being held up by her breast, a piece of it dangling over her bellybutton.

It's cold outside you know.

I know. I'm gonna bring a coat with me.

Aight.

So what time is your friend coming?

Like 45 minutes.

Okay, perfect.

What's perfect?

I've been thinking. And I think I want to try coke with you. Not a lot. But I just want to see what it feels like and if I like it. I don't think I will like it, but I want to try.

Nah, G.

Why not?

Because.

Because what?

Because sorry, I'm not gonna be the one to introduce you.

Why?

Because, man.

Because what? I'm an adult. I can make my own decisions.

Trust me, I hear that, but I aint gonna be the one to give it to you. Say something happens to you?

Then at least you're here to help me. What if something happens to you?

What do you mean?

So you've stopped doing coke? While I've been in Ghana you haven't done any drugs?

That's not what I said.

Well then, that's what I mean. We'll both be doing the same thing. If it's not hurting you, it won't hurt me.

Nah, I dunno, man. You might have a bad reaction or something.

Okay, so?

So if we have to go hospital, then what?

Then we'll go. Okay, if you're so worried, let's do just a tiny bit now and you can sit and watch me and see if I'm reacting badly or not.

I dunno, man.

I just want to have fun tonight, and not be worrying about us and everything else.

Yeah, same, to be honest. But still nah.

So you'll do it with that Belina girl but not me?

Why you keep bringing her name into things?

Because I know what you guys were doing?

How?

Marcus, do you forget how much you tell me?

. . .

I'm your girlfriend.

Exactly why I'm not trying to introduce you.

Marcus, respect me enough to let me make my own decisions.

Look, I understand the baby stuff. At the end of the day it was up to you. I was moving mad.

So why are you saying this now?

Nah, I'm just letting you know I get it.

Okay?

Okay, cool. So my boy said 45 minutes.

I'm not going.

What?

I'm not going.

So why the fuck did you beg me to come?

Don't swear at me.

Okay, okay, sorry. Why did you beg me to come?

Because I wanted to be with you and have fun and forget everything.

So let's do that.

How can we if you're gonna be going to the toilet every 10 minutes and I'm just standing there?

What do you mean?

Marcus, at least let me try and then say no, I don't like it. Which I obviously will.

Adwoa, man.

Look, I'm not gonna beg you. This is weird.

Okay, okay.

Okay?

One line, that's it.

But if I like it, a few more, but no more?

Maybe, man. Maybe.

Okay! So let's try it, then.

Fuck sake, man.

Marcus!

Just one small line, that's it.

Sure. Okay. Let's do it.

I didn't feel good about doing it but I couldn't act like she didn't have a point. She wasn't a yout and could make her own decisions. So, I cut up the tiniest line and just left it on the table so whatever happened from then, that was on her, not on me, then I poured her a fat drink just in case the coke hit too hard.

Okay, how long does it take?

To feel it?

Yeah.

Depends. Just relax, don't force it.

Okay.

Listen, by the time my boy arrived we'd done like 4 lines each and had two drinks and to tell you the truth, Adwoa seemed calm. Like a bit more energy and chatting bare, but she hadn't turned into another person. I wasn't sure if that was a good or bad thing because now she might think it was light work and want to do it all the time. I put down one more line each, told Adwoa to come here, lifted up her top lip and rubbed what was left on the table onto her gums. Then we kissed and I felt like yeah, maybe this could run.

I don't know what it was but as soon as we got in the club, Adwoa was on one. I think she was thinking, maybe she'd seen it on TV or in a film or something, but I think she was thinking when you're on coke in a club, you move reckless and excited and act like every tune is the best thing you ever head in your life. I bought her couple drinks to calm her down but at some points I even wondered if it was the coke making her move like this because even after about an hour, she was still hype and starting to embarrass man, coming up to me and kissing me, trying to get me to dance. The club was even dead so she came across even more extra. Like, it was still ram and the music was decent but my cousin wasn't on the decks and the place just had a vibe like no one really wanted to be there but of course they came through because it's Friday night. Even before we got in the club you could tell something was off because the bouncers weren't letting in any more man. True, I wasn't really looking around like that because I was watching Adwoa but when I did start preeing, the number of guys compared to girls was a bit mad. But you know what, I didn't even have to tell guys to low it when they tried to move Adwoa because she'd be so loud and tell them that her man was over there, or she'd try drag me over so I could chat to them like we'd be bedrins because we checked for the same gyal. I even thought maybe more coke would stop her behaving like this because I swear most of it was just in her head and the real ting might be different, like when we were at her crib. I slipped into the women's toilet with her and we did two more lines in one of the cubicles. We were kissing when someone banged on the door. When I walked out one girl was standing outside screwing. I looked in her face as I walked out behind Adwoa, proper made eye contact and she just kissed her teeth and went in to do whatever had her stressing like that. After that I just thought fuck it and let Adwoa do her ting and be all loved up on me, telling me she was sorry, she'd make it up to me reh reh reh, more drinks and more coke, more lipsing and feel ups and then I found myself outside in the smoking area chatting to one brudda who had this familiar energy but I didn't recognise him and weren't even trying to hear what he was saying, couldn't even, man might as well have been speaking another language because all I was just trying to do was take a break from Adwoa.

Bro, I aint even trying to be rude, yeah, but I'm not really trying to talk about whatever it is you're talking about right now, like, nah, I don't listen to Doctor Octopus. We're in a rave, man. low it.

Dr. Octagon. I was just saying it's a silly album but a classic. Anyway, fair enough.

Sorry, I'm just not in the mood right now.

Where's that girl you were with?

Inside.

She's loving it.

Yeah, too much.

Why not?

Yeah, but when it's too messy it's like, low it.

You looking to wife it?

Wife it?

Yeah, make her your girl.

She already is my girl.

Ah okay. A good girl. We all do things without understanding why.

What?

It was like my man weren't even chatting to me, just bussing convo with someone behind me or in his head, just saying random shit and looking inside like soon as he spotted his people again he'd be gone and they needed to hurry up to be honest because all I was trying to do now was look up at the stars and see if I could clock the ones that always followed me about.

There's your girl. She's calling you.

Is that who you've been looking for? My girl?

No, but she caught my eye and was pointing at you, so 2 and 2.

Four. Aight, bro, in a bit.

I'm coming in as well, dead out here.

I passed through two steps, through man who refused to move, kept my tings away from gyal I had to brush past behind, and then stood in front of the women's toilet looking about for Adwoa. I actually hoped she was dancing in some corner somewhere, away from here, nowhere near where I stood, not inside the ladies' because if I went in there again I knew it meant more coke and she'd be all up on me and I wasn't on it right now, I needed a break, and I swear I was way more sober than she was so it was all starting to feel long. That brudda from outside was walking past me to the back area with a bouncer blocking the open curtain and the red light above it, bare bright this time like say someone had left an emergency exit open, and then, before man went to go chill in the dark, he turned to me and whispered into my ear that he's sorry this has to happen. Next thing you know man pushed me into the women's toilet, my back bussing open the door and as I went flying in I could just about see him standing there staring at me with some offkey look on his face. I almost fell into Adwoa but she held me up and pulled me back into a cubicle and locked the door. She was kissing man all over and I was biting her lips, just going with it, sucking them, moving like say I was drinking the Hennessy off her tongue, then she grabbed my dick through my jeans and used two fingers to undo the top button and then started unzipping. I put my hand inside her bottoms, just outside her knickers, and used my middle finger to start tapping her clit, tryna count how many times it would take till she buss, all while biting her neck, side of her face, back up to her lips.

Marcus, I want you inside me.

What?

Inside me. Now.

Wait, wait, because if someone comes in . . .

They won't. Quick, just do it.

Adwoa wait, hold on, man.

Marcus, I'm so wet. Please, just quickly. Or just the tip then?

I dropped my jeans quick and she rolled down her bottoms and her G-string to her knees and then turned around and reached back and found my dick and pulled me closer, then put her fingers around the tip and found her pussy and I slid inside her so smooth like say she was dripping silk or something. We were beating and I thought I was gonna buss quick but then she was moaning and making bare noise and I thought I was gonna go soft because I was so shook someone was gonna hear us and shout the bouncer and next thing the door opens and we're just there mid-stroke and nah, she was being too loud and messy and I won't lie I started to feel like say I was doing something wrong, like I don't like fucking when I'm not as waved as the other person because then everything just looks and feels fake or like I'm just being used or something and all while I'm thinking this I can feel my dick getting soft so I told her let's just low it, let's stop, let me pull out, but she said no.

No?

No, wait, please, I'm gonna come.

Adwoa, I'm not joking someone's coming, stop.

No, wait, just keep going.

Adwoa, man. Seriously, stop.

Just wait, hold on, wait, oh shit.

I couldn't even move and I didn't wanna start forcing her off man because I knew she'd be embarrassed but I was feeling off, like, something wasn't right. Her hands were pressed up on the wall in front of her in a way that forced me up against the other one, her back-off spread out on man's pubes, my cheeks tensed up in the cubicle. I felt this tingle all through my body and it landed in my stomach, chilling there, them moving about, finding my fingertips and then dropping again, landing around my ball sack. I wasn't cumming, wasn't having an orgasm but something was going through me, I didn't even know what this was. All now I was stuck inside her, she was actually strong, her back arched and all I could do was watch her hands moving slowly up the wall in front of her from the sweat on her palms probably, listening to her telling me she's gonna come soon, making these small movements so man was going in and out of her but in a way where there wasn't enough space between us for me to fall out or stop or escape or whatever. I just shut my mouth, counting her going back and forward on my dick, looking around for anything else that I could focus on. I was somewhere in the middle of being hard and being soft and I was baffled that she was still going and acting like everything was amazing and I didn't even know what was happening. It was weird, I started feeling dizzy, and then all I could hear was Adwoa out of breath and some ringing sound like say I'd left the dance and was in my bed and like my head was filling with air or something, like I was about to float away and my thoughts pulled out my body as Adwoa relaxed and my dick fell out of her and I swear I could see both of us standing there and I wanted to let go, let something else take control, but as I was floating, Adwoa grabbed one chunk of my thigh like she was trying to squeeze out the last bit of her orgasm and as she dug her nails into me it was like a line was cut and next thing I'm falling back into my body, and from then it was as if something was missing, like say something was lost between moments and the night was just flashes before my eyes, like the last thing I properly saw of myself was when I started reaching down my leg with one hand to feel where she'd broken my skin, then tried pull up my jeans but couldn't so I just left it and I was standing there quietly, not like I couldn't speak but like I didn't know how to any more and then I tapped my finger against the skin of my thigh 4 times, 8 times and then Adwoa turned and put her hand around my dick, massaging it like trying to get everything out but there wasn't anything there for her and she'd didn't even clock it, she was so high that maybe she had left her body too, and then she kissed me on the lips and I suddenly felt myself inside my body, stomach and everything else like every organ just became aware, that I was alive or something like it, and I was shook about it so tried to remember another feeling, a feeling felt for the first time but could only think about cruelty, how I wanted to put my hand through the cubicle, through me, how I wanted to push Adwoa off and cuss her out, how I wanted to even hurt myself. Was that good, she said. Yeah, I said. So good, she said, did you cum? Yeah, I said. Inside me? she said. I think so, I said. Marcus, I love you so much, she said, I just want things to go back to normal. Yeah, I hear you, I said. She pulled up her bottoms, moving her thighs left and right to get them all the way up. Marcus? she said. Yeah, I said. What's wrong? she said, and kneeled down to pull up my jeans, zipped them up and tried to do up the button but I finally said more and told her to low it. Her face looking at me at that moment is what I remember most, the innocence of it, a face like say she wanted to love me and I wouldn't let her. Come, she said, and held my hand, pulled me to a corner and then threw it back to dancehall, back to the men's for another line, to the bar for last drinks, to the back with that same guy who looked at me same way my dad did, like he didn't know if he wanted to hold out his hand or hurt me, or something in-between. And then we were out in the garden. We sat on a bench and Adwoa put her head on my shoulder. I looked up at the stars again and remembered we were nothing, this was nothing, me, I, I was nothing. And I always would be. Do you think I should get the pill tomorrow, she said. I didn't answer. I looked straight ahead, seeing, feeling, nothing.

Twenty-Five

In the darkness of my room I knew I could be still until morning with the taste of my sleeping pills holding close to the taste of blood from chewing my inner cheek, but once the metallic urgency of the zopiclone came and went, I also knew I'd submit and be switching from one side of my bed to the other trying to find consistency in my body, my eyes turning against me until being gently put under, a mourning hand sliding down the astonished face of the dead. So I reached for my downers, floated through the house and boiled the kettle, mixed a camomile tea bag with iron fluorine, lavender and lemon. Past 2 a.m., the night made me nervous, knowing the sun would rise in a few hours and with it the day would begin and sleep would become an indulgence rather than a necessity. I walked back upstairs trying not to tilt the tea to spill over my fingers, and when I pushed back into my room again, I noticed, in a corner, some of my books being held up by a small box crushed on one side. I expected unused sertraline or sodium valproate, but my luck leaned more into hands holding back psychosis and into my palm I popped two 100mg tablets of Seroquel. I checked the numbers on the box and they were only out of date by a year and a half, and I knew the potency of the pills would only have suffered by about 20 per cent with gentle side effects, according to something I'd read through Scholar while googling my risk of overdosing on mirtazapine, and so with 1.5mg of Xanax, 50mg of trazodone, topped off with promethazine and my expired anti-psychotics, I drank my tea and sat up against my headboard looking at my bookshelves, waiting to be dropped suddenly into the depths of delirium or woken up by my mum asking why I didn't let her know I was coming home. I started counting my books, 108 on 4 shelves, then began trying to read each of their spines: *Hamlet, The Once and Future King, The Bridge of San Luis Ray, The Lady with the Dog, Madame Bovary, The Invisible Man, Time Regained, Akan-English Dictionary, The Author of Trixie, Alice's Adventures in Wonderland, Ulysses* . . . There was so much I hadn't read, books I knew I'd read one day but for now were only props in the first draft of a diegesis, faux memories included in my evolving personality. My arms felt like they'd fall from shoulders and I started to blink more slowly, wanting to slide down my bedframe and into my covers but I knew I had to wait, needed the pull to be more intense otherwise my body would resist, startled itself awake by the echoes of what I once convinced it was nearing sleep, my desire to go back to *being* without the prospect of becoming. But was it so bad, this bypass and many eyes to see what might have been, only seconds in the time stream of before life and after death, was it so bad to endure life without the burden of immortality? I wasn't even enduring any more, or bearing witness, I was a participant in my own life, and when I thought about moving my hand, it obeyed, and now so too the rest of my life as I thought to walk towards a future with San.

*

I dreamt about her that night, standing in a spotlight tearing out the pages of *Soul on Ice*. I reached for her, to help her, but she stretched out her arm to hold me at a distance, put her fingertips on my eyelids so I would struggle to wake up. I could sense a single question on her lips and as I leaned in for the kiss, the words faded away and she fell into a crouched position, putting her hands around my popliteals and pulling me forward until I collapsed onto my knees, slowly lowering myself to sit between my calves, watching her to make sure she didn't leave me behind. We sat like that with no other occurrence, without the world shifting, presenting an alternative or diaphanous dimensions to walk through, all that was, that remained, was us, in this darkness illuminated by the spotlight that lingered on her. I wasn't afraid to die there, there was enough in our silence to sustain a life, to give mine meaning, the nothingness becoming something when touched by a deity. I became warmer like the onset of so many diazepines and held to the comfort as it cradled me to the floor and my body lost its frame, became boneless, and I looked down to see San, her skin a pile like a mountain mesa in the distance behind her as she crawled towards me, a louse looking for life in skin that wasn't hers. I was then level with her eyes, waiting for her to reach me, knowing, instinctively, that I would finally know who she was the moment she joined me, taking from me as I looked to take from her . . . But then morning came, and I could hear the emerging sound of Edmonton birds chirping as I pulled away, my eyes opening, fluttering outside my window as a lawnmower was throwing up the scent of approaching spring. One side of my body was numb, and with a little more manoeuvring in my sleep, I would have seen the ground, disrupting my dream and the dark rhythm of its deceit. I raised my head from my pillow, closed my eyes and shook my head 4 times. I looked over at my bookshelf and tried to make out their spines again. Then I sat up, spun round, put my feet on the ground, walked over and picked out the book I had found. *In Search of Lost Time*, I read the pages while standing, and then, reflected, closed the book mid-sentence, mid paragraph, on the third page, and put it back on the shelf, knowing then, with more conviction, what I had felt certain of before I had fallen asleep.

Anansi was born in a small village called Jamasi. He wasn't born alone, though, he had like 4 other brothers who were with him in their mother's womb. Anansi remembered his brothers, he thought about them all the time and you'd even see him give them a little wave when he walked past them every morning on his way to school. Because there were so many of them in his mum's belly, and because there wasn't much food in the village, Nyame, the Sky God, was like it's not fair that all these Anansis should come out their mother's tummy and eat all their food when the village is already without. So he only allowed one of them to live, the rest had to return to the earth and maybe come through another vessel of the village. But even though Anansi was allowed to walk the ground and not rest in it, he still needed special treatment, like to go to school every day and things like that. See, his brothers, knowing what Nyame planned, had begun fighting inside their mother's womb, punching, kicking and alla that, and so when the Anansi that survived was born, his body was damaged and he was always in pain. He needed special seeds from a tree that didn't grow in their village. So his mother went up to Nyame and begged him to send a message to Br'er Rabbit, that was Anansi's cousin, the son of his mum's sister, who actually lived where the tree grew, so yeah, she begged that Nyame send a message and ask Br'er to send them the special seeds. And Nyame was like, okay, cool, he will do it, but they have to find these special cowrie shells and send them to Br'er Rabbit for payment. And so now, some weeks later, the seeds arrived in the village and Anansi could go to school without feeling pain and he could still carry on saying hello to his brothers on his way to school. So that's how it went, every time 30 moons would rise and fall, Anansi's mum would send cowrie shells across the seas and then collect the seeds and give them to Anansi. But obviously, soon Anansi got used to the effects of the seeds and needed more and more. And so again his mother, who loved him with the abundance meant for 5 boys, asked Nyame to give her wisdom so she could plant her own tree and collect her own seeds, do her own ting. And Nyame was like okay, cool, I'll see what I can do, but you're gonna have to bop like 23 miles, that's how far away he had already given rise to the tree, because he knew she would ask for it and he told her to bring those cowries as well. And so of course she walked all those miles and Anansi was blessed with seeds closer to his crib. But soon it became Anansi's turn to leave the village and join Br'er Rabbit across the sea. By these times, Anansi's pain was gone but he didn't show no one, especially not his mum, and being the trickster that Anansi was, he said he needed more seeds, so of course again his mother brought more until her feet were red like the colour of chopped beetroot. Then the time came and Anansi said goodbye to his brothers and hugged his mother tight, like, he was actually sad to be leaving but was happy he had saved so many of them seeds just in case there were no trees where he was going. But see Anansi, instead of crossing the sea to meet his cousin Br'er Rabbit, decided to duck out and went somewhere else. He had his own plans that no one else knew. All now he never intended to cross the sea and make a life in the same place Br'er Rabbit, nah, he had his eyes set on another island. See, Anansi missed his brothers so much that he wanted to try and bring them forth, recreate himself, create more Anansis, in a place where Nyame wouldn't be able to interfere. And so he headed for the island where he knew Nyame had no power and started looking for someone to bear his children. In the end, he only had one, broken before birth just as he was.

Twenty-Five

Before I left for London to see my dad, San and I were stood outside a snooker bar and I was trying to take a picture of her posing in front of it. She told me to kneel, and I did. Stand and position the camera so it aligns with our belly buttons, just above your pubes, she said, and I did. Okay, one more, she continued, but stand over there, not in the road, but on the curb almost in the road. I did. You need to learn to take pictures, she told me, learn to bring out the best qualities, what everyone else can't be bothered to notice, because I swear I always look flat whenever you take pictures of me. I said I hear her and tried to remember some of the many photos I had taken of her, realising then that no matter the angle they all looked the same, anyway. The bar in the background had appeared in a music video by a band she was obsessed with but no one cared for any more, making them even more appealing to people like San who took this contrarian pleasure in trying to embrace things the world seemed to have abandoned. This was the first time she'd been anywhere near it since she'd moved to Manchester for uni. I never said it aloud, but I mostly hated the Smiths and could usually only tolerate one song: 'Panic'. When I told her I was leaving for London, she had offered to see me off at the train station, but we'd mistimed the departure and so we were walking around trying to find food, though mostly trying to talk through phrases that tumbled and ascended between us, which meant being confronted by a mass of gibberish as you looked over at the other, eager to see a way through to words you actually felt, not what landed in your lap. From the snooker place we walked towards Cheetham Hill, crossed the road to look into the Indian kebab shops, turned to each other, wrinkled our faces and then decided to keep going until we found a place that was probably equal in quality but a better-packaged poison before I got on a two-hour train. Before a left turn towards the prison, we found a hot dog shop that we thought looked new and agreed to try it out, sat in to eat, and San ordered some chicken wings covered in BBQ sauce and cheese that made my insides turn just by looking at it. I couldn't really taste my meal, and after few groans from my stomach I knew I'd again tricked myself into believing I'd eaten something that would sate me, sat there with San, the two of us I thought like lost children placed around a table with a never-ending supply of imaginary foods. I threw a chip at her and she told me not to be a dickhead.

Why do you keep checking your phone? You're not gonna miss it. The train, I mean. We're close, you'll be fine.

Yeah, I know, I just like to be in the station like half an hour bef—

That's fine. But don't rush me. Let me eat.

I'm not rushing. Just checking.

You looking forward to it?

To seeing my family?

Yeah.

Not really. Well, I guess I haven't seen them in a while. It is what it is, really.

I hear it, I hear it. You want some chicken?

Nah, I'm good.

Yeah, they're nasty, anyway. But I'm hungry so . . .

When you going back to Bristol?

Dunno. Never?

Seriously?

Marcus, I have no idea. Well, actually I have some idea but don't know exactly. Waiting for my mum to go on holiday?

Why?

Let me finish my food and I might tell you.

Cool.

We were silent on the walk back to Victoria Station and San's eyes seemed to linger on the faces of every guy who walked past us, handsome, interesting, unusual looking or not, she made sure to study their features as if she'd need to remember them at a later time in the day. I wondered if she was trying to irritate me but she didn't even glace at me, didn't check in to make sure her wandering eye had registered. I took off my coat and held it across my arm, San quickly taking it off me and putting it around herself. Aren't you cold, she asked me. I didn't respond. We sat down inside the station with 10 minutes before the train. I was sure I was going to miss it or have to stand because of how packed it was going to be but I affected an air of . . . indifference? It was difficult to tell, and I knew my always seeming on edge or somehow without was beginning to irritate her, and I thought it was too early to ask someone to tolerate you before they've learned to love you.

Marcus, I swear you're never listening.

I am listening.

So what do you think then?

About Mbeki?

No, Marcus, I don't care what you think of him, and obviously I can't sum up everything he did for South Africa and the continent, on point economist and all that but basically looking to recreate capitalist classes for melanated people and we can see how that goes, but objectively, and I don't care because it's a big part of his legacy, he is responsible, and believe he was even chatting shit and talking down to the 'pandering' of Pan Africanism without 'practical' applications and how it's living off sloganism, so ironic to me, because at the end of the day, he's the one who utilised well known African paranoia towards the west and their implementation of medicine to further his own conspiracy theories and push his self-interest, and because of that maybe around 400 hundred thousand people died unnecessarily. And my dad still respects him, you know, which baffles me because imagine he was living in S.A at the time. Man wants to talk about sloganims but he doesn't even get that without those compelling colours on theoretical place cards, so many of us wouldn't have found the way in to discuss the finer details, you know things like –

Oh, oh, right, yeah, I think I get you. I agree, you're right.

You love interrupting me. What am I right about, Marcus?

Everything really.

Forget it.

What?

Nothing. I have something for you, before I forget.

Really? What?

Here. It's by Frantz Fanon. Don't say you've read it. Not gonna lie, I wouldn't even believe you.

Thank you.

It's calm. Read it on the train. And then text me what you think.

Is it dense?

No. Are you?

What?

Nothing. But read it. Especially Chapter 3. Actually, I'd even say start there. It will help you understand what I've been saying about black man and mzungus.

Will it?

Yes, Marcus, it will. Because at the end of the day . . .

The bench where we'd decided to sit had a departure screen just to the side of us and I'd made sure to sit to the left of San so I could look past her and follow how much time I had left. She had moved onto double consciousness and I knew from past experiences with her that it was a prelude that it was a prelude to something that had been on her mind the whole time we'd been together, but she was building to the conversation. I wanted to recline and listen, watch her speak as her lips slid up and down her teeth. The wider her mouth became, the better she began to pronounce words with her developing enthusiasm and my silent responses as an extra charge for her spark. But I had to go.

San, I have to go.

What now!?

Yeah, my train is leaving in 3 minutes. I'm gonna have to run.

Fine. But text me. Read that chapter first and then text me, okay?

Sure, sure, alright. Alright, okay, I gotta go.

Bye.

She turned around before I thought to say goodbye, walked away with her arms folded across her chest and my coat still hanging off her shoulders like a heavy cape always struggling to billow in the breeze. I took a deep breath, counted her steps up until 4 and then quickly ran to catch my train. Thankfully I found a seat, sat down, slid my hand from finger to wrist beneath my nostrils and then pulled at my nose just as the whistle blew and the sliding doors to Manchester closed.

San had given me many books to read, it was true, promising they would change my life – well, not change your life, she said, but maybe open up a new personality, humble you or something like that. But I told her, as I believed, maybe more seriously than her comments cared to kindle, that once past your most impressionable, often, the early stages of a life in fiction, it's not possible to be moved by a book into any kind of change. As the train stopped at Trowse Station, on the way to the small village I'd grown up in, where many abandoned seeds were only just sprouting, I was trying to recall the dream from the night before, trying to envision San and the sound of each page she tore from the book, a universal book pulled from a Borges library, though my feeling was that it was my favourite book, a novel, but I couldn't say which one. I frowned to hold the thoughts in place, looked away as someone tried to hold my gaze, lifted my bag onto my seat and let them walk past, then rummaged through it, pace picking up as panic set in, as if that would help salvage whatever I'd lost. I relaxed a little. Took out my last pill of the day, put it in my pocket, broke it from its blister pack and then put my bag down again. I closed the book I was reading, an epic poem by Konstantin Perov, and then focused beyond my dream on a past reverie that wouldn't let go: San must be good for me. Yes, she moved first and I followed, but the poetry could stand with the political, possibly without. At our most hardened, we leaned into each other, San and I, rocky parts coming away with every collision, and even if we didn't reach to piece each other back together, we looked at what was lost, instead of ignoring it. Instead of being like most, San was herself, and that was all I needed. Friendship is easy when it's convenient, love was nothing if not uncomfortable, and I shifted to find space whenever she spoke, but finding myself in her inflections and cadence was intimacy without a kiss, black power without the fist. Just be, and we were, unseen and inert, but building to something to endure from the dirt. As soon as we could speak again, I'd tell her the truth. We both knew it, both saw and looked past it, wanting and waiting for something to replace it. Green landscapes began to emerge, and I knew if I could pass through the glass separating me and the fields brought to life by the cows that grazed them, I would smell something akin to home, greener grass in the air trying to overpower the inevitability of how things end up, used to end up, the sky weighted and threatening rain until the train found tracks bathed in sunlight, light leading to where I grew up, a childhood spent not knowing who I was until the glow of T.V. introduced the shine of darkness, Mr T, my first costume, funny, a reflection of who I knew I could be, though sans fro and gold, still dark and powerful, I'd hand myself to her, grow into her own. San, I listened when she spoke, offered nothing back, looking for ways to relate without her feeling like we're the same, she had to know we were different, I was different, that I fell in and out of the world and couldn't decide how I felt when I found myself once again walking alone in my body.

But being unified helped me, tethered me, not just with her but with the cause, Pan-African, Afrocentric, I'd reach anywhere she'd want to take me, reading about Huey and Malcolm, and Stokely and Shakur, Davis and Du Bois, Frantz and Frederick, finally Boukman over Booker, I could see where I stood, beside her and looking towards where we could scale, to be hidden on the shoulders of giants, doing our work and loving without stirring, avoiding eyes that wondered what we were, as close as the ancestors, our harmony respecting and in sync with their songs to be free. A love built on the concept of blackness, but floating still when ideology collapsed, an outline to be filled with how much it gave us, outpouring, spilling, overflowing with what made us. I could love San without the colour of madness, a lightning bolt in the darkness, a melanated path to her blue eyes. I've read, there are a people in southern Africa who shape their perception and capture their culture, spread their philosophy through tales of a shapeshifting mantis. Khaggen, as it/they are known, may have walked the continent with Anansi, transforming lies into tales, and tales into truths about the world: what is immortality without love? Khaggen belonged to the San people, and Anansi, I finally felt, belonged to me.

Nineteen

I started holding Adwoa tighter at night, it felt good, and while I was laying behind her as she slept, I would count the baby hairs she'd always let tangle up behind her and then pull some through my fingers, over and over, making them straight standing out between the other spirals. I'd fall asleep like that and wake up on my back, still tired, though, like I hadn't fallen deep enough to actually dream. Sometimes Adwoa would be holding my hand when I opened my eyes and I'd squeeze it 4 times but when she moved about and her hand slipped away, I always forgot to try and hold it again. Whenever I stayed at hers, Adwoa would tell me she loved me and I'd tell her I loved her too, but on some days when she moved to kiss me I'd turn to look at the clock, not even realising I was doing it, looking to see how long was left until I had to see a next client. When we did kiss, though, Adwoa said they tasted different. I wasn't really sure what she was saying but I think she could taste the blood from me chewing up my mouth, my tongue sometimes slipping over the inside of my cheek and I'd remember that them sores never fully healed. I told

Adwoa I weren't feeling right, but it wasn't her fault, I was still feeling us, but whenever she tried to touch me my body just automatically moved away, like some reflex even when I didn't feel like myself.

And I never clocked how loud she knocked, how much power she had in her hands when she was banging on the bathroom door asking me to come out. I always opened up as quickly as I could, though, and then we'd just be standing there looking at each other when there was nothing to else to be found out. Honestly, I never knew she could lie like that, after a while of just watching me and then saying how badly she needed to use the toilet, walking past me trying not to touch me, or maybe it was me who moved away from her, I didn't clock I was doing it, and then I know say all she did was sit on the closed lid of the toilet. Maybe she was even doing what I was trying to hide from her. Sometimes I just chilled on the stairs and waited, not sure what I was waiting for but knew I'd know it when it came through. She would find me in the kitchen too, open the fridge whenever I'd turn away but soon as I'd look back, clocking she was leaving, there'd be nothing in her hands, nothing put to the side, just this weird continuing lie, doing shit for the sake of it, living life just to keep an eye on me. So I'd just leave when I heard her coming, try fix my face to smile when I walked passed her, maybe say hey, maybe count the way, just watching the floor and trying not to breathe in when we got close to each other, feeling like I couldn't speak whenever she asked what was going on. Nothing, I said . . .

Do you even care how I feel?

I do, you know I do.

So why don't you just talk?

Adwoa, I am talking.

Marcus, do you know what you're doing to me, how you're making me feel?

What am I doing?

It's like you don't even want to touch me.

I do. You know I've got bare love for you.

Love for me?

You know what I mean. I do.

No, you don't, and you're barely even talking to me now.

I just feel off?

Off? Off how?

I don't know.

Because if we're honest, you *wanted* to have sex?

When?

Marcus.

Adwoa, I don't get it.

At Flashes. You wanted to have sex.

Oh.

Didn't you?

. . .

Marcus? Hello? Can you talk to me please, because this really isn't fair.

No, it isn't.

Should I just leave, then? Should we just break up?

I don't want to.

Neither do I, but you're giving me no choice. Marcus, you're making me feel like I did something wrong.

Did you?

Did I what?

Do something wrong? I don't even know.

So you've been thinking about it? You've been thinking I did something. Me? After everything?

Sorry.

For what!?

You're crying.

Fuck you, Marcus.

After Adwoa left I took my bed to pieces and then left the mattress in the front garden. Imagine, my cousins were just there watching me struggling with this hench thing behind me and all they were doing was running joke. Stephen's hands were always cold and when he put one around the back of my neck, I always got some crazy chill, threw it off and told him to low it. I know it was a minor but for some reason, around these times everyone wanted to touch me. Stephen just laughed and said, You're such a weird yout, Marc, you know that? I bought this new mattress online as well, one of them ones where you can fold it up so you've got more space or whatever. I wanted more space. I won't lie, I was starting to feel like everything was trying to crush me. So I put my clothes and bare other shit in plastic bags and dashed them into a corner. I gave all my crep away, gave most of them to my cousins, except the youngest one, and I won't lie, I did feel bad but none of them fit him and anyway, I wasn't as fazed as I used to be. Before, I would have probably taken him Foot Locker, let him pick out whatever he wanted. Them days were gone, though. My TV was gone too. I can't really remember what happened but I must have dashed something at it or punched it or something because the screen was fucked so I put it in the skip down the road. So I just sat in my room, up against the door with my mattress so no one could come in. Sometimes I thought about the past and people and how things always seem to be the same no matter where I am or how I move. When I left Norfolk I really thought things were gonna be better, like, I got to see my dad, and my mum would even come visit me sometimes as well. No friends, but that was calm because everything was new. I didn't even realise people felt sorry for me until this one girl came up to me on the playground in primary school. I'll always remember her lips and how they felt against mine, how she was older than me, in Year 6 I think and I was in Year 3, so only like 3 years so it was a minor. But I remember she was the first person I loved. Like, proper loved, to the point where when I came into school and she wasn't there or she was ignoring me, it actually felt like some serious pain in my stomach and then all over my body because I loved that girl so much. I've felt the same again, loved every girl I've dealt with after in the same way. And it's too much, man. I'm too much. That's why one of the main things I remember about Adwoa is how she wouldn't kiss me in the cinema. I never told her but when I went to the bathroom during the film, I wasn't in there to do a madness, wasn't searching myself for my vials, I was in there confused, like I wanted to cry, like I didn't know why she was treating me like that.

I knew I was doing too much, like, I knew I shouldn't be doing as much coke as I was but honestly I felt like there was nothing else to do and sometimes it didn't even feel like Adwoa had bounced, like, sometimes it actually felt like I didn't even know who I was missing, like say there was no one even attached to the feeling. I swear down if I didn't drink or do anything else, everything around me just stared to blend into noise, like I could taste colour or smell the sound of something or touch my thoughts, it was getting mad but I didn't even care, come like say that feeling could burst out my body or drag man somewhere dark and I wouldn't even mind, everything would be calm. And all this noise, yeah, all this confusion turned into these emotions I don't think I'd even felt before. I really didn't know wagwan for me. I missed Adwoa. But she made me feel off, like, there were moments when I could stare at her for time and see how her face would change, how I wouldn't even recognise her, and it even got to the point where I'd be shook sometimes, like I'd be thinking who the fuck even is this person? And she didn't even do anything, that's the mad thing about it, she still told me she loved me and that but I couldn't even say it to her without feeling dizzy and thinking about what happened to man when I smoked that spliff and tried to run home. Things got tense at gym too. During my sessions, I started making excuses and would buss out for a bit, go toilet and then just sit next to the seat with the coke cut up on top of it. If anyone came in that would have been me finished, job done. And honestly, it might as well have been. Bare of my clients had left and I knew it was my fault, like, caring about me wasn't what they were paying for. They couldn't even pretend, and I won't lie, a part of me rated that. Like just be real with me. My nose was proper blocked, fucked, and wouldn't stop running, and more time the back of my throat was numb too. When I was at home, though, if I did enough press ups, 4, 8, 15 or a few more, then my nose would open up a bit and I could quickly carry on.

Strong whisky helped as well, I think it burnt something inside and then it was all good to keep going, keep pushing until my nose bled. I sat in my room with tissue rolled up in one nostril and when I pulled it out it looked like something I'd been stabbed with but hiding something soft. Once, at work, just after Adwoa had bounced, Anton tried it. I was in the steam room trying to relax and he came in chatting about how he knows what it's like reh reh reh. Knows what what's like? Wasn't this the same guy saying how I'm gonna fuck it up with Adwoa?

Look, mate, I've only been kidding about that Adwoa stuff. It's not your fault she left.

Yeah.

Look, I'm around if you wanna talk, have a chat. I know what it's like.

Know what what's like?

Well, I can tell you aint been sleeping much, you've always got a bit of a sniffle. C'mon, mate, I'm the last person you need to hide it from.

Yeah.

You spoke to her at all?

I had goosebumps all over my body when he said that and I swear to God I don't know how I stopped myself swinging for him. I wanted to punch him up, but at the same time I thought, what's even the point? For a second I swear my heart stopped beating and I was waiting for it to carry on running before I got up. Didn't say anything to Anton when I walked out and I know he didn't really care, anyway. Like he didn't fucking replace Adwoa as a client a week after she buss out. Life is fucked, man.

★

It's been a minute since I've spoken to anyone, but then, at the same time, I am a bit pissed no aint here for me, no one's checking for man. I've turned my phone off now anyway so whatever, it is what it is. I've been having that feeling bare recently as well, and really don't know what to do about it because nothing is working any more. You know what, though, now I think about it, people have never really checked for me like that anyway, not properly, and I've never really gotten why, even my mum and dad, and you know what, when I actually deep it, my dad has actually shown me the most love out of anyone. Yeah, he was semi strict but he never licked man and spent most of my punishments just telling man stories, like at least he chatted to me like he liked me. I used to see him sitting on the top step just outside my door drinking and talking to himself, sometimes I even thought he was out there waiting for me, like, so we could both chill together and drink and buss joke or whatever, but nah, when I'd clock that he stopped talking for a minute, I'd get up to go toilet just so he knows I'm awake, so he knows man's there behind him, but he'd just say sorry when I'd brush past him down the stairs, too shook to even look back at him. And when I'd be going back up, my man would be gone, like I couldn't hear him sleep and so I wouldn't be able to sleep either. Life is fucked, man. Adwoa, man, where even are you now? I don't even know what I did? I actually thought that was it, you know, like, I'm actually so lost. Sleep is even more fucked now as well, I wake up randomly and when I can't get back to sleep I feel to do something mad, like say after I've done it I know I'll feel better and will finally be able to rest. I swear I don't even know what I'm pissed about or who I'm pissed with. But nah, I'm clocking it now, that it's actually me, always been me, just weren't tryna hear it before. My room is basically gone now as well. I cleaned it up, it was all just random shit anyway, just things. I can't even get anything up my nose again. And alcohol takes too long to lick man. Shit, man, what am I even saying.

Twenty-Five

My arms went around my foster mother. She was so slim my hands could have come back toward me to rest on her ribs. Laying my head on her chest I felt her collar bone pushing on my temple and above me her chin sat where my hair was beginning to thin. I couldn't acknowledge her aging without bearing witness to my own and as we walked into the kitchen I had to slow my steps to respect her pace and was able to swallow two more pills, that's it, for the nerves she'd never known about but suspected. I was still so tired from the night before and the smell of coffee on her breath made me think I could take on the caffeine and win, but I didn't want to take more of my pills than necessary, didn't want to swallow something so numbing in front of the children. Upstairs, I could hear them, hear children who would have been in school earlier in the day, the holiday batch away with their parents, waiting to come home. My room used to be on the left side of the stairs and I shared it with a younger boy who used to shake in his sleep and wake up as if someone had surprised him. Instead of parents, social workers visited him, but when we huddled and discussed what gifts we'd been given or where we'd been promised we'd go, we called them his mum or dad and stared expectantly, waiting on the lie that would bind him to us, the storyteller's spirit so essential for children in foster care. I learnt to read in this house, or to understand the meaning of words, each one sounded out but discarded in favour of phrases said in whispers even though the adults thought they were alone. Foster parents were perennially old so the signs of their approach were understood from a distance: sliding feet and groans of effort, popping limbs and words with themselves. It wasn't often we were found out, but the most important proof of approach disappeared and for a while we were pinched on the ear while caught in acts of adult imitation or gluttony, but soon added again to the signs of the times. Can you imagine, children disappointed by a mother ceasing to cough? Even now, when we speak, the silence still feels unfamiliar, no sounds of organs dying for relief, a mother survives and a world never ends. We sat down at the dinner table and she reached over and put her hand on top of mine.

It's lovely to see you, dear.

Sorry, I know it was short notice.

Don't worry about all that, dear, just happy to see you. And your dad would be happy you still pop by.

Yeah.

I'll tell you what, if you feel like it later, we'll take a walk and we can put some flowers down?

I'm not really sure how long I'm staying.

Go on. He'd appreciate it.

Maybe.

Alright then, luv.

Thanks, Mum.

I won't put any pressure on you.

Thanks.

Still working things out with your old man, then?

Yeah. Saw him before I came here, actually.

You'll get there.

Yeah.

And how are you?

I'm okay.

Any more problems, then? You still on the medicine?

Nah, I'm okay now.

Being kind to yourself, then?

Trying to be.

Well, that's good to hear.

Yeah.

And your mum, how's she doing?

She's okay. Worried.

As usual, then.

Yeah.

I'll tell you something, when you were a baby, you'd never think things would be like they are now.

Like what?

You know what I mean, luv. Just a bit strained.

Yeah.

In the early days, you two were stuck together, peas in a pod, they called you. He had one of those what-do-you-call-it? Those carriers you can put little ones in. You don't see them nowadays but everyone had them back then. You two were a pair.

When he came to visit, maybe. I've seen some of the pictures.

And his stories. Gawd, he went on and on.

He still does.

I'll tell you what, though, he only started going on like that once you came out the hospital.

Hospital?

Nothing serious. You were a cheeky little bugger. You'd hold your breath until you went blue.

Blue?

Don't be silly, dear, you know what I mean.

Yeah. I do. I didn't know that, though.

I've told you enough times. Had to take you up the hospital because you wouldn't stop.

And the stories helped?

I believe they did. He stayed here for a while after that.

I see.

Telling 'em and hearing 'em. Almost the same, I'd say.

Not really. But I understand.

I'll tell you something else.

What?

Sorry?

Oh, right, sorry, I mean what else will you tell me?

I'll tell you if you stay for dinner?

Yeah. Alright.

Lovely.

So I learned to read and I learned to count. But numbers were in more places than the words that defined them. I saw numbers in everything, and they spoke to me, in my own voice, predicting something bad or appeased and promising everything would be okay now. It was a different time, my foster mother said, they did things differently back then. She was caned, so were her children, and if we ate the same food and slept under the same roof, we could expect the same punishment. Thinking back, it's unlikely those of us with parents were beaten without their consent, but social workers were left in the dark, never seeing the bruising of the children in their care. When we all knew one of us was in trouble, I had to find out what they'd done, and once I did, I listened from the top step and counted how many canes they got, remembering the number in case I wanted to, or found myself doing something similar. Group punishments, I had to expand my foresight, hiding myself in places until everyone else had taken their licks, needing to listen and count the number of times the cane came down before I could endure it myself. So many times afterwards we all had to sit around the table and eat with each other, our bodies sore and our mum avoiding our eyes and depth of darkness in our faces. Once, San compared me to Toussaint Louverture, not for anything other than my foster mum, a woman I would always run back for even as freedom was looming. Waiting, I listened to the sounds of the kitchen, my foster mum talking over her shoulder, not really expecting a response but needing to keep me tethered to a conversation in case I got up and walked out the house while her back was turned and never came back. I remembered trying to ignore the kitchen rattle and other intrusive sounds as a child, sometimes running around playing with my hands pressed over my ears. I wasn't really hungry but thought I'd eat something to be polite, but then the smell of baked sea bass and butter got me and it was served with peas and lightly seasoned potatoes, bread-and-butter pudding for desert, if I fancied it. My mum and I, we didn't go for the walk but sat in the living room watching DVDs of *Goodnight Sweetheart* I'd given to her for Christmas years ago. I wasn't convinced she'd be watching it if I wasn't there, but with her feet up in her recliner chair, she seemed comfortable, satisfied with this ritual. I could hear the DVD skipping every now and then, the disc struggling to be read, and began counting every time it sounded like it slowed down and began spinning again. After dinner, one of the children decided we were friends and lodged himself in the space I opened up for him in my chair. He hadn't said a word to me and had quietly summed me up during dinner as with shaky hands I used my fork to squash from their skin the split bodies of individual peas on my plate, skewering each half, sliding them off the fork with my teeth, leaving their translucent shells to one side. He was watching the TV as intently as he had watched me eating and I wondered how this memory would play out for him when he was old enough to want to remember his time in care.

He seems to like you, doesn't he?

Yeah. I like him too. What's his name?

Bertrand.

Bertrand!?

Yes, dear.

Where are his parents from?

Zimbabwe. But let's not talk about that, alright, dear? He doesn't speak but he listens.

Oh right. Okay. Just like me.

You, listen?

I always listened!

Not when I was having a word with you.

I wasn't the naughtiest.

That's right, you weren't. But you were still a little terror.

Yeah, probably.

You came around, though, didn't you?

I did. Then ended up back where I started.

We all have rough patches, dear.

I guess.

We learn from 'em, don't we?

We do.

Sometimes from others, an'all.

Yes, Mum.

You taught me a lesson.

I know, Mum.

Don't be cheeky.

Sorry. What lesson?

The day I walked in 'ere and you all had my fags in your mouths. I'll never forget the look on all your little faces.

I remember. Not it happening, but you telling me this story.

Well, I wouldn't be surprised if you didn't, you were only a littl'un. Last time I left you lot with a sitter. But to this day, for the life of me I still don't know how you got your hands on my cigarettes. I think you'd tried lighting them an'all. You all took notice of a lot more than you let on.

Yeah, some of us.

Well, it stopped me in my tracks.

Yeah.

Couldn't let you all grow up smoking like me.

Yeah.

Glad none of you lot smoke, otherwise I'd only blame myself.

I don't smoke, Mum.

I know, dear, I know.

I was on my knees in front of the settee and 4 children were seated in front of me. Only one smiled and the others were shifting from one expression to another, looking at the clock, then their mum, then me again. They were probably bored, but listening to me meant they could stay up and wouldn't have to be alone, thinking thoughts that didn't make sense to them yet. Our foster mum was trying to stay awake to listen but I wanted her to fall asleep before I told my final story, a story my dad used to tell me, I'm sure his favourite more than it was mine.

A small spider crawled in the rain and knocked on a big door...

When I finished, the kids stared silently. Maybe they realised I was like them. Maybe they were waiting for more. The one who had become my friend opened his mouth as if he was about to speak, then closed it without saying anything. I hear it, I thought, and wiped my brow, the stories having taken a lot out of me. I looked over at my foster mum. She was awake and trying not to smile, hands resting in her lap, reclined, tear drops collecting and then falling from her ear. For the first time that day, I noticed her hair.

Your hair looks nice, Mum.

Thank you, dear. I only had it done recently. Are you staying then?

Yeah, I think I will. Maybe a couple of days, if that's okay?

Of course it is, dear. We'd be happy to have you.

Nineteen

It was raining outside but I didn't mind getting wet so walked to the shop in my T-shirt, socks and sliders, 42 steps and bossman was still serving me but he did it slow like, and watched me as if to say he had something for me but I'd have to ask him for it before he would pass it over. I felt as if I could touch his face, like, just wipe my hand down it, smudge his features or something, I felt like he'd allow it, too. Outside, I could see those couple stars, or what, constellations that follow man around, but tonight it was like all the stars in the sky were moving too, like, every time I took a step, they took one as well, so by the time I was back at the yard it would be like say most the stars in the sky were just chilling above the house watching man. My head was gone, getting wet and watching the sky, blowing the rain away from my lips, spraying like say I was blowing away all the aches before the pain, but man kept crying and you wouldn't even clock, shit soaking up my moustache. When I actually got inside, I looked into the living room where mostly everyone was chilling. There was a dog on the sofa with my cuz, Kane, and he was feeding it bits of chicken from his chicken and chips box. Crazy, cos we didn't even have a dog. Stephen and one of his boys were smoking and watching a film, a man stepped into a puddle on the screen and then I swear the TV was looking like it was stretching towards me, like I could climb into it. I closed my eyes and shook my head and looked back again. Everything was the same. I could only see the back of Nii, though, sitting on cling film to one side of the living room with his scales and vials and whatever next to him. I could even see Renner, the guy we don't really see again, down from his room and *Halo*, opening the rice cooker and adding more water. Everyone seemed calm. My cousins were actually good people, still, it actually weren't right that I thought they should be worrying about man. People have their own problems. I walked into my room, closed my door and sat on the floor. Then put that hench bottle of whisky in front of me and just looked at it for a bit. I was too weak to change my mind, drained, even, I just wanted to sleep, like, switch off my brain, forever maybe. Whatever happens, happens. To be honest, I don't even like whisky like that, but it makes me tired and I can drink it straight. I opened it up and sniffed it. Couldn't smell nothing. That would make it easier, too. Calm. Sometimes, it's like you can see the thought in your head, like it's there trying to make noise but you aint trying to hear it, you just ignore it, try switch it up with something else, act like you aint clocked it. I won't lie, it was hard not to let any of them distract me from what I was coming to do. I lifted the bottle quickly and started backing it like it water. Shit still burned. Then someone was knocking on my door, a random voice I didn't even know, calling my name. Who let someone come to my room like that? I put my tongue over the mouth of the bottle but didn't put it down, just let it stay there while I was still, silent, and listening to try see who was at my door. I stayed like that while they knocked and knocked and knocked for like 4 minutes. Then it stopped and I moved my tongue away and was downing the whisky again, I wasn't going to stop till I blacked out, just firming it, and if I die, then I die.

Nineteen (Again)

My head was gone, getting wet and watching the sky, blowing the rain away from my lips, spraying like say I was blowing away all the aches before the pain, but man kept crying and you wouldn't even clock, shit soaking up my moustache. When I actually got inside, I looked into the living room where mostly everyone was chilling. There was a dog on the sofa with my cuz, Kane, and he was feeding it bits of chicken from his chicken and chips box. Crazy, cos we didn't even have a dog. Stephen and one of his boys were smoking and watching a film, a man stepped into a puddle on the screen and then I swear the TV was looking like it was stretching towards me, like I could climb into it. I closed my eyes and shook my head and looked back again. Everything was the same. I could only see the back of Nii, though, sitting on cling film to one side of the living room with his scales and vials and whatever next to him. I could even see Renner, the guy we don't really see again, down from his room and *Halo*, opening the rice cooker and adding more water. Everyone seemed calm. My cousins were actually good people, still, it actually weren't right that I thought they should be worrying about man. People have their own problems. I took the first step to go upstairs now and then heard someone trying to open the front door, bare force trying to push down the handle. At first I thought fuck, feds are coming to raid the house again, but when I got closer and looked through the distorted glass I seen it was only one person standing there trying to break into the yard. I shouted for my cousins and Stephen was the first one through the living room door, on a mad one and asking the brudda if he was dumb. Then everyone else came out and it was over. Kane ripped open the door like say it didn't have a handle and then I was gone, didn't even wanna see what was gonna happen, so just left them there and quickly walked back to my room.

I closed my door and sat on the floor. Then put that hench bottle of whisky in front of me and just looked at it for a bit. I was too weak to change my mind, drained, even, I just wanted to sleep, like, switch off my brain, forever maybe. Whatever happens, happens. To be honest, I don't even like whisky like that, but it makes me tired and I can drink it straight. I opened it up and sniffed it. Couldn't smell nothing. That would make it easier, too. Calm. Sometimes, it's like you can see the thought in your head, like it's there trying to make noise but you aint trying to hear it, you just ignore it, try switch it up with something else, act like you aint clocked it. I won't lie, it was hard not to let any of them distract me from what I was coming to do. I lifted the bottle quickly and started backing it like it water. Shit still burned. But I wasn't going to stop till I blacked out, just firming it, and if I die, then I die, the mandem would understand.

(No, Again!)

There was a dog on the sofa with my cousin, Kane, and he was feeding it bits of chips from his large portion spread out between them. It was crazy cos we didn't even have a dog. Stephen and one of his boys were smoking and watching a film, a man stepped over a puddle and then I swear the TV was looking like it was stretching towards me, like I could climb into it. I closed my eyes and shook my head and looked back again. Everything was the same. I could only see the back of Nii, though, sitting on cling film to one side of the living room with his scales and vials and whatever next to him. I could even see Renner, the guy we don't really see again, down from his room and *Halo*, opening the rice cooker and adding more water. Everyone seemed calm. My cousins were actually good people, still, it actually weren't right that I thought they should be worrying about man. People have their own problems. I walked into my room, closed my door and sat on the floor. Then put that hench bottle of whisky in front of me and just looked at it for a bit. I was too weak to change my mind, drained, even, I just wanted to sleep, like, switch off my brain, forever maybe. Whatever happens, happens.

To be honest, I don't even like whisky like that, but it makes me tired and I can drink it straight. I opened it up and sniffed it. Couldn't smell nothing. That would make it easier, too. Calm. Sometimes, it's like you can see the thought in your head, like it's there trying to make noise but you aint trying to hear it, you just ignore it, try switch it up with something else, act like you aint clocked it. I won't lie, it was hard not to let any of them distract me from what I was coming to do. I lifted the bottle, was backing it, but next thing now I heard the window fly up but catch on the latch bit and turned to see someone trying to climb in.

Oh shit, what the fuck!

Oi, Marcus, man.

Stephen?

Yes, man. Oi, I beg you help me and stop just standing there.

Aight, one sec.

I put the bottle down, lifted my mattress with one foot and then quickly kicked my mirror with my bank card and coke on top of it underneath. Then I jumped to the window, flicked open the latch and pushed up the window. I know say there was a moment from the outside where it looked like the yard was trying to swallow Stephen, this brudda always on something.

Fucking hell, man, you scared me. Wagwan, man, why you climbing through the window?

Bruv, didn't none of you man hear me banging on the door?

What? I didn't hear anything. Hold up, I swear you were downstairs?

Downstairs where? Bruv, you just seen me come through the window.

Nah, wait, hold on, I swear I saw you.

Marc, I beg you don't start this shit again, not right now, man.

Shit, what the fuck, man?

Bruv, why you sitting in here on your ones backing rum?

It's whisky, man. Stephen, though, seriously, so you weren't downstairs?

Marcus, big man ting, does it look like I'm trying to buss jokes?

No, but you man are always—

Ahh, allow it, man.

Fuck it, whatever, man.

Oi, what a fucking mad ting.

What?

Someone was licking off shots in Flashes.

Seriously?

Fam, it was mad. Everyone trying to buss out the same door and I know say some people got trampled over.

Shit.

Listen, man.

Do you know who it was?

I didn't even see, you know. But I won't lie to you, obviously man had to quickly bury something in the back garden.

What!?

Ay, relax, man.

Nah, Stephen—

Nah, Stephen, what? I beg you low it. You weren't even there.

Yeah, but—

Oi, Marc, I'm not gonna lie, you're actually starting to piss man off. This is why no one don't tell you nothing.

Rah. Okay.

Nah, I'm just saying chill, init. Everything's cool, trust me.

Aight.

Do you hear feds?

No.

Exactly. Just relax, man, drink your rum.

Whatever.

Shit, man. What you saying, though?

Just here.

I beg you give me some of that rum please.

It's whisky.

Yeah, whisky, whatever, just pass it.

Don't drink it all.

How am I gonna back all this? Shit. Bro, look, I'm still shaking, you know. My head coulda got licked off.

You're lucky.

Nah, not even luck, man. Timing.

What do you mean?

My boy was parked outside so once I got past everyone I just jumped in his whip and he dropped me off down the road.

Who?

You know what's crazy, Marc? I don't even know my man's name. I see him about but we don't roll like that. He knew I was strapped, though.

And you just jumped in his whip? Where's your car?

Marc, do you live on another planet? My car got written off tiiime ago.

Oh swear?

Yeah, man. Oi, this whisky is aight, you know.

Yeah.

And you were gonna back it all on your ones. Oi, Marc, wagwan, though?

What?

Don't think I aint seen you walking around the house looking all sad and shit. I was gonna say something but I aint really seen you in a minute. What, did you break up with that ting?

Adwoa?

Yeah, Adwoa, what's she saying?

Yeah, she's gone.

So that's why you've moving like this, backing whisky on your ones in your room?

Not really. I'm cool, man, don't worry.

Ay, Marc, remember when Hannah buss out and left you sitting in that church? Don't think I don't remember. And even Layal. Oi, I won't even lie, though, that one would have man stressed out too. But nah, man, you can't be moving all sad like this whenever a girl says she's not on it any more.

So I said I'm cool and you've still come to chat shit?

How am I chatting shit, though?

Bro, you don't even care, just low it. You don't even know what's like.

What, what's like? Chat to me, then.

Fuck you, man, you don't care or even know what man's going through, what I'm always going through. I swear, everyone just takes me for a dickhead.

How do I take you for a dickhead? Ay, low it, man. If I don't know, tell me then, init?

Let's just leave it, man.

Marcus, stop chatting, man. Seriously, what's going on? Fuck everyone else, you know you can chat to me.

Whatever, man. It's nothing, let's leave it.

A man said whatever, you know. Cool. Oi, I'm buzzing. Come to my room and let's drink this. Oh yeah, ay, remember that girl I was linking? That Spanish ting from Seven Sister? Tell me why she's telling me she's coming to have a yout.

Isit?

Yes, man, it's all mad. Already started stacking, though.

And she's having it?

Yeah, obviously she's having. Oi, what do you think this is?

And you're cool with that?

I have to be, c'mon. Anyway, why not? But at the end of the day, it's up to her, init. Anyway, come, man. I aint sitting in here on that tiny mattress. Listen, gyal come and go, get me, but you see family.

I hear you, man.

Oi, Marc, man, you actually make me laugh, you know, like, you know I got bare love for you, but you're actually cracked. Come, let's go, man. And ay, don't even try it. Don't think I didn't clock what you were doing. Dash that shit down the toilet and let's drink this ting. I'll holla my girl to bring some of her girls through.

Whatever.

Again man's saying whatever. Marc, I love you my bro, but listen, the way you chat sometimes I'm like who even is this guy.

Twenty-Five

San met me at the train station and said I could stay with her as long as we didn't have sex. I lay behind her on a single bed, my shorts and T-shirt pressed up to her bare skin, Adinkra patterns tattooed all over her body, listening to her whisper, telling me to come closer. Incense burned and with every drop of ash, a new turn in our talk and stone picked up and examined. Neither of us could sleep so we sat outside her building, passing a bottle of Baileys back and forth. When we kissed, she tasted of milk and honey. San was a paradise I could adapt to, without wondering if there could be more.

There was a forest behind our campsite and as I heated spaghetti hoops, San collected sticks for the fire. There were logs for purchase from the reception but San wanted to ignore what this place really was and imagine we were free to do whatever we wished. In our tent with the wind outside like a furious squall trying but failing to force us out of this delusion, the cold was unbearable. Embracing, I felt San's toes curling over and over, 16 times before I reached down and started massaging them in my palm, then letting go of her above, sliding down and rubbing one foot and then the other between both of my hands. Sensitivity rolling back up her body, she reached down with one hand and pulled me up to kiss her. Her lips were warm and slick, could swallow me with a deep breath, and we lay there, extending the most tender points of our bodies, close, silent, a prayer seen in the other, communing in confidence, our tongues below the surface, and I remembered my favourite type, lips full and moisturised, no one knowing it but me. In the morning we got up early and walked to the coast, climbed a jagged rock and wished we'd brought our phones to take pictures of ourselves posing like African gods before the rolling waves behind us.

San and I moved in together. As students, it made sense, she said. I was only half listening, trying to draw her attention to the 4 stars always visible from wherever I looked. After a bottle of wine, I pointed to those striking lies, already dead in the sky or showing us the last throes of their demise, naming them Set and Apate. San said she lowkey liked that, and she leaned into my chest, then lowered her head onto my stomach. You're hungry, she said. I am, I said, and downed the rest of the of wine, noticing as I put the empty bottle back on the table in front of us that the gesture felt empty even before I had finished it.

San, unlike every other object or person or insight or being, was not just an assembly of impressions compressed to time. She was independent of a pendulum, so that I could go on loving her indefinitely. My anxiety interrupted the rules of the world and the world resisted, but I was grateful for those moments of absurdity, motion unfastened, floating, because San would be still, approaching like she dissolved and reformed, every time a little bit closer to me.

We sat facing each other, her legs crossed and mine beneath me, one hand of each with fingers interlinked, the other sliding and drying itself over the settee when we took turns to speak. I loved him and followed him around the playground, and when we kissed behind a hill, there were eyes that found us from a window above and after a teacher told us we were wrong but were allowed to make mistakes, all the children avoided us, then just me, because I had told him to come and look at something and then put my lips to his before he could run away. But I didn't resist, I let the lie stand and I sank into my sadness, fabricating in the class and outside of it, created myself, secrets or fictions, sheltered who I wanted to be from the brush strokes of the departing artist. As we sat together, our grasp became tighter and San began to speak as our cells interlinked and either she or I used the word inamorata.

From lectures to trains, from station to bus. From there, I walked, I scurried along, everything a sign of how close to being home, so when I turned, corner of the wholesale district, before Cheetham Hill, aware of the dormant prison in the distance, and the high road no longer in view, I was no longer in view, I ran the rest of the way, thinking about sitting with her folded into me and my head resting on her shoulder, in silence, before the window, beyond which the trees that lined the path in the roaring breeze leaned heavily one way and then other, almost lifting from their roots it seemed, separating like stars grew them apart to widen my path to the sky, and I kicked through their leaves and made the leap to our door, stopped and caught my breath, calmed, walked in and saw her sitting on our sofa, legs up beneath her, on the phone, waving at me with the smile that led me home. And I told her she had no idea how much I missed her.

Some nights, I didn't sleep, I sat in bed and read until I could slide my hand down her back and watch it swell and then fall. There was nothing to count on these nights, her braids swept back before bed, no mention, no ceremony, a new ritual soundlessly enacted. We both knew. I was stripped too, timidity peeling off me, the words I love you no longer pushed out in a rush of more air than soul, more breath syllables. They were now solid and set, and I could kiss her forehead and say them and mean them and tell her goodnight knowing the morning would no longer feel like rebirth into a world that didn't make sense. And even if there were days when it didn't, San taught me that chaos wasn't always a terrible thing to wake up to.

She asked me to dance today but I made a move at night, slight, watching as she slid out of the bed like her fragile body falling out of a silken dress, and we danced on the golden records of Al Green or Billy Paul, two-stepping with her tiptoeing on the tops of my feet, curling her toes to the cold and securing herself, dreaming in my arms, the pastor singing our psalm. The moon shifted, and if the stars could think, our room would have lit up with cosmic envy, a glow only Poe set to poetry, but I was the seed, Anansi, swaying godlike in a world of my own making, unchallenged by those who watched, except her, in my arms, San, she looked up at me and I was no more, annihilated.

When the sun was in the sky and let the winds roam free, San and I would go for walks, often passing allotments, and she would try and name each plant she could make out through the crate fences and cardboard barriers. I pulled open the wire fencing for her and she slipped through. I followed her and we stopped in front of a patch, nothing yet growing but sticks to acknowledge their potential. She pulled seeds from her pocket and told me to choose some. Then we knelt down, breathing life into our laughs as we passed them back and forth and reached out into someone else's land and planted our seeds. I was still patting my part of the soil when I looked up and saw San already walking away.

We were sitting across oak floors, sofas and single chairs, tipsy and excited for more to spill over, holding back nothing to this group of strangers, hoping for familiarity, a reach to be touched or accepted upon hearing our stories. Some writers, some editors, some authors, some journalists, the party had condensed into the singularity of us and no one could leave until we'd all discussed what we did and how we'd managed to get there. I was asked about myself and everything slowed down while I thought for a moment and then decided to say I was a poet. I waited for follow ups but they didn't come until we'd left the house and San, pulling me closer to keep warm and holding onto my arm, said, don't say you're a poet please, it makes me cringe.

There was a child in the park with me. They were scared to come over to the swings. While they played on everything else, they'd watch me, and I wanted to get up and let them have everything to themselves. But I couldn't. I took a bottle of brandy out of my inside pocket and covered my face with the side of my coat like the wing of a creature transformed, ashamed. My hand shook and my throat burned, my nerves turning my stomach until I wanted to shout, scream, roar, until I was back in sync with the time of the world, till my internal clock ran smooth without skipping. I was exhausted, could see our house from here, knew if I looked long enough I would see San moving around inside, picking up her phone to check a reply, maybe phone me again to see where I was, how long I'd be, sat here watching her, so beautiful, she was God's flourish after so many familiar outlines, lips like no other, I remembered, recalled how she'd always touch mine like she was saying goodbye, always planting a shorter and gentler kiss on me after each long one, a kiss with no secrets, so I let go of the chains and stepped off the swing, put two diazepam in my mouth and threw my last blister pack in the bin, making my way home, making my way back to San.

The train had stopped moving, something was wrong, my delusions dissembled and I opened my eyes to a world in which I could feel the presence of San drifting away, fading slowly with the flashes of the dreams I vaguely felt above me. I took out my phone and checked to see if she'd messaged me. My thumb hovered, shaking above the apps like it was unsure which to open, the anxiety of a choice already made, occasionally tapping the screen as if to ask for help. I was without my meds for the first time in a long while, so sure I'd packed more and had them secure in my pocket, and almost broke down at the thought of being without them for so long, throughout the night and for such a stretch as my journey back to Bolton. I hoped the kids hadn't gone through my things, but then, it was possible my foster mum had. I'd left Norfolk soon after I'd realised, and in the daylight, when I'd hugged my mum goodbye, I was gritting my teeth on her shoulder, tense, feeling I could crumble her in my arms while I strained and tried to cast away the building tremors and twitches conflicting under my skin, that crawled beneath the night before, a night I'd contorted my limbs, turning continuously, cocooning myself in my covers and panicking when I slipped out of sleep and couldn't move my arms. I lay awake on the top bunk belonging to a missing child and listened to the children many times removed from family whispering, wanting to figure out who I was and if I'd be staying, their voices often seeming to me like a chorus I had conjured myself to see me into the chimeric conclusions of a night without my pills, a night without sleep, any vague soporific feeling of drifting remaining on the surface, my closed eyes seeing the eternal approach, anxious for it to snatch my awareness. But on the train, for a time, sleep seemed easier, but I'd opened my eyes to the startling anxiety of my reality dissolving and reforming, the feeling of a high that kept souring until it found dreams to cut through, pouring fancy onto the uncertainty of sane ambitions. I was losing, felt shaky but excited, blinked 42 times, I think, forcing back the manic thoughts trying to spill from my eyes as they looked around the train, staining it with shades of delirium. The prospect of madness felt exciting, for once knowing the limits of my thinking meant I understood some things were real and others could never be. Reality is more static than we care to admit, and we often call crazy a perspective that recognises and tries to break free from it by doing something unexpected, unconventional, running down a street naked or jumping in front of a moving train with no intention of dying. I felt light and had so many ideas, for San and myself, life beyond this odyssey. I straightened my hand in front of my face and couldn't stop the shaking, suggesting I was somewhere in the middle of my pain. I was desperate for the journey to end but felt fascinated by everything passing the window, the life beyond the glass, by the bodies packed into the back of the train, talking myself down from standing and approaching someone no longer a stranger. I shook my head 4 times and tried to shake off the daydreams insisting upon themselves, not too much but just enough, seeing that I wanted to return, return to San, once I'd found my bearings and calmed myself down. I was beginning to sweat a little and put my head inside my jumper and sniffed hard at my underarm. I was good, felt good, but knew something was off, had always been off, really. I counted my blinks again until 42 and then lost the count, worrying myself, increasing my heartrate so I sat for a while holding my chest, waiting for something to fail or burst through my ribcage, heartbeats like the fist of someone trapped pounding against a corner of the flesh that's encased him. I looked out the window again to distract myself, at the large houses in the distance, remote, some places with no cars so intentionally stranded, a back turned on the world. I felt I understood, but through an act of God or my own stupidity, I could feel, like tiny hands under my skin, that I was slowly being turned back to face it all. I leaned over and held my stomach. The sudden pain was fucking insane. I smelt something burning so lifted my head, lifted my head and looked out the window across the aisle some distance from me, struck by the feeling of déjà vu, and then tried to speak the words I thought I knew were coming. Excitement touched me again and I forgot about the pain, just this feeling of knowing or being before anchoring my attention. The familiar arrived again and again and I kept trying to outpace it, change something that I could sense was supposed to happen. Then, suddenly, the train stopped at a red signal. I lifted my hand to my face again, held it flat horizontally, and then put it down only to lift my other hand to wipe the sweat from my brow. I was glad there was no one around me for a few seats down. I looked into the sky and saw the holding-back blue, disguising the truth, the truth of emptiness all around us, something reassuring in the thought, in the thought of being alone now. I tried to adjust myself in my seat and it expanded for me, the headrest now a pillow, rough seating now a supple mattress cradling me to the floor, my intention modifying the soft world just to appease me and lull me back to my half sleep, my half dreams. But I couldn't go back, San would have to accept me and my world as it was, for what it was. San would have to? My eyes flickered as if trying to trail back to themselves, and with a force of will I managed to keep them closed and still. But then I could feel, like my dreams peeking, glancing at life, looking for a place to settle, somewhere to colonise, I could feel someone watching me, closer than they were before. And I had to see. I took a deep breath and tried to get myself back to equilibrium, steady, and in the seconds before I turned, I pushed to the back of my mind the trick of time insinuating it had foreseen this all before. So as I turned, slowly, I saw a face, there as if disembodied, one unafraid to be looking so directly into my own, one I didn't expect to know but could see that with a change in the size and distance of features he would be vaguely familiar.

Huh.

What's up.

You're looking at me.

I am.

Okay. You good?

I am. You good?

Yeah, fine.

You don't look it.

Trust me, I'm good, bro.

Kweku?

Huh?

Yeah, yeah, Kweku.

You know me?

Yeah, we've met.

Have we? You know what, maybe, you know.

You were coming from an ACS meeting.

Oh shit, yeah!

Yeah?

Yeah, nah, nah, it's coming back to me, actually. I'm not gonna lie, I was looking at your face thinking, where do I know this guy from.

Yeah, on the train. I think it was the same day as well, Sunday.

Yes! That's it. Oh shiit! Nana?

One and the same.

Oh, shit. How you doing, my bro?

I'm good, you know. Just out here. How you doing?

I hear it, man. Shit. Good to see you, man.

I'm glad.

Rah, how random.

Right?

Nana, you know.

I'm not gonna lie, I thought our last meeting was a bit awkward so I thought you'd brush me off.

You think so? I remember it being calm. Like, I felt like it was cool. Nah, man, I'm actually happy to see you.

Ah, me too. What are the chances, ay?

What are the chances? Man like Nana, you know. Sorry, I'm sweating bare.

How are you doing, though? You sure you're okay?

Yeah, yeah, it's all good, man. So what you saying? How's things?

You know, I hoped I'd see you again. So much I wanted to say. But now you're in front of me, all I can think to say is, keep going. Like, keep trying.

Love, my bro. Appreciate that.

Where you off to?

Yard, man. Been in London. And Norfolk, actually,

Oh yeah?

Yeah, man. Went to see the fam, still.

How's your dad doing?

He's calm, you know. Just there.

Yeah, I hear that. You still going to your ACS meetings?

Not even. That was just a one-off. I go to Pan-African meetings, though.

Oh swear?

Yeah, man. The struggle continues.

I hear it. I miss London, I won't lie.

Yeah?

Yeah, man. I lived there most my life. Well not most my life, but a significant time.

Whereabouts?

Tottenham?

Oh shit, same here!

Look at that.

Where in Tottenham?

Near Seven Sisters. A bit farther up from where Flashes used to be, one night club I used to go to.

C'mon, of course I know Flashes.

Yeah?

Yeah, man, my cousin used to DJ there.

You sure you're okay, bro? You want some water?

Ah, bless, man, yeah. Thank you.

No problem. Here.

Safe, man.

Cool. So who is your cousin again?

Erm, fucking, DJ Kane.

Hmmm. Maybe I know him.

I mean, they had bare different DJs so—

Yeah, you do look familiar, though. Not familiar because we met before but like I've bumped into you or something.

Maybe, you know.

Yeah, maybe.

So where you going now?

To see my partner.

Oh swear down you're married? You look young, boy.

Well, I spend a lot of time away from my own age. Looking into the past, I mean. Less stress. And yeah, married.

Bro, I hear that. I'm always thinking about the past.

Wishing you could change things?

Yeah, semi, but there's a part of me that believes whatever's happened, happened, if you get me?

I get you. But the way I read things is that sure, there are fixed events in life, but when they happen, like the order in which they occur, can be changed, if you follow? Like let's say you were supposed to die by being struck by lightning or drowning or something.

God forbid.

Yeah, God forbid, sure, but say that was the way things were supposed to happen, I think we can put it off or change when it happens, and so then we've affected the consequences but allowed the events to remain, get me, keeping the cosmic forces happy.

I hear you, man.

Do you?

Yeah, man, I think about this shit a lot.

I know. I know, champ. You feeling better?

Yeah, a bit. Still feeling dizzy but it's nothing. So what, you and your wife—

There's some distance between us, yeah. But not for long, hopefully. I've had a few chances to make things right and I think I'm nearly there, to make myself better before her, you know.

I hear you, man. I always wish I could change shit.

You married?

Married!? Nah, G. I'm hoping to wife someone, though.

Yeah?

Yeah, man. You know when everything just feels right?

Yup. I know that feeling.

God willing and everything, though, I'll see her when I get back.

Yeah?

Yeah, man, but I'm taking my time. Not tryna rush it, letting everything breathe.

How long you not seen her?

Only like a week and a bit but that feels like time! But good things come to man who wait, get me.

Yeah, but only the things left behind by those who hustle, though. It's all relative, is what I mean. Imagine years.

Crazy. I can't even. Being away from people drives me nuts.

I hear you, man. Well, this is my stop. It was good to see you again, Kweku.

Yeah, you too my bro. Nana.

I hope you look after this girl you're coming to wife. Take it slow.

Yeah, me too, man. Her name is San.

San. A nice name.

Proper, init?

Yup.

But yeah, safe, my bro, honestly, was good to see you.

Take care of yourself, Marcus.

He slipped out of the train just as its doors were closing and I watched him stop, pick something off his shirt, examine it and then rub his fingers together to discard it. By now I was certain something was up and I even thought maybe I should just go hospital and see what they say. But I felt like there was something for me to do and I knew San would be waiting for man at the station and I couldn't wait to see her and just lips her for the first time and tell her how I felt and then we could try and work things out, I had a good feeling, and just thinking about her made my entire body tingle and I swear I could see flashes in my eyes as if a lightning bolt was close, and I was shaking a lot now and wished my man was still on the train, distracting me and actually he was a cool guy and I'm not even sure why he thought things were awkward before. The train started moving and I slid up against the glass, put my fist to it to spud Nana if he turned around. Man like Nana, you know. Listen, you see Oscar Wilde, I remember they used to say he was a great conversationalist because talking to him, he made you feel smarter than you were. Man like Nana made me feel more me than I had in a long time. Crazy. Those are the typa man you gotta keep close, I should have got his number. I watched him walk down the stairs and he did look back but while he was turned is when he disappeared. So then I just sat back and I let my head fall onto the headrest again, closed my eyes, my body feeling like it was spilling out to fill the carriages before and after me. Marcus. I really hated the name Marcus. I wanted to be someone else. And that was my last thought as my entire body began to tremble, my brain telling every muscle in my body to fight and free me from my fixed point in time . . . and then there she was, purple eyes appearing in front of me only so she could disappear again, they could disappear again, I'm disappearing again, walking through the empty seats on the train, stumbling toward an earlier phase of my life. The world began to turn and the name I tried to cry out was snatched from my breath as I hit the floor, the flashes becoming darkness, and the rest becoming silence.

Epilogue

Belina told me to open wide and then put half a tablet of Xanax on my tongue like it was an ecstasy tablet or something. I backed it with this Moscato wine she got me that's proper fruity going down compared to other ones I've tried. Belina was sitting cross-legged in front of me, bending almost in half doing lines of cocaine off the book she was supposed to be reading aloud. These days it don't really phase me when I see people doing it, like, I won't lie there's still a bit of temptation there, but it's not strong enough to pull man in again. I thought I might even give up drinking as well, but I like the way the wine licks me with my medication, proper calm, and always with wine, you'll never catch me drinking whisky again, nearly choked man to death and I swear it feels like my throat is still burnt.

Sorry, Belina said.

It's, cool, man, trust me, do your thing.

You sure?

Trust me.

Okay, just one more and I'll carry on reading.

Calm.

She snorted the last line and put the little baggy in the bent waist line of *my* tracksuit bottoms.

Okay, I'm good now.

Cool.

You ready?

Yeah, do your thing.

Okay, should I start the chapter again or just continue from where we were?

I think just continue?

Okay, one sec. Erm, okay, here. So, *'I wouldn't ask too much of her—'*

Wait, wait, hold up, is this where we were?

Yes.

Are you sure?

Yes, Marcus.

Okay, cool. It's just that it doesn't sound familiar. And don't say my name like that please.

Probably because I haven't read it yet? And yes, my prince. Thank you.

Anyway, so, again, *'I wouldn't ask too much of her,'* I ventured. *'You can't repeat the past.' 'Can't repeat the past?'* he cried incredulously. *'Why, of course you . . .'*

DSM-5-TR Categorical Criteria for BPD

A pervasive pattern of instability of interpersonal relationships, self-image, and affects, and marked impulsivity beginning by early adulthood and present in a variety of contexts, as indicated by 5 or more of the following:

- Frantic efforts to avoid real or imagined abandonment
- A pattern of unstable and intense interpersonal relationships characterized by alternating between extremes of idealization and devaluation
- Identity disturbance: markedly and persistently unstable self-image or sense of self
- Impulsivity in at least 2 areas that are potentially self-damaging, for example, spending, substance abuse, reckless driving, sex, or binge eating
- Recurrent suicidal behaviour, gestures, or threats, or self-mutilating behaviour
- Affective instability due to a marked reactivity of mood, for example, intense episodic dysphoria, anxiety, or irritability, usually lasting a few hours and rarely more than a few days

- Chronic feelings of emptiness
- Inappropriate, intense anger or difficulty controlling anger, for example, frequent displays of temper, constant anger, or recurrent physical fights
- Transient, stress-related paranoid ideation or severe dissociative symptoms

Acknowledgements

I would like to thank my editor Ellah Wakatama and my agent Crystal Mahey-Morgan for their patience with me. I know it isn't always easy. I'd also like to thank Korkor Kanor, Symeon Brown, Yvette Henry and Melissa Adler for reading early manuscripts.